NIGHTINGALE

BOOK TWO

A CHARADE OF MAGIC

HELEN HARPER

RECAP OF BOOK ONE

The Story of *Hummingbird*

Scotland is a troubled land ruled by the Mages, men with magic who abuse their power and position. Each Scottish city has its own Mages and its own Ascendant at their head. Every night, as soon as darkness falls, the Afflicted take over – men and women who were once human but who have been transformed by disease into something very different.

Mairi Wallace lives and works in a small tartan shop in Glasgow, owned by Belle and Twister, a humourless and unkind couple. Mairi dreams of studying at university to become an apothecary so she can use her knowledge of herbs to help people, but she is held back by her lifelong inability to speak.

Mairi's best friend, Isla, sends word that she needs help at the orphanage where they both grew up. Mairi risks venturing out at night to go there and help a young, orphaned girl who is sick. Isla tells her that a baby girl has gone missing and she suspects that the Mages have taken her.

On her return journey to the tartan shop, Mairi is confronted by a daemon called Nicholas who has been enslaved by the Mages. Instead of giving her up to his Mage companion, he helps her hide by way of magic. As a slave, Nicholas is physically unable to refuse a direct order from a Mage, but there are often loopholes and he possesses some limited freedom.

The following week, Belle and Twister are given a large order for tartan to be delivered to the Mages at the City Chambers. A woman called Fee comes to the shop and tells Mairi to visit her because she possesses secrets about Mairi's true nature. Mairi decides to ignore this, but then Isla is publicly executed for asking too many questions about the missing baby girl. Devastated by grief and shock, Mairi resolves to avenge her friend. She walks away from Belle and Twister and her apothecary dreams and seeks out Fee.

Fee, together with her two wards, Flora and Jane, and a strange old man called the Gowk, tell Mairi that they are part of a resistance movement against the Mages. They also reveal that women can wield magic just like men, but the Mages prevent them from doing so.

Mairi learns that she possesses magic; although she cannot speak, she can pull on her considerable power by humming. However, strong emotions can dampen the effects of magic and a magic-wielder must be in control of themselves to control their power.

After learning this, Mairi sneaks away from Fee and the others to go to the City Chambers. Using a connection she has already made with a Mage called Noah, she gains employment as a servant.

Once working there, Mairi meets Billy, a young man who tends a garden inside the Chambers. She also meets the daemon

Nicholas again, who initially appears displeased that she has found her way into the City Chambers. Mairi learns that Nicholas's real name is Laoch; the Mages renamed him when they enslaved him. She also meets a grumpy old Mage called Angus, who is very different to his cohorts.

After a secret message is passed to her by Trish and Lottie, two servants who also work for the Mages, Mairi meets the Gowk in a local park. He tells her that she cannot kill the Ascendant on her own but, if she can find incontrovertible proof of the Mages' wrongdoings, the city might be spurred into action against their magical leaders.

Mairi reluctantly agrees. She tries to find incriminating evidence but doesn't discover anything useful until she follows a small group of Mages one night. She realises that they have captured and imprisoned one of the Afflicted, though she doesn't understand why.

Noah continues to flirt with her and asks her out for dinner. There is a rumour that if a male Mage has sex with a woman who possesses magic, some of the Mage's magic will transfer to her during the act. To test this knowledge, Mairi has sex with Laoch. She discovers that the rumour isn't true, but their intimacy results in a sudden and unexpected ability for them to communicate telepathically. Laoch tells her that he's on her side and he will help her.

Mairi finds a strange garden inside the City Chambers, macabre, reeking of death and powered by magic. Laoch gifts Mairi with a spell that allows her to transfer herself into the body of a mouse, which she christens Mungo. While in Mungo's body, she finds a hidden basement beneath the Chambers.

After she returns to her human form, she finds the Afflicted man who was taken prisoner inside a tiny cage. He has obviously been tortured, but Angus confronts her before she can release him from the cage. Instead of raising the alarm, the old Mage helps her to free him. As she escapes the basement with the Afflicted man, they go through the strange garden where the man digs up some loose earth and uncovers the mutilated corpse of Mairi's friend, Isla.

Shaken by the gruesome discovery that the Mages use female corpses to boost their magical powers, Mairi takes the Afflicted man to a back door near the kitchens. The house-keeper, Ailsa, is there and, after some discussion, helps Mairi to free him. Ailsa tells her that the Mages don't kill the baby girls they kidnap; she doesn't know why they take them, but she knows that they are adopted by good families. Mairi later finds out that the Mages drain the babies of their natural magic.

The following day, Mairi witnesses the Ascendant blaming a Mage called Ross for the Afflicted man's escape and brutally punishing him. The Ascendant mentions someone called Farris, who has provided crucial information about the resistance. The Ascendant has received details of a powerful female, and he instructs the Mages to find her. Mairi initially believes he is talking about another baby girl but later realises that she is the target.

When Mairi goes to meet the Gowk again, she overhears him being called by his real name, Farris; *he* has been passing information to the Mages. Mage Ross appears and discovers who Mairi is and what she can do. He immediately attacks her, but Belle and Twister appear and stab him in the back.

Ross's death and the revelation about the Gowk mean that all the Mages are now after Mairi, but several people in nearby streets help her escape. She learns that the Gowk didn't knowingly pass on information, and that the Mages have been using him for years. She also realises that those who have helped her, including the Gowk, Belle and Twister, may now be the Mages' prisoners. She resolves to return to the City Chambers and try to release them.

Using Mungo the mouse's body, Mairi returns to the City Chambers and persuades Ailsa to help her. They locate the Gowk and the people who helped Mairi escape, but, before they can escape, they are confronted by the Ascendant and Noah.

The Ascendant tells Mairi that women are not permitted to do magic because the existence of female Mages was the cause of the disease that affects the Afflicted, then he orders Laoch to kill her. Before Laoch attacks her, he tells her telepathically that he loves her. Something inside Mairi breaks, and she finally finds her voice. She uses her magic to hold back Laoch and kill the Ascendant. Noah is wounded and beaten back.

Mairi frees Laoch and he disappears back to his own realm before she and her companions escape into the night.

CHAPTER

ONE

There was nothing more evil or destructive than a Mage. I reflected on that fact as I shivered inside the dark, damp cellar with its moss-green walls and rotting floorboards.

It certainly wouldn't have been my first choice of hideout, but beggars couldn't be choosers. We were here because of the Mages, and we had to take what we could find if we wanted to stay alive and hidden from them.

Belle had refused to sit down for the first five hours; eight days later, she was still keeping her arms crossed over her chest most of the time, as if she were in peril of catching a terrible disease if she touched anything.

Her husband, Twister, wasn't much better. His eyes darted continually from side to side at the flickering shadows. When someone passed near him, he flinched with characteristic melodrama.

The others were gathered in small groups, their chatter muted; even the Gowk was quiet. Perhaps I was rubbing off on them, which wouldn't be a bad thing. Since discovering my

1

voice a few weeks ago, I'd found few opportunities where speech had improved my situation. Silence allowed me to take stock, to consider possible plans, and to pay attention.

It was the latter that meant I was the first to be alerted to the imminent danger.

Above our heads, the front door of the small, terraced house banged shut with more force than usual. The noise was followed by rapid steps along the hallway towards the trapdoor concealed under a rug in the back room.

I was already on my feet by the time the trapdoor was raised and the taut anxious features of John McAllan, the middle-aged homeowner, were revealed. 'Mages,' he hissed. 'They're going door to door. They'll be here in less than ten minutes.'

Aye: there was nothing more evil or destructive than a Mage – and nothing more relentless, either. Although I'd been expecting them, my stomach still tightened with fear. It wasn't only my own well-being I was responsible for now; the fate of the motley crew in front of me – not to mention the anxious man who owned this house – were tied to mine. Any mistakes or errors of judgment on my part could see the lot of them executed in George Square.

Every face turned to me and I swallowed. I didn't want to lead them. I didn't want to be responsible for their lives – I could barely look after myself. If Laoch were here... I hastily pushed the thought away. He wasn't here, and I couldn't afford to think that way.

Lottie, who until now had remained stoical, flapped her hands in alarm. 'What do we do? What do we fucking do?'

Ailsa glared at her. 'Wheesht!' Her eyes returned to me. 'What *do* we do, Mairi?'

I didn't get the chance to answer.

'She'll use her magic,' Twister said. He tried to sound confident, but his voice was shaking.

'She cannae use her magic!' the Gowk said. 'Those fuckers will sense it in a second and they'll be all over us.' He was right; we didn't just have to escape, we had to escape without the Mages realising we'd been here. Any attempts at magic on my part would alert them.

I stood up, grabbed my small bag with its pathetic collection of belongings, and rolled up the blanket I'd been using as a makeshift bed. We couldn't leave any trace of our presence . 'You know what to do,' I murmured, my voice barely audible. 'We've discussed this.'

Several heads nodded in agreement, but the flickerings of fear didn't dissipate.

'Someone tattled – one of your bampot neighbours.' Belle turned her head towards John McAllan, who was still staring down at us with a wide, owlish gaze.

This was hardly the time for accusations, even if they were the result of terror rather than anger. Besides, if someone *had* told the Mages where we were, they'd have come straight to us. They were doing what they did best: inciting fear to keep people in line in the hope that sooner or later someone would inform on us.

I thrust Belle's bedroll into her hands, and she jerked back. I pretended not to notice that she was almost as afraid of me as she was of the Mages, then I headed for the ladder without bothering to check that the rest of the group were following. They knew what was expected of them.

As I hauled myself up, my eyelids prickled painfully from the bright sunlight that filtered through the kitchen window. Time had lost all meaning while we were underground but, from the strength of the sunshine, it had to be somewhere around midday.

'Where will you go?' McAllan asked.

I shook my head; it was better if he didn't know. I reached for his hands and squeezed them. 'Thank you,' I said softly. The words, still unfamiliar when spoken aloud, scratched my throat but John McAllan didn't seem to notice. Instead, his cheeks turned pink and he bowed. Actually bowed. I stared at him.

'Anything for you, ma'am. Anything. You're going to save us all.'

I wasn't sure what disturbed me most: the impending approach of the Mages, McAllan's unshakeable belief in me, or the fact that he'd called me ma'am. I gave a tight smile then tilted my head to listen to the muffled shouts and running feet outside.

The others emerged from the cellar. 'Fuck me,' the Gowk growled, rubbing his eyes. 'That's bright.'

I opened the back door. We hadn't hidden in this house because of the comfort of the dank cellar, or because John McAllan had been brave enough to let us in; we were here because it offered several avenues for escape. Plan for the worst and hope for the best. Alas, now the worst was upon us.

I squinted up at the clear blue sky. Nothing more than a lazy pigeon flapped past. Exhaling, I glanced back. Everyone was ready.

There were ten of us in total. The Gowk, Fee, Flora and Jane were from the local resistance. Trish, Lottie, and Ailsa had worked at the City Chambers. Belle and Twister had been my employers in the tartan shop.

Jack, Ewan and Jenn, who had previously helped me escape and been arrested by the Mages for their efforts, had departed days ago to find friends and family with whom they could hide. They knew that the Mages weren't interested in them – our magical overlords wanted the rest of us to torture, hang and make a bloody example of – but we couldn't stay together because such a large group would be noticed within seconds.

'Six hours,' I said. My voice still sounded disembodied and strange to my ears. 'When the sun sets, we'll meet at the next location.' I paused, then added, 'Good luck.' I pointed to the Gowk. 'You and Fee go first.'

Belle's lip curled. 'Just because he's disabled and she's old doesnae mean they should get to go first.'

When I looked at her, she blinked as if she hadn't realised she'd spoken aloud. Her head dropped and Twister gave me an apologetic shrug. It wasn't important.

The Gowk turned his wizened face to mine. 'Don't take any unnecessary risks, lass. If we get caught it'll be pure shite, but it won't make any difference to the fight. If *you* get caught, it'll be a different story. You're the face of the resistance now. We need you.' He snorted, a phlegmy sound that wasn't particularly healthy. 'The whole city needs you.'

'The whole country,' Fee corrected. Her voice was quiet, but her gaze remained intent. 'You're the figurehead we can all get behind.'

A figurehead was a token, nothing more than a symbol, but I couldn't disagree. Much as I hated it, I knew what they meant. The Mages' campaign against me, which had gained considerable traction after I had killed the Ascendant, was creating a groundswell of feeling amongst the ordinary folk of Glasgow. The city's passive acceptance of a shitty situation was beginning to change, and we could all feel it happening. If my face helped with that, I couldn't argue about it.

The Gowk squeezed my shoulder with his clawed, misshapen hand, then grabbed Fee. Without another word, they walked out of John McAllan's back door to the snicket at the right of the house. I held my breath and waited for several beats until they were out of sight. There were no cries of alarm. Not yet.

I gestured to Flora and Jane, who slipped out silently and took the side street to the left. Ailsa, Trish and Lottie followed them, and a moment later it was Belle and Twister's turn. After they had departed with stiff backs and hurried steps, I adjusted the bag on my shoulder and nodded to McAllan.

That was when there was a loud thump on the front door.

'Open up in the name of the Mages! We must search these premises!'

I reached for the trapdoor and closed it, and McAllan hurriedly pushed the rug on top to hide it. The Mages would find it within seconds, but that was okay. There was nobody down there, not any more.

'Go,' McAllan said to me. 'Go now.'

I nodded, and then I was out in the fresh air. It was tempting to pick up my grubby skirts and run as fast as my legs would carry me, but that would only draw attention. I forced my feet to maintain a steady pace as I drew out a dark scarf, wrapped it around my head and knotted it under my chin. The dye I'd used to cover my natural red hair ten days ago was already fading, and there was danger from overhead as well as from street level.

I altered my gait to a shuffle; it wouldn't hurt to cover all bases. It was as well that I did because a few seconds later I heard the harsh caw of a raven above me. I bit the inside of my cheek, drawing blood, but my pace remained steady. As long as the bird believed I was nothing more than an old woman out to do her messages, I'd slip by.

There was another caw. The bird passed over, flapping its heavy wings as it circled away in search of more interesting prey. I heaved a shuddering breath and kept moving. I'm nobody, I projected. There is nothing to see here.

I reached the end of the first street and crossed over. Less than two hundred metres away, the weekday market would be full of people at this time of day. I could easily lose myself in the crowd and I'd be safe. I could only pray that the others were safe, too.

As I prepared to turn right towards the market square, three black-cloaked Mages appeared from the next cross-roads. I faltered. If I kept going, I'd pass right by them. Shite: now I'd have to go the opposite way and take the long way round.

Before I could turn, however, one of the Mages raised his head and clocked me.

There was nothing to suggest he'd seen my face, and at that distance the headscarf was enough to keep me safe, but if I didn't change direction I'd pass within five metres of the sinister trio. On the other hand, if I altered my course I'd draw their attention. The Mage would be bound to follow and inves-tigate – and he'd bring his chums with him. More would prob-ably appear.

I could take one down in a fight, even two; in fact, I could probably hold my own against all three of them if I had to. But there were too many other magical bastards nearby, and it wouldn't be long before I'd be confronting three dozen Mages, instead of merely three.

I was between a rock and a hard place. Perhaps there was something to be said for hiding in plain sight. I'd have to keep going and hope they didn't notice my face and recognise me. I cursed silently and shuffled towards them.

I wasn't the only person out on the street, and I certainly wasn't the only person who was nervous of the Mages. Several other passers-by were giving them a wide berth, and a small child screamed and hid in his mother's skirts. As I drew closer, an older gentleman with scraggy grey beard and tattered clothes spat on the ground when he saw them. He was fortunate that they didn't notice.

Once I was close enough, I sneaked a quick glance at the Mages' faces. I recognised two of them: Alex, who was one of the nicer ones – if that were possible – and Michael. He had been a friend of Ross, and he possessed a similar cruel streak to the now dead Mage.

The third was older, and I couldn't recall seeing his face before. When I heard his voice, I realised why: his accent suggested Edinburgh. Either he was in Glasgow on a casual visit, or Mages from other cities had been drafted in to find me and my group of renegades. I hoped that wasn't the case although, given that I'd killed the Glaswegian Ascendant a mere three weeks earlier, my hopes were likely forlorn.

'You!' the third Mage barked at a young woman hauling her shopping along the street. 'Halt there!'

She dropped her bags and stared at him, wide-eyed and trembling. 'Aye, my Lord?'

'What's your name?'

She looked terrified but she stood her ground and resisted the temptation to flee. She licked her lips and lifted her chin. 'Kate Stewart.' Then, 'I'm not in the resistance. And I'm not the one who killed the Ascendant.' She paused. 'But I would have slit his throat and pissed on his corpse if I'd had the chance.'

Oh no.

The Mage reacted instantly, raising his fist and punching the side of her head. She went reeling and her head cracked against the wall behind her. Alex stepped forward and, for one optimistic moment, I thought he was going to stop his companion from hurting her again. Before he could say anything, however, Michael spoke up. 'Let's take her in for questioning.'

'She doesn't know anything,' Alex said.

The Edinburgh Mage sniffed. 'So? This city has gone soft. If you don't deal with this sort of insolence now, especially from a female of all creatures, there's no telling where it might lead.'

I closed my eyes. I should get involved. The Mages were doing this because of me, but the Gowk's warning flashed through my mind. I glanced at the woman and noted the blood trickling from her nose, then shuffled past with my head down. Shame and guilt marked my soul with a heavy stamp.

Coward. Fucking coward. I couldn't deny it, least of all to myself. I turned the corner while hot tears of impotent rage filled my eyes. I was nobody's saviour and nobody's hero. In fact, given that woman was attacked because of my actions, I was quite possibly the villain. I should go back, I should do something, *any*thing. I clenched my fists – but then I sensed another Mage approaching, and this one was heading right for me.

My tear-laden eyes flicked towards him and my heart stopped. Noah. Oh fuck.

He had a raven perched on his shoulder and his cloak was swirling behind him. He was going to pass within inches of me. There was no chance of escape. Once upon a time, he'd wined and dined me; now he'd move heaven and earth to strike me dead.

The raven's glassy eyes glittered with fixed, beady malevolence. I held my breath, certain that either the bird or Noah would glance at me and the game would be up, but with my hunched shoulders, bedraggled dress and aged appearance, I was apparently beneath their notice. Neither of them looked at me, not for a second.

When they drew abreast, I could have reached out and touched Noah or plucked a midnight-black feather from the damned bird, but I kept my hands by my sides. Noah's familiar scent tickled my nostrils.

And then somewhere behind me, Kate Stewart cried out, her voice filled with pain and anguish. Noah's face spasmed with vicious satisfaction. He didn't know who she was but her terror pleased him. Then he passed by, sweeping down the pavement and away from me.

I shook my head. The sensible thing was to get away from this place and the swarming Mages, but the expression in Noah's eyes had tipped me over the edge. My tongue darted out and I licked my lips, then I pivoted and hummed to draw on the power that lay deep in my belly. *Ins Veil.*

It wasn't a breeze that stirred the sunlit air, it was a powerful, cold whoosh that rattled nearby windows. It had enough force to rip the scarf from my head and lift my skirts up to my waist; it also knocked the four Mages, Noah included, off their feet. Their bodies slammed to the ground. Even the raven spiralled backwards.

Kate Stewart was unharmed by my magic because I'd made sure she wasn't included in my attack. I raised my eyes to hers and she stared straight back. She was cradling one arm and even from a distance I could see it was broken. My jaw tightened. The Mages had done that.

She nodded, her face white, then spun away, fleeing the scene and the fallen Mages as fast as she could. As soon as she'd vanished, I sprinted in the opposite direction.

If I didn't escape now, I'd be dead within the hour.

CHAPTER

TWO

The passers-by had scattered, running and ducking for cover to avoid getting caught up in the attack. I didn't look at their pinched, scared faces, I simply ran, my feet slapping hard into the dirt and dust.

The magic strike had taken a lot out of me, but I was far from done yet. It was just as well; the Mages wouldn't stay down for long.

From the outraged shriek that tore through the air, it was clear that the raven had recovered first. I didn't look back – I didn't have time. Instead, I spun right to cross the street and immediately I felt a rush of magic chasing after me. One of the Mages, probably Noah, had thrown something in my direction. I couldn't tell what the spell was, but I knew it wouldn't be good.

I hummed a single note in the nick of time: *Vaz*. My body juddered and shook when the attacking magic slammed into the invisible wall I'd created. I gasped with the effort of maintaining it and the wall held – but only just. It wouldn't protect me against a second attack, and I still had to get away.

I changed direction, swerving left out of the Mages' line of sight. The raven screeched again, filling the air with its fury. I had to hide somewhere the damned bird couldn't see me from above, but there was nowhere obvious. The streets here were too wide and there was no cover, and I couldn't slip into a building because I'd be putting the inhabitants in danger and making myself a sitting duck. There had to be somewhere to go, somewhere I could hide. I wasn't dead yet.

I squinted. There was a deep alcove next to the greengrocers on my right. It was far from ideal but it was the best place on offer. Anyone passing at ground level would see me in an instant, and it wouldn't be long before Noah and the others caught me up. Fool the bird first, I told myself, then worry about the Mages.

I darted towards the recess and all but threw myself into its limited shelter. Was it enough? Would the raven see me? Eejit, Mairi, a voice in my head chided me. You could have gotten away. You've risked everything for one person.

I suddenly smiled. One person counted; one person was enough. No matter what the Gowk said, nobody was irreplaceable. If the Mages caught me now, others would take up the baton because the momentum was already there.

Then the raven cawed in triumph as it spotted me and my heart screamed panic. I was human enough to still be afraid.

I drew in a ragged breath and twisted my head to stare upwards. I doubted I had the precision to hit the bird with my magic while it flew overhead, but I had to try.

There was a flicker of movement in my peripheral vision and I glanced down. A boy was standing less than twenty metres away from the grocer's with a sling in his small, grubby hands. He couldn't be more than ten years old – but that wouldn't matter if the Mages caught him.

I flapped my hands at him urgently. He had to stop, to get

away and hide. With the misplaced confidence of youth, he ignored my pleading gestures, flashed me a cheeky grin and aimed the sling. A single white pebble pinged forward and the boy smirked with satisfaction. A beat later, there was a strangled squawk followed by a dull thud. Bloody hell, he'd done it. His confidence hadn't been misplaced after all.

I stared, then bowed in his direction because I couldn't think of what else to do. His face broke into a wreath of smiles and he raised his hand in a smart salute. I saluted back.

A shout drifted over from the street behind us and my blood turned to ice. 'She must be this way! Move it! Where are the fucking ravens?' That was Noah.

I waved frantically at the boy, but once again he was a step ahead of me. He stuffed the sling down the front of his stained shirt and turned away, walking casually towards the Mages rather than away from them. He was going to use the same trick I'd tried earlier and stroll right past them, a perfect picture of childish innocence.

He turned the corner and vanished. Holding my breath, I waited another beat.

'You boy!' It was the Edinburgh Mage. 'Have you seen anyone run past here?'

'Aye, sir. There was a woman. She went that way, towards the river.'

I was moving *away* from the river. I sent a sincere prayer of gratitude to the lad whose courage and valour were enough to match a dozen Mages, then I slipped out from the alcove and set off at a brisk pace towards the market – and away from my pursuers.

THE THRONG of people around the market stalls made it difficult to get around but easy to hide. Although I sensed that most of the crowd would be on my side, it was wise to maintain my anonymity; after all, not everyone was against our magical overlords.

I averted my face from everyone I passed. The boy had brought down one raven but plenty more would be taking to the skies, and the Mages would soon realise they'd been sent on a wild goose chase and circle back. It was imperative that I was ready to face them again. Nobody possessed an inexhaustible supply of magic, and I'd already depleted a considerable amount of energy.

I wove in and out of the crowd, catching snatches and snippets of conversation as I went.

'Things'll get worse for us. We're all scunnered now. You'll see,' one man said. 'They'll choose a new Ascendant and crack down across the city.'

'I heard it'll be next week,' his companion said. 'By Monday there'll be a new fucker in charge.'

'It takes longer than that. Whoever they choose, you ken that things'll no' be good for us. It's always the wee folk like us that suffer.' He wasn't wrong there.

I grimaced and moved out of their way.

'Mairi Wallace has got daemon blood,' a woman was saying to a group of friends. 'And she's seven foot tall.'

Wait. Was she talking about me?

'I heard her hair turns to fire when she gets angry,' somebody added.

'And she's already killed twenty Mages,' the first woman nodded. 'With her bare hands. Her magic is stronger than all the other Ascendants put together.'

'But – but – girls dinnae have magic,' a young girl interrupted. She hesitated. 'Do they?'

'We've been lied to, lass,' the woman told her grimly. 'For far too fucking long. You cannae trust anything those Mages have told you.'

That part was definitely true, though nothing else was. I put my head down still further. I'd already lingered too long to eavesdrop and I didn't want to draw attention to myself.

I squeezed round a bickering couple and narrowly avoided a yapping dog that had slipped its leash. By the time I reached the opposite end of the market and the crowds were starting to thin, I was breathing more easily.

But suddenly the back of my neck prickled. Somebody was watching me.

I turned my head very slowly. When I saw Ailsa's clever eyes fixed on me, my shoulders sagged with relief, but then I frowned. She was supposed to be with Trish and Lottie.

My thoughts were more obvious than I'd realised. Ailsa jerked her chin and I glanced over, registering both younger women at a baker's stall. I bit back my flash of annoyance that they were risking their lives for a snack. They knew the dangers and had the right to make their own choices, daft as I thought those choices were.

I nodded at Ailsa in acknowledgment, but I didn't dare wander over. Baker's delights aside, the three of them were safe enough for now and we'd meet soon at the next location. It was better for all of us if we stayed separate until then. However, Ailsa jerked her chin again and stepped to the left. That was when I saw the poster.

It wasn't one of the usual ones. The Mages had put up posters around the city emblazoned with a depiction of my face that was designed to make me appear as evil and threatening as possible. They were usually accompanied with metaphorical sticks warning that anyone who harboured me would suffer terrible, torturous consequences, or juicy carrots promising magnificent rewards for information leading to my whereabouts.

This poster was very different. Although it was definitely me, and it was a copy of the version the Mages had put up, in this poster I looked softer. My skin glowed and my eyes were wider than normal. I was ... pretty.

I glanced at the words scrawled underneath: *She Will Save Us*. My stomach tightened. Having someone to front the revolt was necessary to galvanise the city, but if people placed me on a pedestal I'd end up falling. Hard. And then the Mages would win, the way they always did.

Ailsa looked at me questioningly and I shook my head, indicating my unhappiness. She blinked her understanding. Hero worship helped none of us; in fact, it was probably hero worship that had allowed the Mages to rise to the position they were in now.

I gestured to Ailsa that I'd see her soon. She squinted as she tried to decipher my hand movements – she wasn't adept at communicating without words. As I tried again, there was a flash of light and an ear-splitting gong reverberated around the square, so loud that the ground trembled beneath my feet. Several people screamed, others cowered, but most were frozen into inaction.

'Good people of Glasgow.'

My mouth dried at the sound of Noah's voice. Was I never going to be free of him? I whipped around, trying to locate him. Where was he? He had to be using magic to project his words, but I knew he wasn't far away.

I couldn't see him or any other Mages. Ailsa's eyes were wide and fearful as she looked at me for reassurance. I gave her a quick, tight smile as Flora and Jane left the cake stall and joined her. Flora's mouth opened when she saw me, but Jane jabbed her in the ribs and she snapped it shut.

'Do not be alarmed,' Noah's voice continued. 'These are troubled, turbulent times, but I can assure you that the Mages of this fine and beautiful city are continuing to do all they can to keep you safe. There is considerable danger, but together we will defeat it. We are already making progress with our research into the Afflicted, and we are confident that it won't be long until we can save those sorry souls.'

Most of the crowd in front of me appeared to be recovering from the shock of hearing a disembodied voice boom out from nowhere – and few of them looked happy. 'Aye,' someone muttered loudly enough for others to hear, 'well, that's pure shite.'

'Alas,' Noah continued, 'our work is being interrupted by a small but incredibly dangerous group of people who are seeking to undermine our work. These terrorists do not care what happens to Glasgow. They spit on the sanctity of Scotland and would happily see you all dead. They present a very real danger to us all.'

My body rigid with tension, I glanced around again and noted the curled lips and muted snorts of derision.

'They present a danger to the Mages, nay to us,' an old woman shouted in a quavering voice. There was a loud murmur of agreement.

Despite the protests, I couldn't relax. Noah was leading up to something; this was a planned speech that I was certain would go beyond mere propaganda.

'It gives us no pleasure to say this, but we must catch these renegades to keep our city safe. We are counting on you, the fine people of Glasgow, to help us. Our concerns are for the greater good, so we have no choice but to take drastic measures. If the whereabouts of the terrorists are not made known to us, every twelve hours we will select a street at random and decimate its inhabitants.'

Ailsa's face was pale, Flora looked as if she were about to vomit and Jane's lips were pulled back over her teeth in a silent snarl. When he said decimate, did he mean...?

'To be clear,' Noah said, with a note of faked sadness that turned my stomach, 'at dawn tomorrow morning, we will execute every tenth person on a random street of the city. If we still do not find the terrorists, we will select another street at dusk and do the same. Harsh as this may seem, we must do everything we can to keep the city safe. Tell us where we can find those outlaws who are threatening the well-being of Glasgow and the decimation will stop immediately.'

He paused then cried, 'Lang may all yer lums reek.' In other words, may all your chimneys smell for a long time. Good luck and good fortune for the future.

My shoulders slumped. There was a loud crackle followed by another booming gong; Noah was done – at least for now. And we were well and truly fucked.

CHAPTER

THREE

My tight boots were pinching my toes, and my bones felt heavy with fatigue. It wasn't simply the after effects of the magic and the panic of the escape from John McAllan's that were making me feel exhausted, it was the knowledge that whatever we did the Mages would always be stronger. They'd always have the upper hand.

I kicked a small grey stone along the street and watched it bounce a few metres in front of me. Then I kicked it again and it skittered towards the dirty gutter.

I'd left the market not long after Noah had finished his speech, as did most of the crowd. It seemed nobody had the stomach for shopping or gossiping any longer. I avoided looking at Ailsa, Flora and Jane because I didn't want to see the inevitable defeat reflected in their eyes. We'd meet up at the new safe house soon and decide what to do next – although there wasn't any real choice. The Mages had seen to that. I'd wandered aimlessly for a good hour or so, my thoughts churning over what to do. No satisfactory answers presented themselves; there was no sensible way out of the trap the Mages had set.

I side-stepped and aimed my foot at the little stone again, but my frustration got the better of me and I missed it altogether. I cursed inwardly and, in a fit of futile anger, crouched down and scooped it up before throwing it towards a crumbling wall several metres away.

There was a muted thud as stone hit stone. The pebble ricocheted to the left and landed a few feet away, and I gazed at it dully before looking up at the old wall. There was something scratched into the surface of one of the bricks.

I frowned as I drew closer. There were three horizontal scratches with two shorter diagonal slashes branching off them. It was crude but obviously deliberate, like a secret sign or a special rune. I reached out and traced the design with the tip of my finger. Odd.

The bell that heralded dusk was approaching rang out, and I jumped and shook myself. I had to get a move on. I straightened my shoulders and scurried towards the small church that was the location of the next safe house.

The doors were closed. I checked up and down the empty street for any sign of watchers and, finding none, knocked once and made my way inside. The interior was dark and gloomy, and there were no signs of life.

A figure darted out from behind one of the shadowy pews brandishing a small knife in my direction. Fee jabbed the blade towards me before relaxing and dropping her arm. 'Mairi,' she said, relief etching her lined face. 'You made it.'

I raised my eyebrows in question and she nodded. 'The others are all here. Ailsa and the two girls walked in about five minutes ago – they said they saw you at the market. That you were together when…' Her voice trailed off, her jaw tightened and she raised her chin. 'Lord Noah must have used magic to project his voice like that because we all heard him. His words were broadcast across the whole city.'

Aye, I'd figured as much. I nodded and Fee reached out and took one of my hands. 'It'll be alright,' she whispered. 'We're going to find a way to stop them.'

Despite her words, she didn't sound any more optimistic than I felt. However, she pasted on a smile and stepped past me to bolt the church door against the potential horrors of the approaching night. Then she led me up the aisle towards a small antechamber where the rest of my small group had gathered.

When I raised my hand in greeting, the Gowk jerked his head gruffly. Belle, of all people, got to her feet and pulled me into a hug. I was startled enough to remain still, my arms by my sides.

I suspected her sudden show of warmth was as much for the others as it was for me. I knew Belle was afraid of me, but she was afraid of the others as well and wanted to prove her worth. When she eventually realised I wasn't reciprocating, she released me and returned to her place. The wooden chair creaked beneath her weight.

'Here.' Lottie pressed a small package into my hands. 'We saved you a scone.'

I mouthed my thanks, suddenly more than glad she'd taken the risk of going to the baker's stall, and started to unwrap it.

'The priest who runs this place knows we're here,' Flora told me. 'We can stay till Sunday morning.' That was five days away; the Mages could execute dozens of people before then. I didn't think any of us would still be here by Sunday.

My thoughts must have been written on my face because Twister cleared his throat and declared in an unnecessarily loud voice, 'We all made it here, and we're all safe. That's a very good thing.' He wasn't wrong, but he only received several unenthusiastic nods for his efforts.

Jane scowled. 'Aye, we're safe, but the rest of the city isn't.'

Lottie sniffed, her eyes watery. 'Those bastards have never done that before. They've never broadcast to everyone like that at the same time. I didna ken they could, and I worked at the City Chambers for more than five years.'

'I don't know what magic enabled them to do that either.' The Gowk's thin lips pursed. 'But that bampot must have borrowed from the other Mages to gain the surge of power he needed to project his voice.'

Trish fiddled with the cuffs of her dirty blouse. 'They won't really go through with it, will they?' she asked in a small voice. 'They won't really kill innocent people just to find us?' Nobody answered. We already knew the answer, and so did she.

'We'll find a way to stop them,' Fee said.

I knew there was no way to stop them.

'How many Mages are there?' Twister asked.

Too many. My eyes dropped and I bit off a mouthful of scone. It was dry and hard, but it was better than nothing.

Ailsa shrugged. 'Around three hundred.' She hesitated. 'But they seem to have brought in extra from Edinburgh, so there's probably a good deal more of them than normal.'

'Is your magic strong enough to beat over three hundred Mages?' Twister asked me.

As if. I chewed some more.

'We didna ken which street they're going to target first. If we could find that out, we could lie in wait and launch a surprise attack. Mairi's no' the only one with magic,' Flora said with shaky bravado, while nervously rubbing at the birth mark on her wrist.

She had magic of her own, and so did Fee, Jane and the

Gowk, but they didn't have enough – none of us had enough. I swallowed my mouthful and didn't respond.

Fee nudged me. 'We cannae just give up, lass,' she said. 'No' now. No' after everything we've achieved so far.'

Uh-huh.

Ailsa clicked her tongue. 'We've all had a long day and we're all tired,' she said. 'We can't go out now it's dark, so I vote we have a few hours' sleep. When we're more refreshed, we can think of a way around the Mages' plans.' She glanced at me. 'Mairi?'

A few hours' sleep was the best idea any of us could have had. I jerked my head in agreement.

'When we're rested and refreshed, we'll be able to think straight,' Fee said. 'We're nae beaten yet.'

I looked down, while everyone else forced smiles. Laoch's handsome face flashed into my mind. What was he doing right now? Was he thinking of me? I sighed and nodded. 'Sleep,' I whispered to my feet, 'is a good plan.'

Despite the upcoming turmoil and the knot of anxiety that was growing in the pit of my stomach, I slept soundly for three hours on the church floor. I probably had Belle and Twister to thank for my ability to crash out when I needed to. My narrow bed in the attic above their tartan shop had been nearly as hard as this floor, and during my years working for them sleep had been just as precious. I'd learned that you could adapt to your circumstances, no matter how dire they were.

It was difficult to tell what time it was when I woke, but the deep darkness of the room with its one small window high in the far wall told me that there were hours to go before dawn.

I could hear two hushed voices talking quietly in the corner: Jane and Ailsa. I kept my eyes shut and listened.

'She doesnae say much. She couldnae speak before, and she doesnae really speak now.'

'That lass has spent a lifetime in silence. It's a hard habit to break.' Ailsa understood me better than I'd given her credit for.

'If it were me,' Jane replied, 'I'd talk all the time. I'd have so much to say. And whit aboot that daemon? Where did he go?'

'I don't know. We should be glad he's gone. He's no' to be trusted.'

'But we all saw the way that he looked at her. Something happened between them – you must have felt it too. She killed the Ascendant because of something that daemon did, and after that she could talk! Just like that!'

That something had been Laoch silently telling me he loved me. Recently, I'd had a lot of time to think about that moment. His proclamation of love hadn't been real; we didn't know each other well enough for that. And it wasn't his supposed love that had broken whatever was forcing me into silence, it was the knowledge that he had my back, that there was somebody who was completely on my side. Not only did he want to help and protect me, but he also had the skills to do so.

At the end of the day, we all needed to know we weren't alone. He'd done that for me, and then he'd gone because he was needed elsewhere. The Mages had enslaved him and he had to return to the family he'd not seen for years. I couldn't blame him – we all had our own responsibilities – but selfishly I wished he were here now.

I didn't dare demand it or pout about it; he'd been mine for little more than a few days. I had to be satisfied with that because it was all I was going to get.

'Like I said,' Ailsa muttered, 'he's no' to be trusted.'

They lapsed into silence for a moment or two, then Jane whispered, 'We're going to have to give ourselves up to the Mages, aren't we?'

'Looks like it.'

'They'll kill us.'

'Aye. They will,' Ailsa said. 'But if we give ourselves up to appease those bastards, Mairi will stay free. There'll still be hope for Glasgow and for Scotland.'

So that was the plan; I'd feared as much.

The problem was that it was me the Mages really wanted. They wouldn't cancel their plans for multiple executions because Jane or Ailsa or anyone else walked into the City Chambers with their hands in the air. They'd only stop when I did because I had the most magic – and I'd killed their leader.

'Wheesht now,' Ailsa said, not unkindly. 'You should get some rest. Tomorrow will be a long day.'

'Aye.' Jane sighed. Several seconds ticked by then she murmured, 'I wouldn't do it differently, you know. If I'd known this was how things were going to turn out, I'd still have helped her.'

Ailsa didn't hesitate. 'So would I.'

Hot tears pricked the back of my eyes, and I clenched my jaw so tightly it was painful. I had to stay quiet; I couldn't allow myself to sob aloud.

By the time I had control of myself again, Ailsa and Jane were exhaling the soft regular breaths of sleep. I swallowed hard, stretched my legs and stood up carefully. It was time to go.

As I tiptoed to the door and placed my hand on it, a voice drifted across the darkness. The Gowk: of course it was him. He'd understand more than the others; long ago he'd been in a similar position himself. 'Good luck, lass,' he whispered. Then he added shakily, 'When the martyr dies, her power begins.'

I hoped he was right. 'Thank you,' I replied. I swallowed. 'You should all leave at first light. I won't be able to hold my tongue for long.'

'No,' the Gowk said sadly. 'You won't.'

I sighed, and then I left.

CHAPTER

FOUR

There was something about walking on dark streets that provided a fearful thrill. The night belonged to the Afflicted, and it was rarely wise to wander around after the sun had fallen, but needs must.

I had the power to protect myself as long as I didn't stroll into a nest of the sorry pock-marked creatures, so I didn't cower or skulk. This was the best course of action – shite, it was the *only* course of action. What happened afterwards would be up to the others.

I followed the river for a long time. The murky water and faint reek of sewage weren't particularly pleasant, and neither was the glimmering layer of oil that lay restlessly on the surface, but there was a decent breeze that rippled through my hair and cooled my skin. It reminded me that I was alive, at least for now. It also helped clear my head and clarify my thoughts.

I hummed quietly as I walked, allowing the air around me to shiver with unfocused magic. I only fell silent when I turned away from the water along the wide street that led directly to the City Chambers. That was when I started to take more care and keep an eye out for any patrolling Mages. I didn't want to get caught until I was ready. This was going to be on my terms, not theirs.

When I turned the last corner and the spires of the City Chambers came into sight, stark against the bright moon, I heaved in a breath and squared my shoulders. My hands were shaking and there was a churning nausea in my belly. Death didn't scare me, but torture was another matter.

I closed my eyes briefly. Somewhere to the west there was a guttural scream, but it sounded far off. The Afflicted rarely came this close to the Mages' stronghold; they had their own good reasons to be wary of the Mages.

I cricked my neck first one way then the other, stretched out my arms, opened my eyes and gazed forward. I was as ready as I'd ever be. Time to go, Mairi. Time to do this.

I darted across the street, keeping low and moving swiftly. The ravens, with their watchful beady eyes, would be asleep with their heads tucked under their wings. I couldn't risk waking any of them up because I didn't want to alert the Mages to my presence. Not yet.

Within seconds, I'd reached the imposing stone walls of the City Chambers. I pressed my back against them and waited for several seconds. There were no caws of alarm – I'd not been spotted. I was still safe.

I swallowed hard and scurried round to the heavy oak doors, hoping that my decision to enter through the front entrance was a sensible one. Surely it was the last thing they'd be expecting?

I reached for the ornate iron handle and pushed, and there was a jarring creak as the wood strained against my touch. I winced – and the doors remained resolutely closed. I hissed under my breath. They were locked. That was not what I'd been hoping for.

I'd have to spin some magic to get in, and there was every chance that the hundreds of Mages inside would instantly sense me. I didn't even know if I had the right word; I'd not tested it out before, but I'd read it in one of the spell books I'd snooped through when I'd worked here.

My muscles tensed. I crossed my fingers then hummed a single note. *Brashar.* Open.

Both oak doors burst open with such violent force that they slammed against the stone walls and splintered. Shite – I'd thrown too much power at them. I gulped hard and ran, sprinting into the City Chambers at high speed. At least I knew where to hide.

My boots slipped and skidded on the marble floor as I heard shouts from deep within the building and the sound of running feet. With blood roaring in my ears, I dived into the dark alcove where I used to hide and watch the Mages – and Laoch – then I whipped round and waited, my heart thudding painfully against my ribcage.

Less than five seconds later, dozens of black-cloaked Mages swirled into the entrance hall. My breath sounded painfully loud and I clamped my hand over my mouth. Fortunately the Mages were yelling loudly enough to mask the sound, but I wasn't taking any chances.

'What the fuck was that?'

'The doors!'

Several of the magical bastards rushed over. The door on the right had a crack running down its centre, and the left one was hanging off its hinges. I didn't know my own strength. That was some spell.

Noah appeared from behind the grand staircase and strode forward, his expression thunderous. He stalked up to the doors and sniffed. 'It's her,' he said shortly. 'It's her signature.' He glowered out into the night and jerked his hand towards a half dozen of his cronies. 'Get out there and see if you can find her. She won't have gotten far. You might yet catch her.'

They nodded eagerly and ran outside. Noah turned to the others. 'She's sending us a message,' he bit out, angry blue flames licking at his fingers as he clenched and unclenched his fists.

'What message?' a younger Mage asked, his eyes wide.

'She wants us to think that she can attack us. She's obviously trying to put a stop to the decimations tomorrow. Well, we can send a message back. We won't target one random street, we'll target *three*. Let's see what she does then. Stupid bitch – she's not going to win against us. Once we start killing three times as many people, someone out there will tell us where she is.'

I gazed at him from my dark corner. The trouble with Noah was that he believed I thought in the same way that he did. He believed that I'd never willingly give myself up because he would attack if he were in my position, so that's what he thought I was doing. He really wasn't particularly intelligent.

Unfortunately for me, Noah wasn't the only Mage with authority. The older Mage from Edinburgh swept forward. 'She might have sneaked inside.'

My mouth went dry.

Noah shook his head. 'She wouldn't dare.'

'She dared to break open our front doors.'

Noah's eyes narrowed. 'Lord Aspen...'

There was a polite but insistent cough from the staircase. 'Lord Aspen is right. We need to check inside the City Chambers as well as outside.'

I turned my head and stared. Mage Angus. What the hell was he doing? He smiled at the cluster of Mages and walked down the rest of the stairs. 'I have just the spell,' he said, bowing towards Lord Aspen.

The Edinburgh Mage nodded sharply. 'Get on with it. If the magic bitch is inside these walls, we need to know about it.'

Oh no.

So much for my other plans. It appeared the game – such as it was – was already up. I dropped my head, closed my eyes and waited. Maybe, I thought hopefully, they'd strike me dead when they found me so we could skip the whole torture section of tonight's show. That would be the best outcome.

I reached for the tendrils of magic within me and prepared myself. If I attacked them with all I had, they'd have no choice but to attack me back. It could work.

Angus coughed again. '*Fel za tum,*' he intoned. The air crackled with his magic and for the first time I realised quite how powerful he was. His magic rushed towards me and wrapped invisible hands round my throat. It knew I was here, and so did Angus.

I stifled a choke. I wasn't going to show any weakness, not to these bastards.

'The building is clear,' Angus declared. 'Nobody is inside these walls who shouldn't be.'

I frowned and lifted my head.

'See?' Noah said, with enough of a sneer in his tone to sound insolent. 'She wouldn't *dare* enter the City Chambers. Mairi's teasing us from outside. She's too cowardly to come in. She knows what would happen to her if she did.'

Lord Aspen gave him a cool glance. 'Your uncle may well have been the Ascendant, Lord Noah, but I am in charge here until a replacement is chosen. You would do well to remember that.'

Noah stared back defiantly, then looked away. I almost laughed aloud.

Aspen approached the doors and looked them up and down. 'She has power,' he mused. 'That will help us once we get hold of her. We need more magic.' He flicked his wrists at the broken wood. '*Finza.*'

There was a crack and a shudder, the doors righted themselves, the splintered fissure sealed over and the hinge reattached itself. Aspen reached across and closed them.

'We should wait,' Noah said. 'The others might find her outside.'

Aspen had already started walking away. 'They won't. This one is too smart to get caught.' He paused. 'Yet.' He turned. 'Go back to your rooms. Tomorrow will be a long but necessary day.'

The other Mages immediately dispersed, melting away to whichever grim corners and shady work spaces they'd sprung from. Angus turned on his heel and marched back up the stairs. Noah stared after Aspen with a glint of hatred in his eyes, then he also whirled away.

Only moments after I'd stormed the entrance to the City Chambers, I was alone again. Unbelievable.

I stayed there for several minutes, each second filled with almost unbearable tension. I didn't know if the Mages who'd been dispatched outside would return soon, or if any of the others would come through the entrance hall on their way to another part of the building. But nobody appeared again; for now, my way was clear.

I shook my head, still amazed that I'd not been clapped in chains, then I straightened my shoulders. Onwards and upwards, Mairi, I told myself. You know where to go.

Despite my good luck so far, I wasn't daft enough to risk the main stairs. Instead, I twisted to the left and made a beeline for the servants' staircase. At this hour none of my old workmates would be around; after the commotion that just occurred, none of them would want to be, either. I reckoned I'd have a free run up to the second floor.

I sidled over to the small door and nipped inside before tiptoeing up the narrow curving staircase. I paused at the door to the second floor and listened for any signs of life. Eventually, when there was nothing but silence, I stole out and scurried towards the far end of the hallway.

When I reached the final door, I raised my fist. Should I knock or not? I decided to open it without announcing my presence; after all, he already knew I was coming .

Angus was seated in a high-backed chair facing the doorway. As I stepped inside, he raised the glass in his hand and took a sip. 'Well, you took your fucking time.'

I closed the door behind me and eyed him.

'Cat got your tongue?' he enquired. 'And here was I thinking you'd found your voice. That's what I was told.'

I glared at him; he was as irritating as ever. I folded my arms and squinted. 'Why didn't you tell your chums where I was? Why did you lie?'

He appeared to consider the question. 'Things have been rather dull here since you left. I thought I might spice matters up a little before I handed you over.'

'You think planning to decimate a street tomorrow is dull?'

'It's three streets now, darling,' he drawled. 'Besides, that's not happened yet.' His eyes gleamed. 'Who knows what might occur between now and then?' He put down his glass and leaned forward. 'So go on, then. Why are you here and what are you planning?'

I walked over, picked up the glass and drained it, then I choked. Shite. That was strong stuff. I returned the glass to the side table. 'I'm going to give myself up to prevent anyone else from dying,' I said matter-of-factly. 'But before I do that, you're going to help me.'

For a brief moment, Angus looked satisfyingly nonplussed, then he shrugged. 'And why,' he asked, 'would I do that?'

'Because if you don't, I'll tell the lot of them that you've helped me before. I might even embellish the truth and make things worse for you than they already are.'

Angus tilted his head. 'You know, I liked you better when you didn't talk.'

I smiled at him; my smile didn't reach my eyes.

He sighed. 'What do you need?'

'You're going to help the resistance. You're going to make sure that after I'm dead the rest of your little magic friends leave them alone. You're going to pass the resistance members copies of your best magic books so that those who have magic – including the females – can practise it and improve. And you're going to do whatever you can to help the people of this city survive.'

The old Mage stared at me unblinkingly for several long seconds. 'There are several flaws in your plan.' He stood up, rubbed the small of his back and picked up his glass before walking to the sideboard and re-filling it with amber liquid from a cut-glass decanter. He took a long draught and turned to me.

'First of all,' he said, 'you'll be dead, so any threats or blackmail will no longer work because you won't be around to check up on my efforts. Secondly, what's the actual end game here? What do you want to happen? You can't rid the city of all the Mages because, whether you despise us or not, you need us to keep the Afflicted at bay. Frankly, you need us more than we need you.'

'You're supposed to serve the city of Glasgow, not subjugate it,' I spat.

'That's as may be, but it doesn't change the bottom line.' As he gazed at me, a tiny smile played around his mouth. 'The

Ascendant told you, didn't he? Before you killed him, he told you why we don't allow female Mages to exist.'

I stilled. 'He was about to die. He would have said anything to save his sorry skin.'

Angus threw back his head and laughed. 'The Ascendant wasn't afraid of you. He had no need to be afraid. Until you stabbed him, he didn't know what you were capable of. None of us did.' He took another mouthful, swirling it around his mouth and finally swallowing. 'And he didn't lie. We ensure there are no female Mages because they created the Afflicted in the first place. Those creatures are out there suffering a terrible, tragic existence because of people like you.'

No. 'That can't be true.'

His expression didn't alter a jot. 'Believe what you want, but it *is* true. It wasn't deliberate and nobody meant for it to happen, but that doesn't change the fact that if female magic had never existed there would be no Afflicted. We didn't manage to curb the numbers of the diseased until we made sure there were no more little girls with magic running around.'

He paused, drank again then went on. 'It started more than a hundred years ago, well before my time. Almost every child born to a strong female Mage becomes Afflicted, and those children infect others. If it weren't for your sex, the Afflicted wouldn't exist. If the male Mages hadn't taken drastic steps, the whole country could have been annihilated. We *saved* this city by preventing females from practising magic.'

He eyed me. 'So I ask again: what is the end game of the resistance? Because I don't think any of you have really thought this through.'

I pulled over a wooden chair and sat down in front of him without taking my eyes away from his for a second. The more I spoke, the easier it became, and I discovered that I wanted to speak to Angus. Maybe it was because he was a Mage; maybe it was because I liked him, despite my instinctive hatred of his position. Whatever the reason, I wanted him to listen to me and that helped to strengthen my voice. 'We want to be treated like people, not cattle.'

A smirk curled his mouth. 'That's a vague desire. How will you measure your success?'

'When people aren't executed for voicing their opinions.' I gritted my teeth. 'When the Mages don't walk around the city taking whatever they want just because they can. When babies aren't kidnapped because they are girls who have magic.' I paused. 'That would be good for a start. There's plenty more.'

'The populace needs to be kept in check for its own good,' Angus retorted. 'We Mages work hard, and we deserve some sort of reward for our efforts. And, as I have just pointed out, if we don't take those poor little baby girls, the numbers of Afflicted on the streets – on *your* streets – will double. Then triple. Glasgow will be over-run.'

Angus's tone was calm, but there was a glint of a challenge in his eyes. He wanted me to step up, to answer his question and give him an achievable demand. Very well, then.

'Elections,' I said clearly. 'Hold elections where people – *all* people – can vote for leaders who aren't Mages and who don't have magic. Let them vote for citizens who will have overall control of the city, and who will curb the excesses, the executions and the summary judgments that leave the rest of us in constant fear for our lives.'

Angus leaned back in his chair and eyed me for a long moment. 'That's better,' he said finally. 'That's a specific goal.' He wagged his long, bony index finger at me. 'But you still need to address the issue of females with magic. If you don't allow us to take their magic – magic we need to keep the existing Afflicted at bay – are you prepared to tell all the women with any spark of power that they must promise never to reproduce?'

I wasn't sure if I believed that it was female magic that created the Afflicted, but I didn't know enough to argue otherwise. Not yet. 'It's something we could discuss. It's better than what we have right now.'

'And what if someone – perhaps even you – falls pregnant by accident? What then?'

'That wouldn't happen.'

He laughed. 'Why? Because accidents never happen? Or people never change their minds? What if you say you'll never have children when you're sixteen, then at twenty-six you long to have a wee baby in your arms?'

My jaw tightened. 'You're talking about hypotheticals.'

'I must talk about them, and you must consider them. There's more at stake here than the future of your little resistance group.'

I licked my lips and swallowed. My throat was beginning to hurt. I'd probably spoken more to Angus in the last few minutes than I'd ever spoken aloud to anyone. Apart from Laoch at least. 'Is there proof?' I asked.

'That the existence of female Mages causes the Afflicted?'

I nodded.

Angus shrugged. 'I could probably get evidence to prove it to you, but you're about to hand yourself in to be executed so there's not much point.'

The heavy weight pressing down on my shoulders increased. 'If I don't hand myself in,' I whispered, 'others will die.'

Angus scratched his chin, his fingers rasping against his grey stubble. 'Others will die anyway.' A new gleam lit his eyes. 'And you're not seeing the big picture.'

My brow creased. 'I don't know what you're talking about.'

He grinned. 'I know you don't.' He threw the rest of his drink down his throat. 'You heard the words I used to search the building for you?'

I nodded slowly.

'Try them for yourself,' he said.

A tendril of suspicion uncoiled itself. 'Why?'

'Do it.'

I had nothing left to lose, so I tugged on my magic and hummed. *Fel za tum.* The atmosphere thrummed, and I gasped. There were pockets of energy across the City Chambers. I felt Billy, the Mages' gardener, hefting something dangerous in his hands. One of the cooks was reaching for a knife. A maid was spilling kerosene. And outside, a strange pressure was growing in intensity, pushing towards the building with rage and terror – but also hope.

Angus quirked an eyebrow. 'Your latent talent is really quite extraordinary.'

I barely heard him. I screwed up my face as I continued to feel the strange stirrings around the building. 'What's going on?'

'I tried to tell the others.' Angus started gathering some books and papers. 'I tried to warn them that this is what happens when you go balls out to create a martyr.' He gestured to me once more. 'This is why you can't give yourself up. And,' he added ruefully, 'why we all have to run.'

That was when I felt the maid strike a match and bend towards the kerosene, the cook leave the kitchen with a deter-mined stride, Billy sneak up behind a Mage with an axe raised – and the crowd of people outside on the dark streets that surrounded the City Chambers surge forward as one.

CHAPTER

FIVE

I sprang to my feet and stared at Angus. He had turned away to a chest of drawers and was taking out several folded items of clothing. 'What – what – what's happening?'

'What was always going to happen when we Mages push an entire city to breaking point,' he responded with irritating calm. He bent down, picked up a bag and tossed the clothes, books and papers into it. 'Get the cage, would you?'

I remained where I was, gaping at him like an eejit.

'Cage!' he snapped. 'Over there!' He pointed and my eyes followed his finger. Then, on shaky, uncertain legs, I walked to the small cage on Angus's dressing table and gazed down at it.

The tiny mouse inside yawned and squinted up at me. 'Mungo?' I whispered. Was this the same mouse whose body I'd transferred myself to all those weeks ago?

It merely yawned again.

From somewhere below us, there was the sound of splintering glass, then a roar from outside followed by more glass

39

breaking. I grabbed the small cage, darted to the window and peered out.

Even though the magic I'd used had told me what was going on, seeing it with my own eyes made me gasp. There were hundreds of people outside, perhaps even thousands. Some held burning torches aloft; others were carrying sticks and batons. As they surged towards the building, I heard pounding feet and the alarmed cries of the Mages outside Angus's door. The cries of startled ravens waking from their sleep filled the air.

Angus hefted his pack onto his shoulder. 'Let's go.'

I looked away from the window, my confusion continuing to get the better of me.

'If you die this night,' the old Mage said, with only a trace of impatience, 'the whole city will burn. If you live, with luck it will only be this building that goes up in flames.' He stalked over and gave me a tiny shove. 'Now move.'

He spun away. Still holding the cage, I stumbled after him.

Angus opened the door, and I glimpsed several more Mages running towards the stairs. There was an acrid stench in the air: smoke that must be coming from the fire the maid had set below. If someone didn't put it out soon, the whole City Chambers would burn. The books and papers and wooden furniture crammed into every room provided the perfect kindling.

Angus whirled out of the door and marched down the hallway without looking back. All I could do was follow him.

I'd walked this path hundreds of times when I'd worked here as a servant, but it had never been like this. I'd never felt the Mages panic or imagined that people outside would try and attack. There was a series of muffled booms and more cries and, as I stumbled after Angus, his words echoed in my ears: *others will die anyway.* And likely soon. It was that blood-freezing thought that galvanised me into action.

I tightened my grip on the cage and ran, overtaking the old Mage. My boots skidded on the smooth wooden floor, but I didn't falter. I kept going until I reached the head of the stairs and saw the carnage below.

There was no longer just one fire; smoke was billowing into the grand lobby from several directions. The grand oak doors, which Lord Aspen had magically fixed less than an hour ago, had burst open again and the chants and jeers from the crowd outside were pouring in, together with furious screeches and caws from the dive-bombing ravens.

'Kill them!' I heard Noah scream. 'Kill them all!' Then, '*Meshar al*!'

The ground shuddered and the building groaned as the magic rushed out of him towards the people outside. My stomach tightened and I hummed once, doing whatever I could to protect those souls out there. '*Vaz!*'

I was a split-second too late, and I heard cries of pain and horrified shrieks. Several people died on the spot, and several others were sent into spasms of agony. Even so, Noah's magic didn't diminish the attack. Instead, it spurred on those who were unharmed.

I felt pockets of magic flare up across the City Chambers. Some Mages were working to put out the fires, others were fighting the servants who were attacking from within. As one problem was dealt with, another appeared in its wake.

Several people burst through the gaping maw of the doorway, at least three of them dripping with blood. One man let out a roar and charged at the group of Mages. I saw Mage William, who'd once yelled at me for moving a pile of books so I could dust his desk, raise his hands and bellow at the intruder '*Alsh cheen!*'

The man crumpled, and his eyes rolled back in his head as he dropped dead. The spell didn't do William much good, though, because the effort of making it made his knees buckle. A second later, a whirling dervish of a woman ran at him and raised the rusty iron shovel in her hands. When another Mage stepped in to help, I hummed a counter-attack. The Mage fell back, and the woman brought the shovel down on William's skull.

More Mages sprinted into the entrance hall from all directions. In the chaos, nobody noticed me. One eejit even pushed past me, knocking my shoulder as he threw himself down the stairs.

I heard a shout from the other side of the hallway and saw Billy grappling with yet another Mage. His hands were soaked with blood and the frozen grimace on his face told of pain and rage. 'Decimate?' he spat. 'Decimate? I'll fucking decimate *you*!'

I half-turned, the hum already on my lips to help him, but the Mage fell back, horror and shock flashing across his face in the split second before his eyes rolled back in his head.

Angus: it must have been him. I held my breath and glanced around. His bag was still on his shoulder and his features were tense, but he'd done it. He'd used his magic to attack his own kind. His eyes met mine and he bared his teeth.

I nodded, then flew down the stairs to join the fray. I dropped the mouse cage behind a pillar and spun to face the carnage. Despite the fires breaking out across the City Chambers and the number of people who were flooding in, this was still going to be a suicide mission for anyone who wasn't a Mage. I had to help them. These were *my* people.

'There are more of them coming in from the rear!' a Mage shouted, his voice rising above the chaotic yells.

'Deal with it!' Noah threw back. He turned to a trio of teenagers who were climbing in through a broken window while fending off a raven. This time, I was prepared. As I hurtled down the last few steps, I hummed towards them. *Vaz.*

The invisible wall sprang up just in time and whatever Noah's spell was, it smacked into it and saved the young trio from being blasted. Noah's eyes narrowed and his head turned, eyes piercing the smoke and running figures. Then he saw me, and his mouth formed one word. *Bitch.*

I pulled back my shoulders. Come on, then. Come and get me.

Noah started forward, his attention wholly on me, but he'd forgotten about the teenagers. They pushed through the magic wall I'd erected for them with only one thought in their heads: kill all the Mages.

The first one jumped on Noah's back and the other two started hitting him with sticks. I saw him struggle and his lips move. But as I started to hum, something hit the side of my head and I staggered, my spell interrupted. A split second later, the three youngsters were flung backwards and Noah struggled back to his feet.

I turned to my right and spotted the Mage who'd attacked me. In the panic, he'd forgotten to use his magic and reverted to throwing things. He reached for a priceless vase and hefted it upwards, preparing to fling it in my direction. I threw myself aside in the nick of time, rolled on the floor to avoid it and hummed a single attack towards the porcelain-wielding bastard.

He fell backwards, but I didn't have time to celebrate because another movement caught my eye. Looking up, I saw Lord Aspen striding through the hallway gathering together Mages as he went. Oh no. This couldn't be good.

My eyes were stinging from the black smoke that seemed to be growing thicker by the second. A hand reached down and grabbed my upper arm. Without thinking, I swung up my other arm to defend myself before realising Angus was helping me to my feet.

'The Mages are going to join together,' he muttered. 'Aspen will use their magic to gain the strength he needs to repel the crowd. This isn't going to be pretty.'

I heaved a shuddering breath, then I reached for all the magic and power inside me. My hummed note this time was low but full of intent. *Kall moy.*

I felt the magic leave me and spin through the air towards Aspen, but he sensed it before it reached him. His lips moved and my spell, for all its might and power, smacked uselessly into his defences. He turned his cold eyes on me. One Mage was gripping his elbow, and another held onto the second Mage. More joined the chain.

As I stared, Aspen's eyes turned black as he took the power from each Mage. Oh no.

'Mairi.' Angus's voice was filled with warning.

I grasped inside myself for more magic but I'd almost depleted my reserves; there wasn't enough, and I didn't have the power for any useful defence. The only thing left to do was to run and duck for cover. I hissed under my breath – and that was when more screams sounded from outside.

These cries were different, guttural and forced, and they spoke of twisted bodies and fragmented minds. This wasn't about us versus the Mages; another group had joined the battle. My stomach dropped. Now I was truly afraid – and not merely for myself.

I couldn't tell whether a Mage or someone else shouted the first warning, but whoever it was yelled loudly enough for everyone to hear. 'Afflicted! The Afflicted are here!'

Aspen's black eyes narrowed on me and he glared with such intense hatred that I almost staggered. Then he turned away and drew on all the power he could take, not to attack me or the people of my city but to defend against the impending onslaught from the ravaged, diseased folk who were approaching in mighty numbers.

We all felt his magic ripple out. The stone walls of the City Chambers cracked, a fissure opened in the floor beneath our feet, and the world seemed to shudder.

Angus gripped my arm even harder. 'We have to go.'

I nodded, turned and leapt for the stairs, scooping up the cage and clutching it to my chest. 'Leave!' I roared. 'Everyone leave now! Run!'

I couldn't tell if anyone heard me or not, but they didn't need to heed my warning to know that it was time to go. Wherever the urge to attack the City Chambers had come from, it melted away in the face of the peril that the Afflicted presented. It wasn't simply the fear that the Afflicted could attack and kill, it was that they could pass on their terrible disease. For many, that would be a fate far, far worse than death.

I looked at Angus and he looked at me, then we joined the stampede to escape from the building into the night.

I expected a rush of cold air as soon as we got outside, but the heat from the fires inside the building that the Mages hadn't managed to extinguish was far greater than I expected. Ferocious temperatures scorched my bare skin.

People were running from the building in all directions, and scores of ragged, pock-marked, screaming Afflicted were running after them. The street was littered with bodies – whether they were alive or not, I couldn't tell. I couldn't even say whether they were normal people or Mages or the Afflicted.

'Angus!' I yelled.

He didn't look at me. His grey hair was plastered against his grey skin and his eyes were unfocused. '*Bristash.*'

His magic made me stumble. As I righted myself, I saw the

movements of the fleeing people change; instead of the Afflicted gaining on them, they started to run faster and pull away. Angus's magic blast had affected dozens upon dozens of them, his power enabling them to get away.

I turned to him, my eyes wide and a question on my lips, but before I could say a word he collapsed at my feet with a heavy thud. Shite. *Shite.*

I put down the cage and tried to haul Angus up so I could drag him away safety, but my actions were slow and ponderous, and I couldn't move quickly enough. I heaved his limp arm around my neck and grabbed his waist with one arm, then I picked up the cage.

A sprawled figure only metres away, who'd likely been affected by Aspen's magical attack, started to stir. There was a rasping snort, I heard bones creak – and the body rose up. An Afflicted male.

Panic endowed me with a surge of adrenaline and I moved faster, dragging Angus with me, but I still couldn't move fast enough. I felt rather than saw the Afflicted man turn to me. He groaned once, making my bones shiver. Not for the first time, I cursed my lack of magical stamina.

There was an explosion from the City Chambers. I didn't turn to look at it and neither did the Afflicted man because his wild eyes were fixed on me. He lunged forward, claw-like hands outstretched. I released my grip on Angus and carefully placed the cage on the ground, then raised my head to meet the man's eyes. His thin red lips drew back over his yellowing teeth and his hands raked towards me.

I stiffened, ready for the pain – but the man hesitated. He wasn't coherent enough to savour the moment; the Afflicted weren't like that. So why had he stopped?

I stared at his face, unable to see much beyond the rat-tailed hair that hung over his cheekbones and the mad glint in his eyes. His naked body was covered in scars, more than I'd seen on any other Afflicted man or woman. That was when I looked more closely at his outstretched hands, long, sharp, dirty fingernails still frozen in mid-air as they curved towards me. Three of the fingers on his right hand were missing.

My gaze snapped back to his face. 'It's you,' I said softly.

He didn't answer, which was no surprise, but his head jerked as if he were nodding. He had been the Mages' prisoner; he was the one who'd been held in a cage in the basement of the City Chambers. He was the one I'd helped to escape.

With very slow, very deliberate movements, I reached for Angus and pulled up his unconscious body once more. Still in his cage, the mouse squeaked – and the Afflicted man twitched. His mouth opened. 'He is,' he groaned while his whole body trembled, 'coming.'

I froze, waiting for more, but when he didn't move or speak again I picked up the cage. Then I dared to take my eyes away from him and glanced at the shell of the City Chambers.

It looked as if half of the east wing had collapsed in upon itself. Dark figures, some with cloaks and some without, were silhouetted against the flickering flames. I looked towards the entrance and saw Lord Aspen walk out. He wasn't moving quickly; in fact, he was holding himself in such a way that suggested terrible fatigue and perhaps pain. Good, I thought. He deserved to suffer.

An Afflicted woman bounded out from behind a shadowy building on the other side of the street as another Mage appeared at Aspen's side: it was unmistakably Noah. He said something and the woman stopped in her tracks, suddenly wavering before collapsing.

Aspen and Noah turned to stare at me. I didn't need to be able to read minds to know that they were hoping the Afflicted man in front of me was about to attack. I stared back at them, mouse under one arm, Angus under the other.

'Thank you,' I murmured.

This time, the Afflicted man didn't twitch or even blink. I wet my dry lips, slowly turned and limped away. There were more Afflicted out there, more Mages to contend with. We still had to get away.

CHAPTER
SIX

The journey back to the little church was agonisingly slow. The further we went, the heavier Angus seemed to become, and I had to stop several times to hide from groups of howling Afflicted who were running wildly through the streets.

Fortunately, once I left the immediate area around the City Chambers there were few other people to be seen. Anyone who'd not been seriously hurt must have run for cover as soon as the Afflicted appeared, their temporary bloodlust abandoned. I kept my face averted when people passed me; things were bad enough without more people getting caught up in my drama.

The one good thing was that none of the Mages followed us. They likely had enough of their own problems, considering that the smoke spiralling upwards from the City Chambers didn't appear to be dissipating. There were hundreds of them, and they possessed more magic between them than the rest of us could dream of, but it seemed that even the Mages' power had limits.

The agonising tension didn't leave my body, though, not for a moment. It had settled deep into my bones and echoed my every pained footstep.

By the time the church spire came into view, dawn was well under way. Relief had flooded through me as soon as the sky had started to lighten because the Afflicted never emerged during the day. Whatever happened to their bodies when they were infected meant that they found daylight unbearable.

I glanced away from the pink streaks and mauve glimmer in the sky and down at Angus, whose eyes remained resolutely closed. I had the horrible feeling that he'd been telling the truth about the Afflicteds' origins – and that the Ascendant had been, too. Whether that terrible knowledge would change anything remained to be seen.

I shook off my dark thoughts and dragged Angus's unconscious body the last few metres before shoving open the church door with my shoulder. I hesitated on the threshold and listened carefully for any signs of life. I probably needn't have bothered; everything about the church's interior screamed emptiness.

Whether they were aware of what had gone down at the City Chambers or not, my little gang had gone. I curbed my disappointment. The Gowk had done well to get them out. The important thing was that they were safe.

I heaved Angus into the antechamber and made him as comfortable as I could. He had no obvious injuries and his skin was cool. Presumably the force of magic he'd used to propel the fleeing people away from the Afflicted was so great that he'd passed out.

I didn't know how long he'd be unconscious – or if he'd recover. Neither did I know of any herbs that I could collect to help him, or if I'd do him more harm than good by trying to revive him. For all that I'd learned over the past weeks and months, there was so much more about magic that I didn't know.

I rubbed the grit from my eyes and checked his steady pulse again. The best I could do was hope that nature took her course and Angus revived without suffering any ill-effects.

I sat down on the stone floor with my back against the wall and eyed the cage. Mungo – if indeed it was Mungo in there – was barely visible. He'd burrowed into a clump of sawdust and, if I listened carefully, I could hear tiny mouse snores. I had no idea how he'd ended up in a cage in Angus's room, but he didn't deserve to be locked up.

I leaned forward and opened the cage door. Mungo didn't stir, but that didn't matter; if he wanted to leave when he woke up, he could do so. It was the least I could do for him.

With that one tiny victory accomplished, I leaned back against the wall again and closed my eyes. I was so very, very tired. I thought about what Laoch would say if he knew what had occurred this night at the City Chambers, and how the tattoos that curled across his cheekbones would tighten as he concentrated or his nose would wrinkle when he was puzzled. Then sleep overtook me and I dreamed no more.

As I woke with a jerk, my head bounced off the wall behind me and I hissed with pain. My neck ached, and I didn't feel much better than I had before I'd fallen asleep. I hadn't rested long enough to recover my magic or my usual energy levels because something – or some*one* – had woken me up.

I looked at Angus. There was more colour in his cheeks, which was something. I struggled awkwardly to my feet. Maybe the others had heard what had happened at the City Chambers and returned to search for me. It was even possible that the good priest whose church this was had popped in for a visit. But somebody else might be out there…

I tiptoed to the door of the antechamber and listened. There was a sudden clatter outside as something fell to the floor. I stiffened then twisted the doorknob with slow, silent movements, opened the door an inch and peered outside.

Thanks to the light filtering in through the old stained-glass windows, the nave of the church was much brighter; in fact, the place looked entirely different in daylight. I cast my eyes along the unvarnished wooden pews. Someone had left a tartan shawl on one of them. Tattered bibles, which could do with careful re-binding, were wedged inside specially created shelves. There were no signs of life near the baptismal font at the back of the church and the pulpit at the front.

Not yet ready to relax, I sniffed the air. The faint scent of beeswax tickled my nostrils, but I couldn't detect anything else. I pushed the door open wider.

There was a movement in the far corner near the vaulted ceiling and I tensed, twisting towards the sound. The air shifted and I heard the flap of wings. Fear flashed through me; I was convinced that a raven had tracked me here. When I caught sight of a grey-feathered pigeon high up on one of the water-stained rafters, I exhaled. A pigeon couldn't harm me.

It turned its head and blinked in my direction before cooing softly. I stepped out and squinted up at it. *How did you get in here?* I projected towards it.

'It flew in when I opened the door.'

I spun, raising my fists with a ragged hum ready on my lips. My heart was hammering in my chest and, when I saw who was standing behind me, its staccato beat increased. Oh. *Oh.*

Laoch looked good. Unbelievably good. As I stared at his immaculate white shirt, open at the neck to reveal smooth brown skin, his belted kilt in a dazzling but unfamiliar tartan, his pointed ears, and the sheen of his dark hair in contrast to the coiled horns on his head, I suddenly felt small and grubby and pathetic.

His emerald-green eyes watched me, wary light reflected in their liquid depths. My tongue flicked out nervously as I wet my lips, and his gaze dropped as he tracked the movement.

I opened my mouth, then closed it again. *I didn't think I'd ever see you again.* I thought the words at him, instead of voicing them aloud.

Laoch didn't react. For a moment, I thought he hadn't heard me and that our ability to communicate without spoken words had vanished when my voice emerged.

Finally he answered. *I told you I'd be back.* There was a long, awkward pause. *I am sorry, Mairi, that it took me so long.*

I rubbed my arms; although it wasn't cold, goosebumps had risen across my skin. I took a step towards him. Something in his gaze softened and he moved towards me. We stared at each other, time stretching out between us until Laoch gave a tiny shake of his head. 'Fuck this,' he muttered.

My stomach dropped but instead of striding away, he rushed towards me, gathered me in his arms and pressed my body against his. I clung to him, savouring the warmth of his skin and the taut muscles of his hard body.

'You smell really bad,' he said, his voice low in my ear, humour edging his tone.

'It's been a while since I had a bath,' I told him aloud.

He gazed into my face, then raised a hand only to tuck a loose curl behind my ear. His mouth curved into a broad smile.

'Are you laughing at me because I smell?' I asked.

'No.' He grinned. 'It's your accent.'

'What about it?'

'It's so ... Scottish.'

'What did you expect?'

Laoch didn't answer. He pulled me tighter against him and pressed his lips against the nape of my neck. Shivering, I turned my head, pushed up on my tiptoes and kissed him. He groaned as he tangled the fingers of one hand in my hair and used his other hand to curve around my waist while he deepened the kiss.

His hand stole upwards, sneaking underneath the coarse material of my dirty shirt until he found my bare skin, and I burned wherever his fingers touched. His insistent fingers reached for my breast and brushed against my nipple. I squeaked and he chuckled mid-kiss.

'I'm not sure,' Angus said faintly from the side, 'that this sort of conduct is what churches were designed for.'

In a single breath, Laoch pushed me to the side, whirled round and leapt towards him. '*Tez moy.*'

Angus was thrown backwards, his body flying through the air and against the far wall of the church. He smacked into it and collapsed. I cried out and ran forward until I was standing between the pair of them with my hands raised. 'Laoch! No!'

His voice echoed in my head with one terse word: *Mage.*

I answered instantly. *I know.* Then, *He's on our side.* Kind of.

Laoch clenched his fists and his body quivered with the effort of holding himself back. It wasn't only rage that was affecting him but also fear. His hands unconsciously went to his throat where once a slave band had resided.

I looked from Angus's crumpled form to Laoch's tense features, then I went to Laoch and reached for him, my hands cupping his jaw. *It's alright,* I told him. *I promise.*

I felt him tremble beneath my touch, but he gave a juddering nod of agreement. *I trust you. But you need to explain.*

I will. I heaved in a breath. *Just give me a minute.*

I turned away and went to kneel beside Angus. He was still breathing. As I touched his arm, his eyes fluttered open. 'Fuck me,' he gasped. He flicked a glance up at Laoch. 'How did we ever enslave you?'

'You black-cloaked bastards don't usually believe in a fair fight,' he bit out.

Angus grimaced. 'Aye, I'll admit to that.' He groaned. 'I'm fine, lass,' he said to me. 'Dinna fash.' He held out his arm. 'But you can help me up.'

As I pulled him to his feet, he clutched his side and pasted on a pained smile. 'Good to see you again, Nicholas.'

'It's Laoch,' we replied simultaneously.

Angus blinked. 'If you say so.' He heaved himself over to the nearest pew and sat down. 'I could really do with a very stiff drink,' he remarked to nobody in particular. 'Do you think there's any communion wine going spare?'

Laoch's eyes spat green fire. 'Isn't that just like a Mage?' His voice was soft as velvet. 'Thinking of themselves and their own comforts.'

'Says the daemon,' Angus returned, 'who fucked off the moment he could and left this one here to hand herself over to us so we could hang her in George Square.'

Laoch's gaze moved to me, and I shrugged helplessly. *It's not been an easy few weeks.*

His jaw tightened. *I can imagine. I am sorry I was not here.*

You had your own family to worry about, I replied. *Are they okay?*

They're fine. He folded his arms across his chest. *What's this about handing yourself over to the Mages?*

Before I could decide where to begin, Angus interrupted again. 'Are you two communicating by thought? Truly?'

Laoch's lip curled. 'It's none of your business.'

'Sure.' Angus waved in irritation. 'I'm only the person who saved her skin last night, along with the skins of hundreds of other people. Don't mind me.'

'Whatever you did, it doesn't make up for decades of despotic behaviour,' Laoch snarled.

I expected Angus to snap back, but instead he passed a hand across his face and sighed. 'You're right. It doesn't.'

From Laoch's expression, that answer surprised him too. For a long moment, he said nothing; when he did speak again, his tone was different. 'What *did* happen last night? I was planning to return from my realm in the next day or two, but then I felt the ripples of power surging from here and I knew something was going down.'

'It still is.' I bit my lip and gazed at Angus. 'What will the Mages be planning in response to last night?'

Angus's face darkened. 'The decimation won't have gone ahead. The devastation at the City Chambers will be too much to deal with at the same time as reprisals – at least for today. If we're lucky, my former colleagues will have finally realised the danger in continuing their course of action, given the current atmosphere and the strength of feeling against them. The city is on a knife edge and one wrong move could lose them Glasgow forever.'

'So what do you think they'll do?'

Angus looked tired. 'I don't know, lass. This situation is unprecedented. Anything could happen.'

A growl rumbled inside Laoch's chest. 'You still haven't explained to me what happened.'

I rubbed the back of my neck. 'It might be easier to show you. We need to find out what the Mages might be planning next, so it makes sense to go out and poke around.' And I also needed to find my tiny group of resistance fighters. I pointed at Angus. 'You stay here. You're still recovering.'

'Aye.' He sniffed. 'And which horned fucker's fault is that?'

Laoch growled again. 'Watch how you speak to her. Show some damned respect.'

I was starting to believe I'd have to knock their heads together but before I could, we were distracted by a faint chirrup from the floor. Mungo.

I looked down. The little mouse immediately scurried towards me, his paws skittering across the church floor. When he reached my foot, he leapt upwards, ran up my breeches and disappeared inside my shirt.

Angus pouted. 'Three weeks I've taken care of that rodent. So much for rat loyalty.'

'He's a mouse.'

'He's a wee fucker.'

Aye, whatever. I shook my head. 'Stay here,' I told him. 'If we're not back in four hours…'

He rolled his eyes. 'I've looked after myself for this long without your help, lass. I'm a survivor. I'll be fine.'

That much, I decided, was definitely true.

CHAPTER

SEVEN

I purloined the discarded tartan shawl, wrapped it around my head and knotted it under my chin before we left. The same disguise would have worked yesterday if it hadn't been for sheer bad luck, but hopefully today would be better.

Despite my fatigue and gnawing anxiety, having Laoch by my side made me feel more energised, confident and relaxed. It would be hours before my magic returned to its normal levels, but he possessed far more power than me. And the Mages wouldn't be expecting his return. I certainly wasn't.

We walked side by side along the cold, grey streets. There were fewer people around than usual, and the faces of those who were braving the outdoors were pinched and frightened. Nobody looked at us as we went towards the still-smoking City Chambers; in fact, nobody dared to look anyone in the face. They were probably afraid of what they might see if they did. Even so, I was careful not to draw attention to myself.

Public displays of affection were rare and, despite our all-too-brief engagement in the church, I remained unsure of

Laoch. I didn't drift too close to him, and I certainly didn't hold his hand, although I occasionally brushed it with my fingers as if to reassure myself that he was still there.

I couldn't tell what he was thinking. He'd found an old brown cloak abandoned or lost by a previous churchgoer, and he'd covered both his body and his head. We certainly didn't want anyone to notice a daemon strolling around the city, so his face – and consequently his feelings – were obscured.

We kept our heads low and communicated through thought. I explained all that had happened since he'd left, and he told me about his family and his home. *They thought I was dead. That I'd been snatched across the border of the realm by your Mages and killed.*

Nobody came to find out? I questioned, faintly disgruntled on his behalf.

Daemons are not as prolific as you might think, Mairi. We are wary of the Afflicted and how their disease might affect us. And the Mages' power, at least when they take the magic from females and combine it with their own strength, is more than a match for ours. My mother told me she begged permission to cross the border to find me. I am glad that her pleas were denied, he said grimly.

I shuddered. The Mages had so much to answer for. We hurried past the smashed-up windows of a tiny greengrocer's shop and I prayed that nobody had been hurt when it was attacked. *Do you know how the Afflicted came into existence?* I chose my words carefully, unwilling to put ideas into his head. When Laoch didn't immediately answer, however, I knew that what both the Ascendant and Angus had told me was true.

The evidence suggests that the progeny of female Mages gave rise to the Affliction, he said eventually. Obviously I wasn't the only one choosing my words carefully.

My shoulders slumped. *So our magic is taken from us for a reason. It's not vindictiveness or evil, it's for the greater good.*

This time Laoch didn't hesitate. *Perhaps it began that way, but it's not that way now.* The hood of his dirty cloak fell away for a brief moment and he glanced at me. His gaze shimmered with intensity. *We have a saying where I come from: 'A man can get rich from more than digging for gold.'*

I thought about it. *You mean there's more than one way to skin a cat.*

Indeed. There are more solutions to this problem than taking magic forcibly from girls. And, he added darkly, *whether the Mages' original intentions were pure or not, there is nothing pure about their behaviour now.*

That was certainly true. The face of my old friend Isla flashed into my mind; she'd been executed for asking questions about the disappearance of a baby girl. That wasn't the official reason offered for her death, of course. Laoch was right: this was about much more than magic.

I don't know why the Afflicted attacked in that way last night, I said. *They've not been so bold before. And I've never heard of them banding together in such great numbers.*

The noise and commotion would have attracted them, Laoch replied. *All of them. They took advantage of a bad situation, whether they were aware of what was happening on a conscious level or not.*

I nodded. He was probably right.

I hadn't realised how much I'd missed him until now that he'd returned. It wasn't only his physical presence that made my heart skip; I'd missed having someone to communicate with freely like this. The others meant well, but my relationship with them was not the same. I could discuss anything with Laoch. He didn't have tunnel vision, he saw the whole picture, and I needed that.

Something prickled at me, jabbing painfully. I swallowed

hard; I didn't want to ask the question, but I had to know. *How long are you staying?*

I am here for as long as you want me to be, Mairi. I will not leave again. I'm with you against the Mages, and with you in whatever comes afterward. You're my master, remember?

I freed you. I'm not in charge of you. Not now, not ever. You'll never be a slave again, Laoch.

He didn't answer.

WE SMELLED the City Chambers long before we saw it. It wasn't only the acrid reek of burning that filled the air, I could smell death too, its stench overlying everything else. Mungo stirred within the confines of my shirt, seemingly also bothered by the unpleasant scents. I murmured softly and he settled, although I could feel his fur quivering against my skin.

Any corpses must have already been carted away because there were no bodies, not of Mages, of ordinary citizens nor of the Afflicted. Plenty of bloodstains marred the cobbles, though. Even if I hadn't witnessed the events the previous night, they would have shown me that terrible violence had occurred.

Surprisingly, where the streets and alleyways further away had been muted and quiet, the closer we drew to the half-ruined building, the busier it became. Despite the cloud of black fear that hung over the city, there was also considerable curiosity. The City Chambers had been an imposing edifice for so long, towering over us with its dark spires, heavy architecture and threatening power, that it was difficult to accept that a third of the building had been destroyed. The east wing lay in ruins, the front doors of the building had been destroyed, and everywhere there were dangerous looking cracks in the stone.

Although the fires appeared to have been extinguished,

plumes of dark smoke were still belching into the sky. Dust, debris and rubble were strewn across the streets nearby, and every time the breeze picked up, it carried scraps of paper and ash through the air.

More and more people appeared, their shivering fear changing to triumphant defiance when they saw the condition of the Mages' stronghold. Laoch and I took greater care to cover our faces. This was not the time to be recognised – especially when dozens of malevolent ravens were lining the remaining roof of the building.

The birds watched, their beady attentiveness suggesting that they were a mere flap away from attacking, but they stayed at a distance even when an old woman stalked forward and shook her fists at the devastation. 'Tha's what you get!' she yelled. 'Tha's what you get for treating us like this!'

I was convinced that a black-cloaked Mage would swirl forward from nowhere and pulverise her where she stood, but the Mages weren't biting, not today. They had to be inside the City Chambers – there was nowhere else they could be – yet, the building was silent, as if nobody were home.

A group of men in their early twenties pushed through and stood next to Laoch, staring at the building. The nearest bloke, who was jittering around on the balls of his feet, nudged him. 'Ye ken she did this. The Saviour. Mairi the Magnificent!'

I stiffened. I hadn't done this. I'd been in the building, but this hadn't been me.

'We've been waiting for someone like her to come around for too long,' the man continued. 'They cannae threaten us again. Nae after last night. We've got the power now. And so does she.'

I moved away, not wanting to listen anymore.

The toes of my boots scuffed the cobbles as I avoided the bloodstains and veered round the building. Was the garden of death, which lay deep inside the City Chambers, undamaged? It might be possible to catch a glimpse of it through the gaps in the collapsed east wing. I padded round, aware that Laoch was following me. He had my back, even here.

I skirted away from a pile of blackened rubble and squinted towards the building's interior. I could make out one of the grand corridors, together with a scorched wall and a few sticks of damaged antique furniture. As far as I could tell, the horrific, glass-contained garden, with its unnaturally large insects, array of death-soaked plants and mutilated corpses, was in one of the undamaged sections. I pulled a face.

'What's that?' I heard Laoch mutter.

I glanced around, but he was already striding past me towards a large, smooth slab that must have broken away from one of the upper floors. He knelt next to it and frowned.

I joined him and drew in a sharp breath when I saw what he'd spotted. It was a rune. It looked exactly like the one I'd seen beside the church, although this version was larger. I stared at the three horizontal scratches with two shorter diagonal slashes and felt a trickle of unease. If this mark was here, it must have been created by the Mages and it had to contain magical properties. Maybe the rune by the church was also there for a reason.

I shivered. It was a good thing that the others had abandoned the church for another safe house. Then I thought of Angus who was still there and swallowed.

What is it? What does it mean? I asked.

Laoch shook his head. *I don't know. I've never seen anything like it before – but it's fresh.*

The furrow in my brow deepened. *Fresh?*

It was scratched recently. Very recently. He pointed to one of the corners. *See the brick dust here? This mark was made after the slab fell, after the east wing collapsed. Not before.*

Then I was wrong; it probably wasn't anything to do with the Mages at all. 'The resistance,' I said aloud. 'Someone in the resistance did this. One of the Gowk's people.' That would explain the identical mark by the church; it could indicate that this was a place of sanctuary.

Laoch pursed his lips. 'Perhaps.' He sounded doubtful. He straightened up and adjusted his hood. 'We've seen all we need to here. We shouldn't linger any longer. The Mages will emerge sooner or later.'

I nodded agreement; I had no desire to stay. As I stepped back, the flock of ravens squawked and took off, flying up into the air. They circled overhead, dozens of them in perfect alignment. I gaped.

Laoch grabbed my elbow and pulled me close. 'Mages,' he hissed. 'They're coming out.'

My every instinct told me to run, and my feet itched to turn and sprint as far from this place as I could. But there were others here – hundreds of them – and every one was in danger. With the sun high in the sky, the Afflicted wouldn't appear to interrupt this fight. We should never have come, we should have stayed away.

I adjusted my shawl to make sure my face was concealed and held my breath. Drained magic or not, I'd fight again if I had to. I was still prepared to give myself up if I thought it would make a difference, but until that happened it made sense to stay anonymous.

The first Mage to step out from the black hole where the impressive oak doors had once stood was Noah. My stomach turned to stone. Sensing my trepidation, Mungo squeaked beneath my shirt.

Noah ducked out of the opening, his face an impassive mask unmarred by cuts or bruises from the previous night. His cloak billowed out behind him, making him look larger and more imposing than he truly was.

Laoch's voice echoed in my head. *He's afraid.*

He didn't look afraid. *How can you tell?*

I can feel his fear from here.

That was a nifty trick that he'd have to teach me some time – if we ever got away from this place.

There was another Mage directly behind Noah, then another and another. One by one, every single magical bastard filed out until they were lining the steps up to the City Chambers. None of them looked injured, none of them looked scared, but as my eye travelled across the large group I realised that more than a few faces were missing.

The ravens continued to circle over our heads. It seemed that everyone was holding their breath, even the birds. Then someone shouted, 'You magical fuckers!'

The yelled curse broke the spell. A man picked up a small stone and threw it forcefully at the Mages, but it bounced uselessly off an invisible barricade that they must have erected before they stepped out.

I sneaked a glance at Laoch. Could he break through that spell and destroy the barrier that protected them? Dare he do so? And, more importantly, would the Mages retaliate?

Someone flung another stone that thudded pointlessly to the ground. People pushed forward, screaming insults and throwing makeshift missiles. Unflinching, the Mages stayed where they were. They were holding their ground, waiting for the anger of the crowd to die out.

The cold light of day was different to the smothering darkness of the night, and it didn't take long. As the magical wall between the Mages and their people held, the attempts to breach it became less enthusiastic.

A high-pitched shriek rose above the furious murmurs. 'You cannae hide behind that forever!'

Finally one of the Mages answered, 'We're not planning to.'

Lord Aspen stepped forward from behind the long line of stern Mages. 'I kindly request that you quieten down and listen to what I have to say,' he intoned. He offered a benign smile, which chilled me to my core. 'You're going to want to hear it.'

There were more mutters but gradually everyone fell silent.

Laoch's hand reached for mine. *I guess we do want to hear it.*

I clenched my jaw. *But I don't understand,* I answered. *The Mages will be weakened after last night, but they're hardly power-less. They could crush this crowd in an instant if they wanted to.*

Indeed. He paused. *Something else is going on.*

'I am not from this city,' Aspen said. 'I am not invested in its health and good fortune in the way that these good people are.' He motioned towards the other Mages.

His words were met with several jeers. Again, Aspen waited until they died down before he continued. 'But I can tell you that Glasgow is a proud city with a great deal to offer, and the many tragedies that it has experienced in recent weeks truly hurt my heart.'

Aye, right. My lip curled.

Aspen's voice dropped deliberately low, forcing us to strain to hear him. He enjoyed an audience. 'I know the Glasgow Mages have nothing but your best interests at heart, but I also know that they are fallible. They have made some missteps in their attempts to keep this city safe.' Missteps? I snorted quietly. So that's what we were calling random executions these days.

Unfortunately, I also knew now why it was Aspen addressing the crowd. He could distance himself from the Glasgow Mages and position himself as the voice of reason.

But I'd overheard his vitriol in the street, and I knew he was as bad – if not worse – as the others.

'What happened yesterday was wrong,' Aspen said. 'The decision to decimate a street was wrong. The Mages here agree with me.' He bowed his head. 'We have all been humbled by the strength of feeling you displayed. We want to prove to you that we have listened, and we are acting accordingly.'

He swung his gaze across the now-silent crowd of people. The ravens stopped their incessant circling overhead and, one by one, flapped down to the clustered Mages until they rested on their shoulders.

I realised this was another display of power, and it was working. The expressions on the people around me were changing from pure hatred to faint awe.

'This city is ready for change,' Aspen shouted suddenly, 'and so are its Mages! We have tried to keep you all safe, but it may be time for another to step up!'

I suddenly had a very bad feeling about what he was planning to say.

'The Afflicted pose a very real threat. Only last night, they caused devastation. We need to be confident that whoever leads this city has the power to keep them at bay. But,' he paused for dramatic effect, 'it may be that the best person to be in charge is not a Mage.'

There were several gasps. The young man next to Laoch clutched his chest. 'This is it,' he whispered. 'This is where the world changes.'

Or, I thought pessimistically, this is where the world ends.

'In ten days' time, in the grand city of Edinburgh, the Ascendancy Challenge will be held to determine who will lead Glasgow into the future. Several Mages with extraordinary potential from this city will take part.'

I glanced at Noah. His face was impassive, but I'd lay bets that he was one of those who'd be participating.

Aspen continued. 'There will also be contenders from other cities. Glasgow deserves the best person, the strongest person. The most capable person.' He spread his arms out wide. 'And that is why we invite Mairi Wallace to participate.'

There were more stunned gasps. I staggered as wave of light-headedness assailed me. Shite. The Mages were smarter than I'd given them credit for.

'Yes, she is female,' Aspen said. 'Yes, she may not be up to the challenge and, yes, it will prove both dangerous and difficult. But if she is the most talented magic user Glasgow has to offer, then Glasgow deserves to have her!'

The assembled crowd wasn't jeering now, they were cheering. I turned my head and looked round, feeling nauseous. People were pumping the air with their fists, and some were crying with delight. There was even one fellow on his knees, his arms outstretched towards Aspen in abject gratitude.

Fuck. I didn't want to be the Ascendant. I wanted to prevent the Ascendancy from existing. Nobody should possess that much power.

I didn't look at Laoch. *Aye.* I squeezed his hand. *Let's get out of here.*

Good plan.

I started to turn.

'So,' Aspen boomed, his voice in volume rising once again, 'Mairi Wallace, will you accept our invitation?'

I glanced over my shoulder and my blood froze. He was staring at me, and so were all the Mages and all the ravens. Then every single head in the crowd turned towards me.

They knew. The Mages knew I was here the entire time.

Laoch's response was immediate. *Mairi, this is dangerous.*

This isn't a peace offering or an invitation to lead Glasgow. It's a death sentence.

I know. My mouth flattened. *And the last thing I'm capable of doing is leading a city. This is a sham.*

Unfortunately, it didn't matter what it was. The crowd was already starting to chant, 'Mairi! Mairi! Mairi!' Aspen had done exactly what he'd set out to do – and he looked like a hero for doing it.

'They've left me with no choice,' I muttered aloud. I pulled away from Laoch's grip, wrenched back the shawl from my head and face and straightened my shoulders. 'I accept!' I tried to shout but my voice wasn't strong enough.

'Say that again!'

I gritted my teeth and tried harder. 'I will stand in the Ascendancy Challenge!'

The crowd roared its approval. I glanced at the Mages: Aspen and Noah were both smiling.

Aye. Things were truly fucked now.

CHAPTER

EIGHT

It wasn't easy to get away. Laoch did his best, but people kept coming up to me, shaking my hand, clapping my shoulder, and offering heartfelt and well-meaning congratulations.

'You did it!'

'You've beaten them!'

And, worst of all, 'You've saved us! Thank you!'

We extricated ourselves as best as we could as I tried to smile and look gracious. Laoch pulled me away, leading us first down one street and then another. We kept going, putting one foot in front of another until we were no longer being followed.

He led us towards the riverbank and along the edge of the stinking, slow-flowing water. I looked across and saw a bloated corpse floating downstream. A woman, I thought distantly. A well-dressed woman who was now little more than fish food. She'd never know what would happen next. Maybe she was one of the lucky ones.

No Mages tracked us, at least not by visible means. The sky remained clear of black-feathered ravens and even a trickle of sunlight poked through the grey clouds to shine upon us. Neither Laoch nor I paused to appreciate it, although Mungo came out and perched on my shoulder, raising his tiny nose towards the sun with his whiskers twitching. Laoch and I kept our heads down and continued moving.

Returning to the church was incredibly risky but Angus was there, and there was no other place to go. It was unlikely that the Mages would attack us there, even if they knew of its existence. They had different plans for me now, and they no longer needed to come after us. I'd walked straight into their trap with a smile on my face.

We plodded up the final street, past the brick with its etched-out rune and into the church. Before Laoch opened the door, I knew the others had returned.

They were seated in the pews, with the exception of the Gowk who was pacing up and down in front of the pulpit like an irate minister mid-sermon. He stopped when we entered and his hunched shoulders dropped in relief. The others also turned their heads and smiled – but each smile was different. Some were genuinely happy, but the curved mouths of others belied tension and worry.

Fee spoke first. 'You bampot lass! Whit did you think you were doing running off like that?' She shook her head, pale-faced with dismay, then stood up. Wagging her finger and walking towards me, she reached forward and pulled me into a tight hug. 'And you,' she said to Laoch. 'I've heard all about *you*.'

He scratched his head, faintly bemused.

'Good to know you're not deid,' Jane muttered. Flora punched her arm.

Ailsa glowered at Laoch, unimpressed by his return. 'You went back?' she demanded. 'You went to the City Chambers this morning?'

I nodded.

'That was a foolish thing to do, lass,' the Gowk said. The glint of pride in his eyes belied his words. He waved his deformed hand in the air. 'Is it true? Did the Afflicted attack the Mages last night?'

I heaved a sigh. 'They attacked everyone,' I said quietly.

The Gowk's bottom lip jutted out. 'Aye, well, good for them. Equal opportunities and all that.'

I didn't answer.

'We left here after dawn,' Flora told me, looking apologetic. 'But we came back as soon as we heard what was happening. The news is all over the city.'

No doubt.

'The Mages didn't use that magic voice thing,' Twister pointed out. 'You know, booming their words out so everyone could listen.'

'They probably didnae have enough magic left,' Fee said. 'And they knew we'd all hear about it soon enough.'

'The Ascendancy Challenge.' I whispered the words. Out of the corner of my eye I saw Angus, who was in the furthest pew with his head against the wall, flinch.

I noted that the others were keeping their distance from him. My brow creased as I looked at him again. Several rags appeared to have been stuffed in his mouth – and that wasn't all.

'Is that ... rope?' I asked. I peered more closely. He'd been trussed up like a chicken. It was far from the sort of treatment Angus was used to, and I almost smiled.

Ailsa was the only one who seemed uncomfortable. 'The others didn't trust him.'

Angus glowered at her, and I suspected that she hadn't done much to stand up for him. He should have expected that; despite their odd relationship back at the City Chambers, where she hadn't been afraid to tease or snipe at him, he was still a Mage. He could hardly blame anyone for acting like he had the plague, even Ailsa who knew him best.

'Angus saved a lot of lives last night,' I said.

'He's a Mage,' Jane spat. 'I voted to hang him from the rafters.'

The Gowk was equally unenthusiastic about Angus's presence. 'I said we should cut out his tongue to stop him from uttering any magic spells.'

Laoch surprised me by stepping in. 'We should be glad you didn't. We'll need him – and his tongue.'

Ailsa folded her arms. 'Like we can trust *you*,' she sneered.

I passed a hand over my eyes. At this rate we didn't need to worry about the Mages; we'd end up killing each other without so much as a smidge of their interference. 'Let him go,' I said tiredly.

'Mairi—'

I glared. 'Let him go.'

Twister stood up, but Belle grabbed his arm and pulled him back down. Everyone else looked away, too afraid to be the one to approach Angus. I stomped over to him. 'Sorry about this,' I told him.

He let out a muffled moan, which might have translated as a curse or a thank you; at that point, it was difficult to tell. I reached over and removed the rags from his mouth.

He stuck out his tongue like a child, attempting to rid himself of the taste of them. 'If I was truly a danger to you all, I'd have killed you the moment you stepped inside this church,' he grunted,

'Hush,' I told him. 'You're not helping yourself.' I undid the knots in the rope, and he rubbed his wrists and ankles. Wisely, he didn't complain again about his imprisonment.

'So,' he grunted, 'the Ascendancy Challenge.' His watery eyes met mine. 'Check. Mate.'

I sighed. 'Aye. It looks that way.'

Belle peeled away from Twister and looked around. 'I do not understand,' she said, enunciating her words. 'This is what we wanted, isn't it? Mairi becomes the Ascendant, and we all live happily ever after. We've won. As easy as that.'

The Gowk ran a hand through his hair. 'We've not won.' He sniffed at Angus. 'They've won.'

'But—'

Laoch took pity on Belle and explained. 'Half the city revolted against the Mages last night. It wasn't organised by the resistance, and it wasn't a small group of rebel fighters. It was ordinary people who'd had enough and who'd been inspired by stories about what Mairi has done.'

'But the Mages have the magic,' Belle objected. 'They have the power. Ordinary people are no match for the Mages.'

'Sure.' He nodded. 'But a good portion of the City Chambers has been destroyed. If the Mages continue down their current path and the people keep revolting, there's no telling how much of Glasgow will end up in ruins before everything calms down. And magic runs out. A lot of Mages could die if large numbers of ordinary people turn against them.'

Angus got to his feet, shuffled over to the baptismal font and plunged his face into the pool of stagnant water that had lain there for goodness knew how long. He brought his head up, and shook himself like a dog, splattering both Trish and Lottie. 'I can tell you,' he said, 'that the dissent is starting to spread to other cities as well. It's not only Glasgow now. There's been unrest in Edinburgh and Perth, and four Mages were killed in Inverness. What's important to the Mages is that they stop everything as quickly as possible before more damage is done.'

'But they've said that Mairi can be the Ascendant,' Belle objected.

'No.' The Gowk shook his head. 'They've said that she can *participate* in the challenge to *become* the Ascendant.'

Twister frowned. 'So? She can win.'

I lifted my head and looked at him. 'I can't.' My voice was flat but strong enough for them all to hear. That made a change. 'They'll pull out all the stops to make sure that I not only lose but that I die publicly in the process. Then all the Mages will say that I should never have participated, that they gave us the chance but we weren't good enough to meet the challenge. They'll have a mandate to continue ruling in any way they see fit for the next half-dozen generations, and things will get far, far worse for everyone. The Ascendancy Challenge is their game and their rules. I'll never win. *We* will never win.'

Angus snapped his fingers. 'Got it in one,' he said cheerfully.

Flora blinked. 'That's the longest speech I've ever heard you make, Mairi.'

I shrugged. Things were changing in more ways than one.

'The Mages have been badly shaken by what happened last night,' Laoch said. 'They must change the way that they respond. People have never stood up to them in such large numbers before.'

Angus nodded. 'After last night's disaster even Noah, who's the stupidest Mage I've ever met, will realise that if Mairi is killed and becomes a martyr the resistance will be unstoppable. The tide has turned against them, and the Mages need to try something different to bring the city back into line. Their only alternative is to give her a chance and make sure she fails. No doubt they'll invite a section of Glasgow's finest to Edinburgh to watch her falter and relay the gory details back to the rest of the populace.' He grinned at me. 'You're dead, lass.'

Laoch growled. I put my hand on his arm.

Lottie's fingers twisted together. 'So what do we do?'

I cleared my throat. 'I must play their game. There's no choice.'

'There's always a choice,' Laoch said.

'No.' My mouth flattened. 'Not now. If I don't present myself at the challenge, we lose just as much and the outcome will be the same. The Mages will say they bent over backwards and offered the world, but their oh-so-kind offer was refused so they deserve to continue as before.'

Belle stared at me. 'You're saying you can't win. *We* can't win.'

'Pretty much.'

'What happens to the rest of us, then?' Her voice rose. 'What happens to *us*? Are we going tae die too?'

This time nobody answered her.

'YOUR BIGGEST PROBLEM is your lack of stamina,' Angus said. 'To get through the different rounds of the challenge, you will need a lot of energy. The men you're up against have been training for this for years. You've had weeks.'

'Is there a way to fast track myself? To gain extra stamina and build up my reserves quickly?'

'I have a few tricks, but it's not just your overall stamina that will be an issue. Too much emotion and you'll lose control of your magic so it won't work.'

'Are you suggesting that I'm too emotional because I'm a woman?'

'I'm saying,' he replied calmly, 'that you're too emotional because too much depends on you. This isn't about your personal ambitions, it's about what happens to the city. The more pressure on you, the more emotion you'll feel, and that emotion will adversely affect your ability to perform.' He bared his teeth in the semblance of a grin. 'I recommend cheating, wherever and whenever possible.'

Easier said than done.

'If we know what to expect in the challenge, Mairi can prepare,' Ailsa ventured. 'What will she have to do?'

Angus shook his head. 'Your guess is as good as mine. Every Ascendancy Challenge is different. The tasks and competitions differ, depending on who the other Ascendants want to win.'

I raised an eyebrow. 'So the competition is rigged even against the Mages?'

'We're a complicated bunch.'

Jane's lip curled. 'I'd say you're all pretty simple from where I'm standing.'

He ignored her. 'You've got ten days. You can't know what the challenges will be, so you need to spend those ten days building up your magic reserves. If you don't, you'll expend all your power in the first trial and leave yourself nothing to work with.' He drew a finger across his throat. 'And then it'll be cheerio to the magnificent saviour of Glasgow.'

I rubbed the back of my neck. 'You have such a lovely way with words.'

He smirked.

'There is magic I can teach you that will help,' Laoch said. 'Spells that the Mages won't know about.'

Angus looked at him. 'I knew you were holding out on us, despite the enslavement.' He leaned forward. 'What spells?'

Laoch stared stonily back at him and said nothing.

'I'm on your side now. Much good it will do me. If you trust Farris, you can trust me.' He meant the Gowk.

'He's been a member of the resistance for decades. You've been with us for hours,' Fee objected.

'Speaking of the resistance,' I murmured, 'what does this sign mean?' I traced out the strange rune on the dusty floor.

Fee squinted at it. 'Not a clue.'

The Gowk ambled over. 'It's nothing to do with us.'

I looked askance at Angus.

'What?' he asked.

'Is this a Mage symbol?'

'We don't use symbols. We don't need to. And we're wasting time. You should be practising already.'

I sighed and cleaned away the rune with my hand. He was probably right. I dusted off my palms and stood up. 'Fine. Where do we begin?'

'Defence.'

'I'd rather work on attack,' I told him.

Angus snorted. 'Of course you would. But every Mage in the competition is going to be coming after you, and you can't attack them all. They'll want to bring you down as early as possible to prove how weak and incapable you are. If you can't defend yourself from the very start, you're dead.'

I was dead anyway, but there wasn't much point in saying that aloud. 'Then let's get started.'

CHAPTER

NINE

Eight days later, I wasn't any more confident about my chances. If anything, I felt less sure. The days had been filled with practising, learning new spells and building up my reserves. The nights had been spent curled up next to Laoch, although I'd been too tired to do anything more than sleep despite the snickered remarks from Belle about what we got up together once the sun had gone down. It wasn't lack of privacy that discouraged intimacy, it was sheer exhaustion.

Trish and Lottie told me that the during the night the screams of the Afflicted were far louder and more frequent than usual but, if that were true, I was far too sound asleep to hear them.

The barrage of magic that blasted around the wee church on a regular basis should have been a worry because the Mages could have pinpointed our location from the moment I started practising. In my darker moments I wondered if they listened in on my efforts and laughed to themselves about how easy I'd be to beat. I'd gotten lucky when I'd killed the Ascendant; I couldn't rely on such luck again.

Fee, Jane and Flora, who all possessed smatterings of magical power, did what they could to practise too, which stretched their own magic and helped mask my limits. The Gowk, Angus and Laoch did the same when they weren't attempting to teach me.

In any case, our location didn't remain a secret for long at all. Parcels of food were regularly dropped on the church doorstep. The priest cancelled his Sunday service and told us we could stay as long as we needed. There was a steady stream of well-wishers who did nothing for my confidence, although Belle and Twister spent a lot of time conversing with them while boasting of their own involvement and heroic deeds. Nobody stopped them. Given what would happen to them all if – *when* – I failed the challenge, they deserved a brief moment to shine.

Belle particularly enjoyed herself. There was more than one occasion when she snapped at me to tidy up or bring her a drink, forgetting that we weren't back in her tartan shop and that I was no longer her meek, mild and very mute servant. It bothered me far less than the others; truth be told, I almost enjoyed the reminders of a time when life was much simpler.

It was on the final Thursday morning, after the Gowk and Angus had informed me that there would be no magical practice so that I would be fully refreshed for the start of the Ascendancy Challenge, that Lottie appeared.

She ran through the church with panic-stricken eyes. 'Mage!' she gasped. 'There's a Mage coming! He's heading right this way!'

The group sprang to their feet in a coordinated action that would have provoked a smile, even applause, under any other circumstances. But I'd always known that the respite from the Mages' attention would be temporary, and it was almost a relief that the waiting was over.

'Stay here,' I said calmly. 'Stay hidden – there's no point in displaying your faces and identities if you don't have to.' The Mages knew exactly who was in our group, but I wanted to keep their focus on me. It was safer that way. 'I'll go out and talk to him.'

Whoever was approaching wouldn't hurt me, not now, not like this. It would scupper their plans; they'd have plenty of opportunity to smack me down publicly soon.

I thought of something else: if I could provoke a reaction from the incoming Mage, there might be a way to avoid the Ascendancy Challenge. A gleam lit my eyes and I cast around the interior of the church. 'Angus,' I said. 'Do you still have a black cloak?'

He frowned, then nodded as he worked out what I was planning. 'Aye, lass.' He rummaged around in the bag by his feet and pulled out the swathe of black fabric. 'Here.'

I grinned and let him place it around my shoulders and tie it at the neck. I shivered slightly at the sensation of the Mage attire against my body, but it would be worth it. 'Laoch,' I said.

He also understood. 'I'm here.' He strode quickly to my side. 'Hold still for a moment.' He carefully brushed away some dust from my face then fiddled with my hair, running his fingers through its messy curls to comb it. 'You're beautiful, Mairi Wallace.'

I met his emerald gaze. 'So are you,' I whispered back.

He leaned into my ear. 'I know. We're a braw looking couple.'

Ailsa flapped her hands. 'Hello? The Mage? This isn't the time for smoorikin'!'

We should make more time for smoorikin, I reflected as my eyes dropped to Laoch's mouth. Then I shook myself. 'Alright,' I said quietly. 'Let's go and see what he wants.' I spun round and marched towards the church door.

'Wait,' the Gowk said. 'I'll get that. The Saviour of Glasgow doesn't open her own doors.'

I rolled my eyes but let him nip forward and yank on the door handle; after all, we were creating an image and developing our own propaganda. Every little helped.

The door creaked and a gust of wind whistled through, making the cloak billow impressively behind me. No wonder the Mages wore these things. I smiled slightly, then walked out with my chin held high. I wasn't going to allow myself to display a trace of fear or anxiety.

When I saw which Mage was waiting outside, any trepidation turned to satisfaction. Good. I was hoping it would be Noah.

I strode towards him as imperiously as I could manage. Laoch marched a step behind me, his wrists and neck brazenly bare of any slave adornments. Noah did his best to keep his expression blank but he couldn't stop his anger and disgust reflecting in his eyes. 'That cloak is for Mages,' he snarled. 'It is an offence for anyone else to wear one.'

He was pissed off; that was good. If I could increase his rage and make him strike me, the balance of power would shift. It would no longer be his game, it would be mine.

'I think it looks rather good on me,' I said with a small smile. 'Maybe black is my colour.' I ran my tongue across my teeth and leaned forward. 'Unfortunately, it makes *you* look sallow.'

Noah's hands tightened into fists. 'I'm going to enjoy ripping your tongue out and making you mute again some day soon.'

'I'll enjoy seeing you try.' I glanced around him, as if searching for someone. 'When is Lord Aspen getting here?'

His mouth twisted; there was definitely no love lost between him and Aspen. That was useful to know. 'It's me you're dealing with,' he growled.

'Oh? But he's the one in charge. He has more power than you.' I inspected my fingernails. 'I would prefer to talk to him. I don't have time to waste speaking to minions.'

The ugly twist to Noah's face made his feelings clear; his anger was growing – and that was exactly what I wanted. I glanced around. A passer-by had stopped across the street to watch, and several curtains were twitching in the row of houses opposite the church. If Noah attacked me here, I could walk away from the Ascendancy Challenge with my head held high.

I took a deep breath and moved deeper into the proverbial swamp. 'What's happened to your uncle's body?' I asked. 'Did you bury him in your garden of death with everyone else? Did you draw on his dead magic to bolster your own?'

Noah grunted; the sound was more akin to an animal – or one of the Afflicted – than a human. I looked down. Flickers of angry blue magic were dancing around his fingers. He was on the brink.

'My uncle cared more and did more for Glasgow than you could ever do. You think you're something special, but you can't possibly do what he did. He made necessary sacrifices for the greater good. He was a magnificent man, while you,' he spat the words, 'you are nothing more than a woman.'

'But she's a pretty woman, right?' Angus called lazily from the church steps behind me. 'That has to count for something.'

This time, the look in Noah's eyes genuinely scared me. 'Traitor!'

'I'm a fair-weather friend. I go where the power is.' Angus's tone was bright and cheerful. 'And right now the power is with her.'

Beside me, Laoch smiled. 'I can only agree. Mairi doesn't need to put slave cuffs around my wrists to get me to follow her. She's got more balls than the likes of you will ever have.'

I didn't know whether it was Angus or Laoch who pushed Noah over the edge. Either way, I saw the furious light in his face and I knew we'd done enough. He took a step forward and opened his mouth.

I tensed, preparing for whatever he might fling at me. I wanted to take it head on without using magic to defend myself. That would be the best way to prove that the Mages were playing a game and couldn't be trusted.

In the instant before the words of magic formed on Noah's lips, a black shape shot forward. The tip of the feathers from the raven's outstretched wing brushed against his cheek, then the bird circled the air between us and settled on the ground. It tilted its head towards me, mock admonishment in its beady gaze.

I'd never been told off by a bird before, and I glared at it before glancing back at Noah. The raven's interference had done what was required. His fury had been replaced with a blank mask and his arms once again hung loosely by his sides.

'Nice try,' he murmured. 'You almost had me there. It won't happen again.' He smiled coldly. 'Not until we meet in the challenge.' He raised his fingers to his mouth and blew me a kiss.

Suddenly it was my turn to feel a surge of rage. I tamped it down quickly enough, but I caught Noah's triumphant glance as he saw that he'd affected me.

He smirked, stepped back and folded his arms. 'You've never left Glasgow, have you, Mairi?' he enquired, now speaking far more casually. 'It's not a long journey to Edinburgh – half a day by carriage. It's dangerous, though, especially for a woman who's never experienced the countryside. We would hate for something to happen to you before the Ascendancy Challenge begins. We will travel together so the other Mages and I can keep you safe on the journey.'

Wanker.

Laoch moved closer and his arm brushed against me to remind me that he was by my side. I breathed in and the warmth of his body helped me stay calm. Noah's sharp eyes noticed but I couldn't worry about that right now.

'That won't be necessary,' I bit out. 'I shall travel to Edinburgh under my own steam. I have my entourage.'

'Entourage?' Noah laughed. 'A turncoat Mage who's past his best, a horned daemon who's only using you to get back at us, and a group of ragtag idiots from the resistance?' He started to slow clap. 'How utterly wonderful for you.' He snorted. 'Anyway, you can't bring them.'

I drew myself up. 'I'll bring whoever I want.'

Noah was enjoying himself now. 'They won't be allowed beyond the city limits. In fact, *you* won't be allowed beyond the city limits unless you're travelling with us.' He swept an insincere bow. 'My most heartfelt apologies if you thought otherwise.'

The raven between us half turned and started to preen its feathers. Noah watched it for a moment before his gaze flicked to Laoch. 'I tell you what,' he said suddenly. 'We'll tweak the rules this one time because the circumstances are so special. You may bring one person and one person only.'

He spread his arms wide. 'We are not usually so magnanimous, but we want to do all we can to put you at ease. I'd hate for you to claim we acted unfairly in order to gain an advantage in the challenge.' His smile was both sly and calculating. He looked at Laoch again. 'Females are so twitchy and temperamental, aren't they? They have to do everything in groups.'

I wasn't the one who swanned around the city with my bunch of black-cloaked chums. I hissed under my breath and Noah's smile widened. He was in control now and he knew it.

'We depart in three hours,' he said. 'I'll have the carriage stop here to pick you up.' He waggled his fingers in farewell. 'Toodle-pip, sweet Mairi.' As he turned on his heel and swept away, the raven took flight after him.

I glanced at Laoch and then at Angus. It seemed that no matter what I tried, the Mages clung on to their upper hand. I shook my head and walked back inside the church.

WE HUDDLED TOGETHER at the front of the church next to the pulpit. 'It's another trap,' Fee said. 'You won't make it to Edinburgh. They'll slit your throat along the way.'

The Gowk's nose wrinkled. 'I dinna think so. If something happens and she's killed on the way, the resistance will only gain momentum. The Mages cannae afford to kill her out of sight, it's got to be done publicly. Mairi has to be seen to fail by as many people as possible.'

'But why insist she travels with them?' Jane asked. 'There must be a reason for it.'

We glanced at each other. Then, one by one, every pair of eyes turned to Angus. He had taken off his shoes and was picking at his big toenail, his brow furrowed in concentration. Ailsa cleared her throat pointedly and he looked up.

'Hmm?' He seemed surprised by the attention. 'Oh. You

want to know why the lass has to travel with the Mages? It's obvious.' He returned his focus to his toenail.

'I told you we should have killed him,' Jane muttered.

Ailsa got to her feet, shuffled over and whacked Angus on the back of the head. His reaction was instantaneous. '*Ins veil!*'

Her body flew backwards. I hummed a single note before she crashed into the wooden pews and did herself real damage. *Folis.* She juddered to a halt in mid-air, her arms and legs limp and her eyes wide.

'You peely-wally, lairy bastard!' Jane leapt towards Angus. Flora grabbed the back of her shirt and held her back.

Angus bared his teeth at all of us. 'I have every right to defend myself,' he said distinctly.

'It was not exactly a proportionate response, Angus,' I told him.

His mouth twisted, then seemed to remember where he was. 'That was a fast reaction from you, lass. Well done. Maybe there's a smattering of hope for you after all.'

I was truly beginning to doubt the wisdom of keeping Angus with us. He was causing far more problems than he solved. I nodded curtly. 'So?' I asked, surprised by my harsh tone.

'So what?'

'It's not obvious to me, Angus. Why is Noah forcing me to travel to the challenge with him?'

He smirked, his eyes glittering with hard amusement.

I put up my hand. 'The sensible answer, please. Not the facetious one.'

'Facetious?' Angus placed a hand on his chest. '*Moi?*'

I folded my arms.

He sighed. 'Nobody really knows what you're capable of,' he said finally. 'It was a shock when you killed the Ascendant. You had all that power and you'd been under our noses all that time. Everyone wants to know how much magic you really possess.'

'So they can beat me in the challenge,' I said flatly.

'There won't be any worries on that score,' Angus replied. 'They want to know what your limits are so that if any other magically inclined females wander along in future, they'll be in a better position to deal with them.'

'We've got magic,' Jane interrupted. 'We are *magically inclined females* too.' Her lip curled.

'But you're not a problem because your magic isn't that strong.' He pointed at me. 'Hers is. And if there's one woman like Mairi in existence, there's likely to be more, if not now then later. There will be some sort of test arranged en route to see what you're capable of so that everyone can be prepared for what happens during the challenge.' He shrugged dismissively. 'But that's not what you should be worried about. What you should really be considering is why he's permitting you to bring a companion.'

The rest of us exchanged looks. 'Go on,' the Gowk said grimly.

'Noah's anticipating the lass will bring the daemon, and when she dies he'll end up enslaved to the Mages again. He'll be forced to tell them everything he knows about the resistance, including the names of every member. I'm not just talking about you – the Mages know about you lot already. They'll be interested in the names the daemon has heard over the last week or so.'

Ailsa pulled away, putting several metres distance between her and Laoch as if that could help. One by one, the others did the same.

'He's been absent for most of the time. He doesnae ken everything,' the Gowk said dismissively.

Angus met his eyes. 'He kens enough.'

Laoch bristled, his emerald gaze flashing. 'I won't be their slave again. I will die first.'

'While I'm sure that could be arranged easily enough,' Angus drawled, 'it won't happen. You're almost as valuable as she is because once she's gone you can be yanked like a puppet on a string.'

Laoch growled. And nobody else said a word.

Word had gotten around. By the time the Mages' carriage arrived to transport me to Edinburgh – and my almost certain doom – there was quite a crowd. I gazed at the shining faces and wondered whether all these people were truly that naïve, or if hope had got the better of them. We tended to think of hope as something good, something that allowed us to dream of a better future. Perhaps the opposite was true, I thought grimly. Perhaps hope kept us locked in chains.

'You've got this, lass!' somebody shouted.

'Win it for us! Win it for Glasgow!'

Uh-huh. I turned away from the carriage with its ornate gilt trappings and well-groomed horses, which were probably far better fed than the ragged people who'd come to see them. I faced the sea of upturned faces, knowing I ought to say something.

I opened my mouth and my heart stuttered when no sound came out. I wasn't used to this. Speaking to my small group of runaways was one thing; speaking to a crowd was entirely different. My tongue searched for the sounds and I felt the stirrings of panic. Come on, Mairi, I admonished myself. Say something. *Anything.*

The carriage door opened and Noah stepped out. He waved magnanimously at the crowd, ignoring their disgusted expressions, then walked up to me. 'You know, you'll have to speak if you're planning to rule this city at some point,' he murmured so that only I could hear.

The mocking amusement in his voice was designed to sting but it had the opposite effect. I wasn't planning to rule the damned city; I knew I wasn't the right person to do that. My only plan was to stop him and his buddies from ruling it.

I drew in a breath and found the words I needed. 'Thank you,' I said, not to Noah but to the people who were watching me. 'Thank you for your good wishes. I will do everything I can to win the Ascendancy Challenge for Glasgow. *Everything.*' I swallowed hard. 'But I'm only one person. I don't have the experience or the knowledge of the Mages who've been preparing for this all their lives .'

Noah snorted, but I didn't look at him. Instead I lifted my chin and spoke louder. 'Magic isn't the be all and end all. Magic doesn't make you a better person. It's a tool, nothing more. Just because somebody has magic doesn't mean they are better placed to run this city. In fact, the opposite is probably true. We should never allow one group of people to have all the power. No matter what happens in the Ascendancy Challenge, those of us with magic do not have to be the ones who lead.' My voice grew harder. 'The Mages do not have to be the ones who lead.' I bowed my head. 'We should serve you, not the other way around.'

The crowd cheered with far more enthusiasm than I expected. Unsurprisingly, Noah wasn't impressed. 'Managing expectations, are we?' he asked.

Numerous answers sprang to mind, but I decided I wasn't going to give him the satisfaction of a response. I simply shrugged and gestured at the waiting carriage. 'Well? Are we ready to go?'

There was flash of anger in his face when he realised that I wasn't going to rise to his bait, but then he smoothed his features. 'I'm ready if you are. The other carriages are waiting for us at the edge of the city. We shouldn't keep them waiting. Where's your bag?'

I glanced around. The others had come out of the church and were waiting on the steps, watching Noah and me. I'd told them to stay inside where it was safer, but they knew they'd have to make another run for it as soon as I'd gone. The Mages who remained in the city would be after them within minutes.

The Gowk shuffled forward, a small hold-all in his hands. He handed it to me with an unnecessary bow.

Noah rolled his eyes. 'And your companion?' he asked, as if bored. 'Which poor wanker is coming with us?'

My gaze slid across the group. Fee was watchful and wary, with a scowling Jane and a nervous Flora by her side. Trish and Lottie were avoiding Noah's gaze, but Ailsa was staring at him with brave defiance. Belle was muttering something to Twister – from the latter's face, she was scolding him for some misde- meanour. And Laoch – Laoch was as impassive as the stone walls of the church.

I cleared my throat. 'Angus?' Noah frowned. I tried again. 'Angus? Are you coming?'

There was a muttered expletive, then the old Mage plodded out from the depths beyond the open church door, his shoul- ders hunched and his expression morose. 'You don't want to do this, lass. Pick someone else.'

I shook my head. Nope. Angus was the best person to come along. He was the only one of us who'd been to Edinburgh before, and he was the only one of us who truly understood the Mages – probably because, in his heart of hearts, he was still one of them.

I sneaked a look at Laoch's face. A breeze ruffled through the air, lifting one of his inky-black curls. Other than that, he was absolutely still.

'For fuck's sake,' Angus said.

Noah turned to stare at me. 'For once, I agree. You're bringing the traitor? That's who you're choosing?'

I didn't bother answering. A single muscle ticked in Noah's jaw as Angus pushed his way forward. 'Lord Noah,' he said. 'How delightful that once again we get to spend time in each other's company.'

'You'll burn in hell for your betrayal, Angus,' Noah bit out.

Angus rubbed his arms. 'I do hope so. I tire of these chill Scottish winds.'

Noah's eyes flashed. He didn't do well under pressure, and he didn't appreciate being surprised. He broadcast his emotions like a small child denied a sugary treat. His face twisted, then he spoke again. 'You may bring one other person.'

I blinked. I hadn't expected that. The Mages really were desperate to get their hands on Laoch. I looked at the daemon again. His green eyes met mine. *I can help, Mairi. You know I can. Let me come.*

I wet my lips. 'Very well,' I said aloud. 'I'll take Belle.'

This time everyone was shocked; even the watching crowd were taken aback. Twister's jaw dropped open and Belle stared at me. 'Uh...'

'Her?' Noah gazed at her as if she were nothing more than a cockroach. 'Does that woman possess any magic at all?'

Not the sort that he valued. I ignored him and focused on her. 'Belle?' I asked. 'Will you come?'

She puffed out her cheeks. 'Aye.' She glanced at her husband. 'Aye, I will. I always kent that lass was smart. We employed her for a reason. She kens true value when she sees it.' She nudged him. 'Edinburgh. I'm going tae Edinburgh!'

Twister squinted at me. 'You sure about this, Mairi?'

Not in the slightest, but I needed an attack dog and Belle was as good as any sharp-toothed mutt. I nodded and she beamed giddily. 'I'll go and get my things together!' she trilled. She jabbed Twister. 'Come on. You need to help me pack. And when I'm gone, you need to make sure everyone knows that I've gone to Edinburgh to save them.' She jabbed him again. 'Make sure they *all* know.'

The pair hastily retreated into the church. Only then did I permit myself to look at Laoch – except now he was avoiding my gaze. I sighed to myself, walked up to him and reached out to touch his jaw.

'If this is punishment for leaving you...' he began.

'Of course it's not. I can't risk you,' I said softly. 'You'll be needed here.'

'Without you, nobody here will trust me.'

'Then change their minds. You have the charm and wit to do it.' I smiled crookedly. 'Besides, I need someone to look after Mungo for me.'

Laoch stared at me, his expression inscrutable. I waited for him to say something else – anything else – but his lips remained closed. He shook his head slightly, turned on his heel and disappeared back up the steps and into the church. All I could do was watch him go.

'Guess your boyfriend's pissed off,' Noah remarked. 'Can't say I'm surprised.'

'Neither can I,' Angus said. 'I know you don't want to see him hurt, lass, but you need him. Unleashed, he has more magic than I do. And we both know he's more loyal. As for that bloody Belle woman...'

I held up my hand; I'd made up my mind and I wasn't going to listen to any protests. I looked at the church entrance, wondering if Laoch would say goodbye, but he didn't reappear.

After several moments, Belle came out, hefting her bag – and mine – on her shoulder. I turned towards the carriage. 'That's us, then,' I said distantly. I raised my eyebrows at the Gowk, and he bobbed his head. For the second time in as many weeks, he'd have to make sure that everyone got to safety as soon as I'd gone. I hoped he'd manage it.

'Cheerio, Mairi.'

'Good luck.'

'Give those fucking Mages hell.'

I gazed at my bedraggled group of friends. 'Thank you,' I said quietly. 'Stay safe. All of you.'

I COULD COUNT on one hand the number of times I'd been in a carriage. The likes of me usually wandered the city on foot. In fact, the last time I'd travelled anywhere in this manner was when I made the journey from St Mags, the orphanage where I'd grown up, to Belle and Twister's wee tartan shop. The carriage on that occasion had been nothing like this one.

Even Belle was agog. 'This material,' she said, stroking the gold velvet on the seat. 'Where does it come from? Who's your supplier?'

Noah flicked her an irritated look from beneath his eyelashes. 'How would I know?'

Either she didn't register his tone or she didn't care. 'Have you considered tartan? There's a particularly bonnie purple tartan that would set off this gold perfectly.'

'And where would you get this bonnie tartan from? Your stupid wee shop has been shut down. Your tartan was shite anyway.'

Belle pulled back her shoulders and glared at him. 'That didn't stop you fae taking screeds of it without paying. It couldnae have been *that* shite, you bampot.'

Noah's eyes spat fire. 'How dare you talk to me like that? I'm a Mage and you…' he looked her up and down with an expression of disgust '…you're a middle-aged woman with not even beauty to commend you. I could squash you like that.' He snapped his fingers.

Belle looked at him challengingly. 'Go on, then.'

I tried to suppress a smile.

Angus, who was in the corner of the carriage with his arms folded, sighed. 'Is all this really necessary? Can't we journey in peace and enjoy the sights?'

'While you still can,' Noah muttered. 'You won't be enjoying anything soon, you traitorous freak.'

It was curious that he was so annoyed by our presence in the carriage; after all, he had demanded it. I examined his face. It seemed strange to me now that I'd ever considered him handsome. His mouth had a cruel, pinched look, and the light behind his eyes was soulless.

Noah felt my gaze. 'Do you like what you see, Mairi?'

No. 'I wonder if you're more furious that I didn't fall for your charms than that I killed your uncle.'

Angus chuckled while Noah's face reddened. We wouldn't have the upper hand for long, but it was surprisingly good fun to goad Noah, even if it might not be wise to continue in such a confined space. I glanced meaningfully at Belle and Angus, hoping they understood, then settled for staring out of the carriage window at the passing streets. Sometimes I really missed silence.

It took less time than I'd expected to reach the city limits. The narrow streets gave way to more space and fewer people. I'd wandered a fair distance across Glasgow in my time, usually in search of herbs and flowers for my ointments and medicines, but I'd rarely come this far. When the high wall that marked the limits of the city and the start of the countryside came into view, I couldn't deny the frisson of excitement that filtered through me. For the first time in my life, I was going to leave. I was going to see what was really out there for myself.

The men guarding the gate weren't Mages, but they were certainly under the Mages' command. They stopped the carriage with respectful nods and bowed in perfect synchronicity when they saw Noah. They didn't glance at the rest of us; even Angus didn't merit a flicker of attention.

'Lord Noah,' one of them said. 'The others are waiting several miles down the road. They passed by less than twenty minutes ago, so you should have no problem making up time.'

'Thank you.' Noah's eyes twinkled. 'You're doing a grand job, fellas. It can't be easy being out here at all hours. The responsibility of guarding the city perimeter is an important one, and I can rest easy knowing that such fine men as yourselves are in charge of it. Your service and hard work does not go unnoticed.'

Noah's words dripped with glib gratitude, preening the feathers of the guards and ensuring they remained on side. Unfortunately, not everyone in Glasgow could see through the Mages.

The men looked delighted at his praise, like stray mongrels pathetically grateful for rotting titbits of food. 'It's an honour to serve you,' another one said, and they all bowed again.

Noah smiled. 'Tell me, how would you feel about continuing to serve if a woman were in charge?' he asked. 'Could you take orders from a female?'

They didn't need to answer; their shocked expressions said it all. 'A woman?' the first guard asked in disbelief. 'How could a woman rule Glasgow?'

The man next to him shook his head. 'The city would be over-run by the Afflicted within weeks. We wouldnae stay here – we'd go to Perth. Or Edinburgh. A woman wouldnae have the first clue about keeping Glasgow safe. I'm no' dying for a woman.'

I drew in a sharp breath but Angus placed a hand on my arm and shook his head. It wasn't worth engaging with them; they wouldn't listen to reason, and Noah was only trying to annoy me.

Belle didn't receive the warning, however. She pulled back her shoulders and glared out of the carriage window at the men. 'Your mothers would be ashamed of you! Whit does a man have that a woman doesnae?'

The nearest guard cupped his groin with his left hand and smirked. 'Whit do you think?'

Belle burst out laughing. 'A cock? You think a cock is necessary to lead a city? The ability to piss while standing is what makes a difference?' She raised her hand and crooked her pinky. 'I can tell you ain't got much down there. Does size matter, then? Should we raise the man with the largest dick to be the Ascendant, and weed out anyone who's no' big enough to pass muster?'

The guard clenched his fists as his cheeks glowed red. 'Whit would an old woman like you ken about it?'

'I'm fifty-two,' Belle replied. 'I've seen plenty of cocks in my time. I ken plenty.'

His friend jumped in to help him. 'Women cannae do magic.'

'Wrong!' she trilled. She pointed to me. 'She can do magic.'

'Then she's a freak.'

'If she's a freak, so's your Lord Noah.'

'Women dinnae have the strength to lead.'

Belle laughed again. 'Push a baby the size o' a watermelon oot yer body and then come back talk to me about strength!'

Noah glared at Belle. 'Enough.'

'Fuck off.'

He reacted instantly, raising his fist to her. I muttered a swift response. '*Meshar al.*'

Noah's body jerked and he slumped as he lost control of his limbs. The guards gaped in horror while Belle smirked. 'Still think women are weak?' she sneered.

She might have been impressed but Angus certainly wasn't. 'Cease!' he ordered quietly. 'You're supposed to be hiding what you can do, not broadcasting it!'

Anger flashed through me, not at Angus but at myself. I had reacted and waved magic at Noah when I was supposed to be doing just the opposite. I gritted my teeth and released the spell.

Noah shuddered and groaned. 'My Lord,' one of the guards asked hesitantly. 'Are you alright? Should we get some help?'

'Move the carriage,' Noah said. He thumped on the roof. 'Now. We have to get going. We're already late.'

'My Lord?'

He refused to look at the guard. 'Move!'

The driver, who was perched outside, finally heard him and sprang into action. A moment later we trundled away, leaving the group of guards staring after us. Noah crossed his arms and stared out of the window.

'Serves you right,' Belle said, lifting her pointed chin in defiance.

I gave her a warning look and she subsided. Despite appearances, Noah had won this round. We'd not even left the city limits and already he knew too much about what I was capable of.

'That wouldn't have happened if the daemon were here,' Angus said.

Noah's mouth tightened and so did mine as we all lapsed into an uncomfortable silence.

ELEVEN

For all its showy, gilt trappings and expensive fabric, the carriage soon felt incredibly uncomfortable. I shifted position several times, my arse sliding on the seat, and nearly fell off every time we went over a pothole. I'd expected the journey to be smooth, but it appeared the Mages placed little importance on maintaining the roads outside the city.

It quickly grew too hot and stuffy, but when Angus opened a window it felt too cold. Nothing about the journey was pleasant and nobody was interested in chatting. Noah glared out of the window, clearly still smarting that I'd used magic to get the better of him – again. He should have been pleased; he had information about my growing abilities that could be used against me. Soon, unless I was very, very careful, he'd learn even more.

I eyed our bags, which were sitting on the shelf above Noah's head, and sighed. Then I stopped the self-flagellation and, following Noah's lead, gazed out of the window at the countryside I'd only ever previously imagined.

It was greener than I expected. I didn't know why that surprised me, but it was astonishing how many different verdant shades there were at this time of year. Plenty of the trees boasted evergreen leaves, and some of the fields gleamed in the dim, afternoon sun. The rolling hills in the distance provided a stunning backdrop, and the glimmer of water from a deep river was astonishing; it was far cleaner than any I'd seen in the city. After several minutes, it was almost too much to take in.

I dragged my eyes away to focus on the array of plants growing near the road. There were still plenty of pretty white snowdrops, for which I could think of a dozen uses, and all manner of different grasses. There were thistles in abundance, and several plants that I'd never laid on eyes before. When we passed a row of blackthorn trees with tiny buds that were starting to form, it took all my self-control not to jump out of the moving carriage to take samples.

I was so engrossed that I didn't notice the carriage slowing down; it was only when Angus tensed and nudged me that I realised what was happening.

I pretended not to notice and continued to look out of the carriage window, but out of the corner of my eye I saw Noah sit straighter. His expression, which had been dampened after the encounter with the guards, brightened. Aye, I thought grimly, here we go.

The angle of the carriage altered as we ascended a slope. It was gradual at first, before growing steeper. Belle clutched at the edge of her seat, and I felt the small of my back press uncomfortably into the side of the carriage. The sound of the horses snorting reached our ears, then the carriage trundled to a juddering stop.

Noah painted a deliberate frown on his face. 'What's going on? Why have we stopped?' There was no answer. He huffed and reached for the carriage door, pushing past me before stepping out.

Angus and I exchanged looks. I counted to three in my head before Noah let out a sharp cry. 'Careful, lass,' Angus said. 'Don't give too much away.'

I nodded and gestured to Belle. 'Stay here. Don't step outside unless you have to.' There was no doubt in my mind that she would be considered collateral damage. Another thought occurred to me. 'Guard our bags.'

Belle looked as if she might protest but, before she could open her mouth, there was a sharp roar outside. Her eyes widened in fear and she squeaked.

I prepared to meet whatever was out there. It wouldn't kill me – the Mages wouldn't allow it to. They weren't looking for my death, not right now and not without an audience.

I tensed my muscles and ducked my head. As I left the carriage, Angus was on my heels. Another carriage, identical to ours, was on its side with a massive gash along its length. A dead horse lay next to it, and a copse of dense trees stood just beyond.

There was another roar. Noah, who had been peering inside the fallen carriage, straightened up and spun around. 'There were four Mages in here!' he yelled. 'There's none now, and the driver is missing! Whatever is making that noise must have attacked them!'

Uh-huh. I glanced at Angus, who smiled and shrugged, then I joined Noah to survey the damage more closely.

'There's blood here.' Noah pointed at a splatter on the ground. 'We should leave immediately before we're attacked too.'

I looked into the ruined interior. There were no bodies inside, and there was no blood there. I rubbed my chin thoughtfully. 'Four Mages, you say? Which Mages exactly?'

'Why does that matter?' he snapped.

Angus stepped up next to me. 'It matters because if they were new Mages who are untested, it's understandable that they'd be taken unaware by a single creature attacking them. If they were experienced Mages, we'd have more cause to be concerned. What were their names?'

Noah wasn't going to tell us because the Mages he'd referred to didn't exist; this was all part of the ploy to get me to display as much magical skill as possible. If I were drained of power in the process, that would be an added benefit.

As if to prove my theory, there was a loud caw overhead. Three ravens suddenly appeared, flying overhead and circling before settling on a branch nearby and tilting their heads at us.

'I don't know who those Mages were,' Noah said. He nodded at the carriage driver, whose acting skills were less honed. He was sitting placidly on top of the carriage with the reins in his hands; I wouldn't have been surprised if he'd had a picnic in the bag next to him. He knew all about this set-up. 'We should get out of here.'

I pursed my lips. 'Alright.' I swivelled towards our own carriage – and that was when the supposed 'monster' appeared from the trees.

It was an enormous purple thing, some kind of serpent, with a lashing tail and gaping jaws. I eyed the sharp ridges along its spine and the taut glimmering scales that covered it from head to tail. Aye, alright: it was pretty scary. 'Is that thing real?' I muttered to Angus.

His expression was grim. 'Aye. There are a few of us who kept them as pets. They can never be fully tamed but they can be put to...' he hesitated briefly '...use. It's known as a beithir. Its tail will sting you if you get too close. Take care.'

Talk about stating the obvious. I watched the beithir warily. From its flashing eyes to its writhing body, I reckoned it was no happier about being kept as a Mages' 'pet' than Laoch had been about his status as a slave. This beithir was out for blood.

Noah was closest, but the creature chose to go for Angus. No surprise there; it knew who its true masters were, and those masters needed to get Angus out of the way as quickly as possible. In fact, it would solve a lot of the Mages' problems if he were hastily dispatched.

But we already knew this, and we'd discussed at length how to deal with it. The Mages already knew that I could throw up a barrier to block attacks, so there was little point in pretending otherwise. While Angus muttered the word '*Vaz*', I hummed and did the same. With our combined magic, he'd be safe enough.

The beithir lunged towards him, its snout smacking straight into the invisible wall. It howled in rage and took a breath, and a frisson of fear rippled through me. I darted to the side to avoid the blast of flame that the creature spat towards Angus. The magic wall held – but only just. Damn it; the beithir was stronger than I'd expected.

It reared back and blew another flaming jet. I allowed myself a second to glance at Noah; he was standing still, his arms by his side, not watching the beithir. He was watching me.

I ignored the spasm of anger that zipped through me and flailed my arms. 'What do we do?' I yelled, trying to appear panicked. 'It's going to kill Angus!'

'We'll have to fight it,' Noah said. 'We can't escape now.'

Translation: I would have to fight it so Noah could assess my full abilities. Playing along, I nodded nervously, then heaved in a breath and hummed. *Sel ez*.

There was a snap in the air as the molecules coalesced. A split second later, the beithir was doused in cold water that eliminated any further threat of fire. The purple monster hissed angrily and spun towards me. Its jaws snapped and it puffed a cloud of toxic smoke.

I didn't have to fake looking scared now. Those teeth were damned sharp and, from the glistening droplets visible along the ridges on the beithir's spine, it was coated in a viscous fluid that my water magic had done nothing to dispel. A slow-acting poison would be the perfect choice; something that would weaken me by the time the Ascendancy Challenge got under way would be exactly what the Mages were looking for. I'd have to be even more careful now.

In a bid to appear helpful, Noah muttered a spell of his own. '*Sim bra.*'

A cloud of dust rose from the ground, temporarily engulfing the beithir. It didn't contain it for long, and I jumped back as its teeth snapped at me once again.

Angus's lips moved as he uttered a second spell. The beithir writhed in response, raising its head to the sky to scream in pain, but it didn't pause for long. It whipped its tail round and, in one swift motion, knocked me clean off my feet. I landed with a thud on the hard ground, my body jarring in agony. The beithir lunged once more.

I swallowed and hummed yet again, focusing on the words but controlling my power. I had to look as if I were giving everything I had while holding back most of my energy. *Ins veil.*

The beithir's body was flung backwards, landing several feet away. I gasped and made a show of breathing hard from the effort, while Angus used his magic to attack. That allowed me the time to stagger to my feet and face the creature head on.

I hummed a single note and repeated my earlier attack. *Ins veil.* This time there was even less power behind my efforts.

The beithir was tossed back less than a metre and came for me again. Again I hummed. *Ins veil.* Now it merely jerked its head.

'Mairi!' Angus shouted. 'You have to dig deeper!'

'I'm trying!' I pushed my hair out of eyes and panted. 'Let's time our attacks and hit it together!'

Angus nodded. 'Three. Two. One.' He paused. 'Now!'

I hummed one final time. The beithir spun away, blown back by the force of my magic as Angus's spell attacked it from the side. It twisted round, its eyes slitted as it recovered quickly.

I stumbled, tripping over my feet as it came for me, roaring its fury. I took advantage of the deafening noise and hummed as quietly as I could, allowing the newest words that Angus had taught me to fill my entire being. *Fels zor.* With luck, Noah wouldn't notice this final burst of magic.

The beithir attacked, flung itself at me and used its body weight to bring me crashing to the ground. It lay on top of me, the sharp ridges along its spine scraping my skin as I gritted my teeth and prayed I'd done enough. For good measure, I shrieked and threw all my hatred for the Mages into the sound.

And that was when Noah intervened properly. Finally. *'Meshar al!'* he bellowed.

The beithir shuddered and collapsed, pinning me beneath it. I twisted my head to the side and watched its yellow eyes roll back into its head.

My fingers scrabbled on the ground until I found a rough stone. I held my breath and scraped the edge of it against my arm, ripping the fabric of my blouse and scoring my skin. As soon as I felt beads of blood, I kicked and shoved the beast so I could gain enough purchase against its body to wiggle out.

I staggered to my feet, doubled over and made loud retching sounds. I was vaguely aware of the three birds, who hadn't moved from their perch during the fight, taking off into the air and flapping away.

'Mairi! Lass! Are you alright?'

I squinted up at Angus and wiped my mouth with the back of my hand. 'I'm okay,' I said weakly. I looked down at the beithir's inert body before glancing at Noah. 'That was close. I suppose I ought to say thank you.' I offered the words grudgingly, hoping the relief I felt at the satisfaction that glittered briefly in his eyes didn't show on my face.

'When we meet in the challenge, remember that I helped you,' Noah said. 'And that you're only alive because of my intervention.' His gaze dropped to the scratch on my arm, but the only indication that it pleased him was a faint flaring of his nostrils. It was enough.

'What is that thing?' I asked. 'Where the hell did it come from?'

Noah laughed coldly. 'There are creatures like this across the country. The likes of you could never understand the measures we Mages take to keep them away from the cities. No matter what you think, we earn our keep.' He pulled a face at Angus. 'As you know, traitor.'

'We are fortunate indeed that you were here to save us,' Angus said drily

Noah sniffed, then turned towards our carriage. 'Where's the driver gone?' He rolled his eyes and stomped off towards the copse of trees to search for him.

I waited until he was out of earshot then said, 'The driver's probably round the corner having a smoke and a snack.'

'Aye.' Angus nodded to my arm. 'Did that thing—?'

I shook my head. 'No, I did that to myself. I think the beithir was coated in poison. If Noah thinks that is in my bloodstream and will cause me problems, it's all to the good.'

The old Mage chuckled. 'Indeed. How much of yourself did you push?'

'A quarter of my energy, perhaps. There's plenty left, and I only used basic magic to repel the beithir. Do you think it was enough to fool Noah?'

He shrugged. 'Only time will tell. You did the best you could and made a good showing.'

'So did you,' I said quietly.

He snorted. 'I always make a good showing, lass.'

'The birds? Where did the ravens go?'

'Towards Edinburgh. They'll communicate enough of what happened to the Mages there. Noah will fill in the rest when we arrive.'

I was sure that he would. I sighed. 'All those Mages think I'm stupid, don't they? They thought I wouldn't recognise their plan, even with the ravens watching on. They're still underestimating me.'

Angus wagged his finger. 'That's a good thing, lass.'

An odd creaking sound came from the carriage and I stiffened in alarm until Belle popped her head out. 'Are you finished yet? It's hot in here,' she complained. 'And I'm bored.'

I glared. 'Shhh! We don't want Noah to hear you. He has to think that we fell for that idiocy.'

'I'm not stupid.' She tossed her head. 'He's not with you. I checked first that he wasn't nearby.'

No matter what she said, he wouldn't be far away. I gave her another warning look and turned towards the trees. Noah seemed to have disappeared.

'Do you think there are other Mages down there?' I asked Angus. 'Were others watching the attack and taking notes?'

His brow creased. 'I doubt it. I can't sense anyone. The others probably released the beithir then left the area to be safe. It's what I would have done. And besides—' He stopped in mid-sentence.

I stared at him. 'Besides what?'

Angus didn't answer; instead he strode towards the trees. I watched him for a moment then followed. A moment later, Belle emerged from the carriage and followed too.

'I asked you to guard the bags,' I said. I felt her eyes boring into my back. It was the first time I'd openly reprimanded her, even though it wasn't much of a reprimand.

'Who's going to take them?' she returned. 'That dead bampot serpent?'

I thought of a dozen responses but said none of them. Sometimes life had been so much easier when I didn't speak. I shook my head and caught up to Angus. 'What is it?'

He put his finger to his lips, gesturing for silence. Confused, I tilted my head but I stayed quiet. And that was when I saw the human body on the ground in front of him with its ravaged flesh and deadened eyes.

I clamped my hand over my mouth and darted forward.

'This isnae real, is it?' Belle asked, her voice quavering. 'It's an illusion. Another Mage trick.' She hesitated. 'Right?'

I didn't need to check Angus's face to know it wasn't a trick. My eyes travelled the length of the corpse, noting the clothes and the over-sized boots. He was covered in blood and half his face was missing, but I was certain it was the carriage driver.

I was confused. He'd been Noah's man and he must have known about the beithir; that much had been clear from his expression when the carriage first stopped. So why had he been killed? He'd been alive only minutes earlier. It couldn't have been the beithir that did this. Had Noah murdered him? And if so, why?

'I don't understand,' I whispered.

Angus's expression was tight with tension. 'Listen.'

I strained my ears. 'I don't hear anything.'

He waved a hand in irritation. '*Tinza*.'

I hadn't heard that word before and opened my mouth to ask what he'd done, then realised abruptly what had changed. The birdsong around us was louder; I could hear the different notes and changes in tone. The breeze rustling the leaves had altered its timbre, sounding high pitched as it whistled to our left and growing more muted as it hit the denser trees deeper inside the copse. Something was scraping at the ground beneath our feet – a semi-slumbering badger, perhaps.

I swallowed. I could even hear Belle's heartbeat. None of those things were important right now, however; it was the grunts and heaving breaths in front of us that drew my attention. I turned to Belle. 'Get back to the carriage. Look after the bags.'

Her face was white. 'Now!' I ordered. She took off, grabbing her skirts and scurrying as fast as her feet could carry her.

'That sounds like the Afflicted,' I said, each word barely audible.

'Aye lass,' Angus replied. 'It does.'

'But it's daytime.'

He looked grim as he lurched forward towards the source of the noise. I spun round and plunged after him. When I rejoined him at the opposite edge of the copse and peered out at the fields beyond, my heart missed a beat.

There were three hunched figures moving away from us. One was wearing a tattered dress and dragging something behind her, while the other two had ragged trousers but no shirts. Even without seeing their faces, I knew what they were. The grime caking their clothes and bodies, their ratty long hair, their unsteady gait and occasional grunts made it obvious that the trio was indeed Afflicted.

'The fucking beithir wasn't enough? Mages can control the Afflicted as well?' I whispered.

Angus didn't answer immediately and I turned to look at him. I saw something in his eyes that I'd never seen there before: fear. Angus was scared. 'No, lass,' he said. 'The Afflicted cannot be controlled. This isn't another test, and this isn't about you. They must have been drawn here by the beithir's screeching and found easy prey with our driver.'

'It's the middle of the day!'

He shook his head. 'I can't explain that. Maybe these ones have adapted to daylight.'

I was still not prepared to believe what was in front of my eyes. 'If this isn't another Mage test, then where the fuck is Noah?'

Angus raised his finger and pointed. 'There.'

Where? I pushed myself up on tiptoe – and my mouth went dry. I hadn't seen it before because of the long grass but now I could. It wasn't a heavy object that the Afflicted woman was dragging behind her, it was Noah.

CHAPTER
TWELVE

'Is he dead?' I asked.

When Angus didn't move, I gripped his arm and pinched it hard. He yanked it away and glared at me. 'There's no need for violence!'

'There is, if the only thing you're going to do is stand there and stare,' I returned. I'd never seen the old Mage like this before. 'Is Noah dead?'

Angus shook himself. 'I don't know. I can't tell.' His eyes met mine. 'But we have to go and get him.'

'Go and get him?' I couldn't hide my astonishment. 'Are you mad?'

'If we turn up in Edinburgh without that boy, they'll assume you killed him and execute you on the spot. They'll be able to justify your death just like that.' He snapped his fingers

'They're going to kill me anyway.'

Angus's gaze hardened. 'Right now you still have a chance, a sliver of a chance, but a chance nonetheless. Without Noah, you have nothing. And nobody will believe that he was attacked by the Afflicted in broad daylight.'

I knew that Angus was right, but I wasn't quite ready to give in. 'If he's already dead ...'

'Then at least we can show the wounds on his body and explain his death. We have to retrieve him whether he's dead or alive.'

I passed a hand in front of my eyes. 'If he's alive, he might be infected. He might already be one of them.'

'Aye.' Angus's voice was dark. 'He might be. We'll have to hope he's not.'

My shoulders slumped as I struggled to accept the idea that I'd have to risk everything to save Noah. Bloody Noah, of all people.

There was a sudden rustle from behind us. I spun round, prepared to defend myself from the next attack, but it wasn't a monster or a Mage or a member of the Afflicted.

'There.' Belle threw my bag down onto the ground between us. 'There's your precious luggage.' She put her hands on her hips. 'I'm no' your skivvy. You cannae order me around like a servant.' She kicked the bag and I winced. 'Quit pushing me around all the time!'

As if. Belle never permitted anyone to push her around.

'Keep your voice down, woman,' Angus muttered.

'I will not. If I want to shout and yell and scream, I will...' She faltered as she finally caught sight of the three Afflicted. 'Oh,' she whispered.

Oh, indeed. I sighed, knelt down, unzipped my bag and peered inside. Mungo was curled up on top of the neatly folded clothes. He blinked and yawned, then raised his head, saw me and jerked.

'What's that damned rodent doing here?' Angus asked.

Belle smiled smugly.

The air crackled and blessed relief flooded through me. The leaves on the trees rustled and a warm breeze toyed with my loose curls. There was a brief flash and Laoch appeared. His nose twitched, one final indication that a second ago he'd been more mouse than daemon. Mungo squeaked and buried himself into the bag once again as Laoch looked around.

'What the fuck just happened?' Angus breathed. 'Were you *inside* that mouse?'

Laoch's lip curled. 'You Mages don't know everything.'

'What's the spell? How do I do that?' In the face of new magic, Angus forgot our immediate problem and rubbed his hands together like an excited child. He was acting like a sticky-fingered bairn.

'You don't,' I told him. 'That magic is not for Mages.'

'But—'

'Not now, Angus.' I ignored his brief pout and gazed at Laoch. His dark hair was ruffled, his green eyes were tired, and his clothes were creased; he looked wonderful.

He flashed me a quick smile that pierced my heart, then looked around and frowned. 'This is not Edinburgh,' he said

'No.' I pushed away my joy at seeing him. I couldn't afford to act like a giddy schoolgirl. 'We have a problem.'

'The test?'

I shook my head. 'We passed that. I pretended to use all the magic I had to beat down a serpent.' I pointed towards the Afflicted who, despite their lack of speed, were now some distance away. 'We have another issue.'

Laoch turned his head, then stared, slack jawed. 'Shite.'

I couldn't have put it better myself. *I wasn't sure if you were here or not. I thought you might have stayed in Glasgow,* I said to him silently.

He snorted. *Of course I'm here. I told you that I won't leave you again, but I didn't want to signal that to you. Who knows what the other Mages can sense? Angus finally worked out that we can communicate like this. If he can do that, so can the rest.*

'Stop thinking at each other like that!' Angus muttered.

Belle stared. 'Huh?'

Laoch and I exchanged glances. 'Where's Noah?' he asked aloud.

'He's with the Afflicted, enjoying the sunshine over there.' I sighed. 'We have to mount a rescue operation.'

'Now I wish you'd left me in the bag,' Laoch protested.

I grimaced. *I wish I could have joined you.*

BELLE REMAINED BEHIND by the trees while Angus, Laoch and I fanned out, stalking the path the Afflicted had taken. Angus had expelled a great deal of his power to protect himself from the gigantic beithir, and Laoch was equally depleted after remaining in Mungo's body for so long. I'd reserved more energy, but I was far from invincible. We needed to keep our wits about us if we were to retrieve Noah, although I couldn't honestly have said whether I hoped he was dead or alive. At that moment, the only positive note was that the three Afflicted people had no idea we were behind them, but I doubted that would last.

The field dipped into a small valley. We crossed a tiny burn that was narrow enough to jump over, then the slope rose again. I kept my body low, hunkering down. When I crested the wee hill, I saw where the Afflicted trio had gone. There was a small cave set into the next hillside, and I could hear more grunts and snuffles from just beyond it. I prayed that there weren't more Afflicted inside; dealing with three of them would be hard enough.

Laoch and Angus were staying level with me, although both were some distance away. I motioned to them and they nodded, then the three of us moved to the sides of the cave opening. There was a considerable amount of detritus lying around. I avoided gazing at the gnawed bones for too long so I could persuade myself that they were animal in origin and not human. It wasn't the Afflicteds' fault that they were like this; they were victims, too.

I peered around the opening. The cave didn't look particularly deep, and the noises were bouncing back from inside. None of them sounded like Noah, but I guessed that if he were still alive staying quiet was the best thing he could do.

I stared into the gloom, thinking about how to proceed. That was when Angus started to shout and yell from the opposite side of the cave mouth. I stared at him in alarm. He grinned at me and pushed back his straggly grey hair.

'What are you doing?' I whispered. 'Be quiet!'

Angus only yelled louder, then he jumped into the open and waved his arms. 'Oi!' he shouted. 'Beasties! Whatcha doing?'

'Angus!'

He continued to ignore me. I looked at Laoch who was standing where Angus had been only moments before, but he shook his head in warning. I frowned as Angus turned to run back down towards the little valley, flapping his arms and weaving from left to right as if he were drunk.

I'd barely drawn breath when the three Afflicted bounded out of the cave and after him. They loped past me, all their attention on Angus who was whooping and jumping ahead of them. Shite: that stupid bloody bampot of a Mage was presenting himself as bait.

Laoch met my eyes and I nodded sharply. Whether or not Angus was doing the right thing, we couldn't waste this opportunity.

I held my breath and slipped into the cave. It was even messier inside than outside. There were more bones on the rough floor, most of them with visible teeth marks, as well as ragged items of clothing and other rubbish. The stench was eye-watering. A bubble of sorrow rose in my throat; even animals didn't usually defecate where they slept. Clearly the Afflicted were too far gone to care.

I looked at a small headless doll lying next to a pool of rank, algae-infused water. Regardless of what they were now, they had been people once. I thought about the Afflicted man I'd helped escape from the City Chambers and how, in turn, he'd helped me to escape. Not all of them were completely gone; some maintained a shred of humanity somewhere deep inside. I'd do well to remember that.

There was a sudden moan from the darkest corner of the cave. Laoch came up behind me and touched my elbow. *I think that's him. I think that's Noah.*

That meant he was still alive. I told myself to be glad, and nodded. *Let's grab him and get out of here.* I reached for Laoch's hand and some of my tension eased as his warm fingers entwined with mine.

'*Altus ish moy,*' he said quietly. There was a faint judder from the cave walls and a dull light appeared in front of us, enough to illuminate the way ahead. Together we plunged towards the source of the moan.

It was indeed Noah. He was curled in a foetal position, his legs and arms tucked tight against his body. I pulled free from Laoch, darted towards the Mage and knelt down. Other than a large lump on the back of his head, he seemed to have none of the hideous wounds that had killed the carriage driver – but when I touched his skin, I drew back with a hiss.

He's burning up, Laoch. I brushed back Noah's hair before lifting one closed eyelid. Angry red veins bulged from his eyeball and I recoiled instinctively. There was no doubt about what was happening to him.

Laoch's answer was calm and reasoned. *There's nothing we can do about it right now. Let's get him out of here and worry about his ... health later.*

I swallowed, then moved back to let him scoop up Noah's body and put it over his shoulder. Laoch was a daemon and he was strong, but he still staggered slightly under the weight.

Will you manage? I asked doubtfully.

Please! Of course I'll manage. Come on. We must get out of here now before the Afflicted return.

He turned and jogged towards the cave entrance, which gleamed brightly in contrast to the gloomy interior. The spell that Laoch had cast created a cloud of light in front of him, but there was something odd; right behind me, above the spot where Noah had been lying, something was still glowing. It was dim, but it was enough to catch my eye.

I turned my head and my blood chilled when I saw the hatched symbol. It was identical to the runes I'd seen in Glasgow, albeit on a much larger scale. Its presence here in this cave could mean only one thing: it hadn't been created by the Mages, nor was it something that the resistance members had dreamed up. It belonged to the Afflicted, although I couldn't even begin to imagine what it was for.

I backed away, as if putting as much distance between the symbol and myself were the only way to stay safe. A second later, I sprinted after Laoch.

CHAPTER

THIRTEEN

L aoch placed Noah inside the carriage and closed the door. I nibbled nervously on my bottom lip as I watched, then I hummed. *Belzac.*

A tiny flame flickered at the edge of the door. I pushed more power into it until it grew white hot and melted the metal along the edge, sealing the door closed.

'Whit did you do that for?' Belle asked. When I didn't answer, she rolled her eyes. 'Turning mute again, lass? Funny how you only do that when you dinna want to speak to me.'

It wasn't that I didn't want to speak to her, I just wasn't sure I could give voice to what was happening to Noah. It could mean the end of us all.

Angus appeared at the foot of the hill. He waved before he wiped away a layer of glistening sweat from his brow. 'I led those fuckers on a merry dance!' he crowed. He raised his hands in the air and his feet tapped the ground in a jig. 'There's life in the old dog yet!'

'Bampot,' Belle muttered. She dropped my bag, ignoring Mungo whose tiny nose twitched upwards, and turned to

120

peer through the carriage window at Noah. The glass was already steaming up. 'How are we going to get to Edinburgh now? We cannae get inside the carriage because you've sealed it up. There's no' even a driver. And why did those monsters kill the driver and eat half his face but no' do the same to the Mage?'

Good question. Yet again, I chose not to answer; instead I looked down at my feet and waited for Angus to join us.

'Well?' he asked when he reached us. 'Did you get him?'

Laoch pointed to the carriage.

'She's locked him in there,' Belle sniffed. 'But she won't say why.'

Angus paled. 'Oh. Really?'

'Aye.'

He grimaced. 'Shite.'

'Whit?' Belle put her hands on her hips. 'Whit's going on? Whit are you no' telling me?'

I ignored her questions and looked at Angus. 'You shouldn't have done that,' I told him. 'You shouldn't have put yourself up as bait like that.'

'How else were you going to get the boy? It worked, didn't it?' He smiled, although it didn't reach his eyes. 'Maybe you'll trust me a little more now. I can play hero as much as the rest of you.'

'If you're still angling to know more of my magic,' Laoch growled, 'don't bother.'

'You're a humourless horned bastard, you know?' Angus told him, though there was no energy to his insult. Instead, his eyes trailed back towards the copse.

'You remember that symbol I asked you about?' I asked.

He nodded.

Laoch looked disturbed. 'The same one that we saw at the City Chambers?'

'Aye.' I ran my tongue over my lips. 'There was another version inside that cave.'

'Why will none of you tell me whit's going on?' Belle screeched.

From beyond the trees – in fact likely back at the cave itself – there was a rage-filled scream. We exchanged glances.

I hauled myself into the driver's seat. 'Sounds like they've made it back home and realised that Noah has gone. We need to leave before they come back this way – and we don't want to be out here when the sun goes down.'

'Aye,' Angus said, with more than a tinge of sarcasm. 'Because we all ken the Afflicted only come out at night.'

Belle looked fit to explode, so I patted the space next to me. 'Come up here and I'll answer as many of your questions as I can.' Not that I *had* many answers, but I could try.

'Wait a minute.' Laoch walked round the front of the horses and pulled himself up towards me. 'There's something we have to do first.' His head dipped and his hand curled round the back of my shoulders. For one all-too-brief moment his mouth touched mine and everything else faded away. It was me and him; nothing else mattered.

We couldn't remain like that forever, and it was over far too quickly. There was another Afflicted scream, closer this time. 'Are you done?' Angus asked. 'We really have to go now.'

Laoch jumped down and walked over to where Belle had dropped my bag. He crouched next to Mungo and his mouth moved quietly. Angus turned towards him, but I reached down and gently nudged him away. 'It's daemon magic,' I told him. 'You're not meant to know it.'

'Do you?' Angus asked.

I looked away.

There was a crackle and a flash then Laoch was gone, leaving only Mungo and the bag in his place. Angus tutted, but he scooped up the bag without another word of complaint. I offered a hand to Belle to help her up, then Angus joined us and placed the bag carefully on his lap.

There was a deep-throated grunt from inside the carriage. 'If you're going to tell me that the wee fucker back there has been infected and is about to turn into one of those Afflicted monsters, then—' Belle began.

I interrupted her. 'Hold on tight, Belle.' I grabbed the reins. I didn't have the first idea about driving a carriage, but it couldn't be that hard. I jerked hard and the horses took off with an uncomfortable jolt.

I didn't know how we would explain what had happened when we reached Edinburgh. I guessed the only thing we could do was tell the truth. Heaven help us all.

THE CLOSER WE got to the city of Edinburgh, the better the road became. It was smoother, with fewer potholes and muddy ruts to contend with. That was probably just as well, because I wasn't much of a carriage driver; there were at least three occasions where I took a corner too sharply and nearly tipped us over.

Neither Belle nor Angus complained. Belle was too shocked by the confirmation of what had happened to Noah to say much, although she did allow herself sharp indrawn breaths and narrowed glances in my direction. Angus paid my poor driving little attention; he appeared to fall into a snoring slumber within minutes, and his head tipped onto Belle's shoulder despite her irritated efforts to push him off. I noted, however, that he kept a tight grip on my bag, so it was quite possible he wasn't sleeping at all. Either way, I was grateful for the temporary silence.

We passed some farm labourers and, at one point, a line of four other carriages containing well-dressed people who goggled at us. I pretended not to see them and kept my eyes firmly on the horizon and the distant spires that awaited us.

I practised what I would say to the Edinburgh Mages over and over again, adjusting my phrases and sentences in my head. *Lord Noah was attacked. We didn't see it happen, but it was definitely the Afflicted even though it was broad daylight.* It didn't matter how many times I repeated the words, they never sounded credible.

For some reason, I'd expected Edinburgh to look like Glasgow. I'd never seen any pictures of it, and I had imagined that all cities were the same. As we drew nearer, though, it became obvious that it was nothing like my home.

The distant buildings seemed spikier somehow, with more jagged tops and jutting roofs. The stone was different and, despite the massive sloping hill that sprang out of nowhere from the city centre and which I assumed was Arthur's Seat, it looked less green and more densely packed than Glasgow.

The castle stood defiant and imposing, nearly parallel to the large hill. I knew without asking that was where the Mages resided, and I found it hard to take my eyes from it even when a large flock of ravens flew out from the city limits and swooped towards us.

Belle covered her head with her hands and whimpered, but I glared up at the sharp-beaked birds. They came close to the carriage, seemingly determined to escort us for the final half mile or so, but they didn't try to stall our approach. They were more unnerving than the Glaswegian birds; they made few caws or shrieks but punctuated the air with faint squawking sounds, as if they were chatting to each other and planning our demise. I refused to show that they made me nervous; I wouldn't give them or the Mages that satisfaction.

We were less than two hundred metres from the main guardhouse when a parade of black-cloaked Mages appeared, billowing forward from the winding streets beyond the city limits to block the road. I'd expected an unpleasant welcome, so I wasn't surprised to see them, although their numbers were somewhat intimidating.

Noah grunted more loudly from the depths of the carriage and banged on the door. Perhaps some conscious part of him knew that his fellow Mages were nearby. There was no way of knowing how far gone he was; I still hoped that he could explain how he'd gotten infected, although I doubted we'd get that lucky.

The carriage horses huffed, panted and barrelled forward. I pulled back on the reins, but apparently they had decided they weren't going to slow down. 'Uh,' I said to Belle and Angus, 'do either of you two know how to make us stop?'

Belle stared at me. 'Stop? You tell the horses to stop, and then they stop. Whit's wrong with you?'

I gritted my teeth. 'How do I tell them to stop? If I don't slow them down, they'll crash into our welcoming committee and I'll be accused not only of trying to kill Noah but also an entire cluster of Mages.'

Belle paled. As if in answer, the horses picked up speed rather than slowing down. I saw alarm flare on the faces of the waiting Mages. Uh-oh; this could end very badly.

Angus, whose eyes remained closed, opened his mouth. '*Del mar.*'

Both horses whinnied, then pulled up mere inches from the nearest Mage. He held his ground, but I didn't miss the flash of fear in his watery blue eyes. It was good to know that the magical bastards could be frightened; I'd have to remember that.

Affecting an air of nonchalance to suggest I'd been in

control the whole time, I dropped the reins and hopped down from the carriage. 'Good day.'

All the Mages bowed at the same time. I remained resolutely upright. The ravens, who were still flapping overhead, didn't appear to appreciate my lack of forelock-tugging and cawed their disapproval. One particular feathered bastard dive-bombed, claws outstretched and ready to rake across my exposed flesh. I raised an arm to shield myself, but I didn't duck and I definitely didn't bow. Those days were long gone.

There was a cough followed by a muttered command. The raven blinked several times but backed off. The cluster of Mages parted to reveal Aspen, who strode forward, arms outstretched in effusive greeting – although his eyes remained cold. 'Mairi Wallace! Welcome to Edinburgh!'

He was putting on quite an act; they all were. Given that the Mages never did anything without good reason, I looked around to see what I was missing. Then I saw it: beyond the Mages was a cobbled square, and it was packed full of people.

I hadn't noticed them until now, partly because the black-cloaks were blocking my view but also because the crowd was completely silent. They were all staring at me. I couldn't help it; I stared back.

I didn't know any of these people. The faces were different, and so were the styles of their clothing, but even so I recognised them. There were the exhausted mothers with pinched faces, wondering how they were going to feed their children. There were the haggard fathers, some with missing limbs from dangerous work. There were teenagers and young people, whose eyes already reflected the grim truth that they were living in a world where they didn't dare speak out. And there were lots of women, many of whom had clenched fists and barely healed scars; I recognised myself in their expressions.

Most jarring of all was the faint flickering of hope that I regis-tered in every single eye.

I drew in a breath and realised my mouth was dry. Every-thing the Gowk and Ailsa and Fee had said came echoing back: this was not about me, this was about all of us.

Aspen cleared his throat. 'Where is Lord Noah?'

I barely heard him. He repeated his question, and I dragged my attention away from the silent crowd. 'We ran into some trouble on the way here,' I said.

'Oh, yes?' He looked only mildly interested. He knew about the beithir, of course. His gaze dropped to the scratch on my arm, and I didn't imagine the flicker of smug satisfaction in his eyes as he noticed it.

'Our carriage was waylaid,' I said. 'I expect you are already missing four Mages who were travelling here from Glasgow?'

'Indeed. Do you know what happened to them?'

Here we go. 'The Afflicted happened to them.'

Aspen's brow creased. He hadn't been expecting that answer. 'Whatever do you mean? You've been travelling during the day. So were the other Mages.'

'Aye.' I nodded agreement. 'I can't explain it. But we came across their carriage along the way and there was no sign of the Mages inside. First, we were attacked by a giant serpent. Once we'd beaten that back, we were set upon by the Afflicted. They got hold of Lord Noah.' I shrugged helplessly. 'He had gone to search for our carriage driver. I can only assume that the Afflicted killed the driver, sneaked up behind Lord Noah and rendered him unconscious. We retrieved him from their hiding place but,' I shook my head, 'it doesn't look good for him.'

Aspen's eyes had narrowed. Whether he liked Noah or not, he was not impressed by my words. 'What are you saying?' he growled.

Still atop the carriage, Belle started to babble. 'If I hadn't seen them with my own eyes, I'd never have believed it! They were awful, my Lord. Just awful! Their skin was all ... and their hair was all ... and they took Lord Noah and were all...'

Aspen folded his arms. 'This is quite the tale you've concocted between you.'

Angus lazily opened one eye. 'I can assure you it's all true. Lord Noah, or at least what's left of him, is sealed inside this very carriage.'

I felt a brief hiss of magic. Not only were most of the gathered Mages glaring at Angus with undisguised venom, but Aspen had flickerings of angry blue magic around his fingers. He was itching to strike Angus dead. It was quite possible that he hated him for betraying the Mages' cause far more than he hated me for attacking it.

As I took a step back, I noted that not every Mage looked ready to string Angus up from the nearest gallows. There were a few whose expressions were far more guarded who might be more sympathetic to our cause, if not enthusiastic about it. Good to know.

Aspen's curling moustache quivered. He pushed past me towards the carriage without glancing at Angus and Belle, but when he peered in through the window it was too fogged up to see anything. He undid his cloak and let it fall to the ground in a pool of black fabric.

'We should move away,' Angus advised Belle.

She didn't need telling twice. She leapt down from the carriage, landing in an ungainly heap next to one of the horses. I wasn't sure I'd ever seen her move so fast. She heaved herself to her feet and hobbled towards me. Angus followed, my bag – with Laoch-cum-Mungo inside – slung casually over his shoulder.

I watched Aspen. He wasn't the Ascendant of Edinburgh; I

didn't know much about this city, but I knew that the Ascendant was called Fitzwilliam, and that he'd been in charge longer than Noah's uncle had been Ascendant of Glasgow. But Aspen still commanded a great deal of authority; he was obviously somebody important – and somebody with a lot of power.

His lips moved and I strained to hear the words. Alas, I couldn't make out enough of them, although I could certainly sense his magic. It filled the air, humming with its potent vibrancy.

'He's sealing off the area around the carriage,' Angus murmured. 'Creating a bubble so that it can be opened safely.'

'What words is he using?'

He shook his head. 'I don't know. The level of magic that Aspen uses is far greater than anything I can employ.'

'If he's that strong why isn't he Ascendant of this city? Or another one?' I muttered

'Politics,' Angus replied, as if that explained everything. 'Though I wouldn't be surprised if he makes a bid for Glasgow.'

Great. That was all I needed. I sighed and continued to watch. It was galling to think it, but I might learn something.

When Aspen gestured sharply to some of the watching Mages, several things happened at once. Three of them peeled away and walked towards the carriage before turning around and muttering incantations as they threw magical attacks at Aspen's seal, presumably to test its strength.

At the same time, six more Mages marched towards us. Before I could protest, two of them flanked me and grabbed my arms, gripping painfully tight. The others did the same to Belle and Angus while the watching crowd murmured its discomfort.

I'd been confused as to why Aspen had permitted an audience to gather here; now I knew the answer. If he could find any reason to end my existence before the Ascendancy Challenge began he would take it – and he wanted people watching so that he could explain away his actions and bring any resistance-led revolts to an end.

'Whit do you think you're doing?' Belle shrieked. 'Get your clatty hands off me!'

One of the Mages who was holding her dipped his head to her ear and lowered his voice so that nobody beyond us would hear him. 'Shut your mouth, bitch, and behave.' He looked at Angus and me. 'Try any magic and not only is this skinny wench dead but so will be half that crowd.'

Angus rolled his eyes. 'Such unnecessary drama.'

Aspen flicked his hand towards the Mages who were testing his magical security system. They bowed their heads and returned to their places with the others. He turned to us.

'We have extended the warm hand of friendship to you. We have done what no Mages in history have ever done before by permitting you to participate for the Ascendancy of the great city of Glasgow. If you have thrown all that goodwill back in our faces and harmed Lord Noah – who has been nothing but kind and helpful to you – we will have no choice but to act accordingly. We are patient, and we are willing to change if that is what is in our country's best interests, but we cannot allow unbridled terrorism. There must be consequences for unlawful actions.'

He spoke with such calm sincerity that I almost believed him, even though his words were targeting the watching crowd and not me. His silver tongue had allowed him to take full control of the situation.

I couldn't let that continue. I heaved in a breath, swallowed my anxiety and began. 'Lord Aspen—'

He wasn't going to give me leeway to reply. 'We shall open

the carriage and see what has happened to Lord Noah for ourselves,' he interrupted.

No. I had to say my piece, wrest back some control. 'Wait!' My shout was more of a squawk than a command, but I plunged ahead regardless. 'I am not lying about what happened to Lord Noah.' The word Lord stuck in my craw, but I pushed past it. 'It's vital that the Mages look into what is happening with the Afflicted. I can't speak for Edinburgh, but I know that in Glasgow they are becoming much bolder. Our City Chambers has been devastated in part because the Afflicted attacked it. Now they are venturing out in daylight, which they have not done before.'

'The truth of that remains to be seen,' growled one of the Mages who was restraining me.

I ignored him and pressed on. 'There is a symbol. I've seen it etched into stone across Glasgow, and I saw it in the cave where the Afflicted who attacked Lord Noah were hiding. Three horizontal slashes and...'

'...two diagonal ones. I've seen this symbol. More than once.'

I started and turned. It was one of the other Mages who'd spoken. He was only young, perhaps in his early twenties, and he was clearly unused to attention. When everyone looked at him, and several of his fellow Mages glared, his cheeks coloured. But he'd been one of those whose expression indicated potential sympathy for our cause.

I committed his face to memory and carried on. 'People need to know. There must be an investigation. If the Afflicted are changing their habits and growing bolder, it doesn't matter who is the Ascendant of any city. This needs to be looked into now!'

Aspen's lip curled. 'A good leader protects their people. A good leader does not create panic.' He scowled and returned his attention to the carriage, but I knew that the assembled crowd had heard me. I exhaled. At least I'd been able to speak, to warn people about what was happening beneath our noses – and I'd made sure that Aspen didn't hold all the authority. Magic wasn't the only power I had at my disposal.

Whether he was annoyed by my success at speaking out or not, Lord Aspen didn't show it. He threw his arms up into the air in an entirely unnecessary action designed to draw attention to his magic, then boomed out the word to open the carriage door. '*Brashar*!'

The door didn't merely swing open, it flew off its hinges, spiralled through the air and crashed to the ground with a loud clatter. Nobody looked at it, despite its dramatic flight, because all attention was on the inside of the carriage.

We all held our breath, Mages and ordinary people together as one.

At first nothing happened. Nothing moved.

I squinted towards the dark opening. I thought perhaps I could see a foot, or maybe it was an arm. The horrible thought struck me that Noah had died in the last few moments from his infection. If that were the case, it wouldn't bode well for us.

A moment later, the carriage started to rock gently from side to side and there was a snuffling grunt. I glanced up at the sky. Dusk was approaching but it was still light, perhaps too light for Noah to emerge despite the daylight attack he'd endured. I needn't have worried; even now Noah was not the sort of person who shied away from the light.

The carriage rocked some more, and the horses that were still yoked to it whinnied and pulled as they tried to get away. That was evidence enough; all the same, when the crumpled figure half fell out of the carriage door onto the cobbles, there was a loud intake of breath from everyone watching. There was a second gasp when Noah raised his head.

He hadn't looked well before and he looked even worse now. His skin was an ashen, sickly grey, and several boils and blisters along one side of his face scarred his once-perfect skin. His hair was matted with blood and his clothes were ripped where he must have tried to tear them from his body. 'Help,' he croaked. His arms stretched forward and his fingers clawed at the ground.

I took an involuntary step back, my flesh twisting where the Mages were holding me. Part of Noah remained, and he was fully aware of what was happening to him. It didn't matter what he'd done or what sort of person he was, this was a truly horrific fate for anyone to suffer.

I raised my eyes to Aspen. He was as shocked as any of us. 'Lord Noah,' he said. 'How did this happen? Who is responsible for this?'

Noah groaned.

Aspen pushed on. 'Did Mairi Wallace bring this on? Did the traitor Angus cause this?'

Noah's eyes were scarlet red as he stared at Aspen and opened his mouth. 'The Afflicted. The Afflicted did this.' Then he collapsed, his head fell and his body went limp.

I expelled the breath I'd been holding. Noah clearly had no energy left to do anything other than tell the truth; lying was beyond him, even if those lies could lead to my downfall.

I looked at Aspen and felt a rebellious surge of cold triumph as the bells rang out to signal the approach of night.

It was enough. At least for now.

CHAPTER
FOURTEEN

'You are not permitted to travel anywhere within the castle walls without an escort,' the blank-faced Mage told me as he hovered at the door.

'Uh-huh. What about outside the castle?'

He pursed his lips in disapproval. 'It's night time. I don't know what you got up to in Glasgow, but nobody in this city is stupid enough to go out alone once the sun has gone down.'

I bit back my immediate response that Noah's condition proved that it was no longer only the night time that we had to be afraid of. I tried something else instead. 'The Ascendancy Challenge doesn't start for another full day. Can we go out to the city without an escort tomorrow morning?'

'You are not allowed to leave the castle at all.' He gazed at me implacably. 'It's for your own safety, of course.'

I managed to avoid rolling my eyes. 'Of course.'

'A servant will bring you some food later. If you need anything else—' he paused and a nasty grin appeared on his lips '—yell as loud as you can. If anyone hears you, they might come and help.' He stepped back, produced a large, ornate iron key from his pocket and made a show of holding it up. Then he closed the door and locked it noisily, trapping us inside.

'They really want to keep us away from the good people of this city,' I commented. While a burst of minor magic would unlock that door, I doubted it would do us any good to try.

Angus stretched out on the bed. It creaked dangerously but didn't collapse under his weight, which I supposed counted as a success. 'They invited an audience to watch your arrival,' he said. 'That will more than satisfy the populace until the challenge begins. In fact, I suspect that word will be spread that you're unimpressed with Edinburgh and you're planning to spend your time living the high life here in the castle rather than mingling with the common folk.'

I glanced around. 'The high life?' There was a single bed, a bare fireplace and an empty washbasin. I'd enjoyed better quarters when I'd been the Mages' servant.

'Honestly?' he said. 'I'll be amazed if they bring any food at all.'

'No food?' Belle shrieked. 'After the day we've had? I'm starving!'

'We're more prisoners than guests,' I told her. 'Don't fash yourself. We'll sort something out.'

She stalked over to the bed and shoved Angus off it before settling herself down. 'You'd better.' She scowled. 'What's this mattress made of? Bricks?'

I joined her and tested it with my hand. 'It feels softer than the mattress I enjoyed for years in your attic.'

Her response was immediate. 'Me an' Twister did the best that we could! We were poor, and we didnae live in a damned castle!'

Me and my big mouth; I forgot sometimes that were consequences to voicing my thoughts aloud. I still had to get to grips with audible speech. My intention hadn't been to provoke

Belle, although from the look on her face it was clear that was what she thought I was doing. A dozen replies to soothe her bruised ego sprang to mind, but I gave voice to none of them. After all, I had been telling the truth about the bed.

'What's going to happen to Noah?' I asked Angus. 'What will they do to him?'

'I don't know, lass. It's a long time since a Mage became infected. They used to kill them on the spot out of kindness.' He shrugged. 'But whether that will happen now or not is anyone's guess.'

I swallowed. If Noah could turn into one of the Afflicted, anyone could. I hoped the other Mages could see that.

Angus passed over my bag. I placed it carefully on the stone floor and opened it. Mungo was stretched out, his tiny chest moving up and down with steady, regular movements. I reached out with the tip of my index finger and stroked him. His eyes sprang open and he gazed at me.

'It's okay,' I said. 'You can change now.' The Mages inside the castle would register the magic but they wouldn't know what it was. Let them believe I was conjuring up another bed or some food. Whatever they sensed, they certainly wouldn't expect it to be a daemon.

The snap and crackle was starting to sound familiar. In a burst of magic, Laoch extricated himself from Mungo's body. Instead of greeting me with a crooked smile and a heart-stopping kiss, however, he opened his mouth to speak – and crashed with a thump to the floor as his legs gave way.

My happiness at seeing him gave way instantly to alarm. I crouched beside him. 'Laoch? What's wrong?' I gazed at his face, noting that his lips were tinged blue. His eyelids flickered and he looked at me.

'Tired,' he croaked. 'Only tired.'

'He's been inside that wee beastie for too long,' Angus

observed in a calm voice that only made me want to punch him in the face.

'Help me get him to the bed,' I said.

Belle sat up. 'I'm using the bed!' Her face twisted into a snarl, although she subsided when she saw the state that Laoch was in. 'Fine,' she huffed. 'But as a lady, I'm only saying that I should get priority.'

I sent Angus a warning look before he sniped at her. He scowled at me, though he did at least keep his mouth shut.

Between us, we heaved Laoch's body over to the narrow bed and laid him down. 'I'll ... be ... fine,' he managed, 'after ... some ... sleep.'

I smoothed back his hair. He was paler than usual, but he didn't appear to have a temperature. He was right: it was only fatigue from expelling too much magical energy. He'd been inside Mungo for too long. I tried to ignore the stabbing worry and guilt and kissed his brow. 'Rest,' I said. 'We'll look after you.'

'I won't,' Belle muttered. I glared at her. She pouted and I turned away.

Angus scooped up Mungo and held him in the palm of his hand. 'Extraordinary,' he said. 'The wee rat seems entirely unaffected by the procedure. The daemon is half deid and yet this beastie is fine.'

'Laoch is not half dead!' I snapped. 'And Mungo is a mouse, not a damned rat.'

'Whatever he is,' Angus told me, 'he's the best chance you've got of gaining an advantage in the challenge. Tell me what the words are, and I'll enter his body and sneak out of here. I'll find out what's being planned for you in a jiffy. Forewarned is forearmed.' He grinned lazily but there was a spark of animation in his eyes.

I glanced at Laoch. It had taken him only seconds to fall

fast asleep, and I watched the steady rise and fall of his chest. I couldn't tell Angus what the magic words were to enter Mungo's body because long ago I'd promised Laoch that I'd never reveal them. But that didn't mean that Angus's plan wasn't a good one.

He was more adept at reading my thoughts than I'd given him credit for. He stared at me then shook his head. 'Oh no, lass. You can't do it.' He pointed to Laoch. 'Look what happened to him. You need to conserve your energy for the challenge.'

'Forewarned is forearmed.' I repeated his words back at him. 'It's a calculated risk. There's no telling what I could find out.'

'The best information in the world won't do you much good if you're too exhausted by the time the Ascendancy Challenge starts!'

For once, Belle agreed with him. She clucked like a mother hen, and in a manner that didn't suit her personality. 'The old bampot is right, Mairi. It's too much of a risk.'

'Everything about being here is too much of a risk,' I said quietly. 'But we're backed into a corner. This is the best plan.'

'Tell me the words and I'll—' Angus started.

'No.'

'Why not?'

'Because I promised I wouldn't.' I held his eyes. 'And I will honour that promise.' I nodded at the door. 'Just be careful if any Mages come calling, or any servants. There's no telling where people's loyalties lie. You'll have to pretend I'm sleeping. If anyone tries to come in...'

Angus rolled his eyes, but at least he knew when he was defeated. 'Fine,' he muttered. 'If anyone comes to the door, Belle the bulldog can deal with them. She's scary enough to send Aspen away quivering in his boots.'

'Oi! You!' Belle sounded pissed off, but there was a note of pleasure in her voice at the old Mage's words. Aye, annoying as she was, I'd made the right decision by bringing her along.

'You must have been here before,' I said to Angus. 'Where am I going? Can you describe the castle layout?' We hadn't seen much of anything when we'd arrived; we'd been hustled directly to this room via a narrow curving hallway and staircase.

He sighed. 'Aye. I can do that.'

I thought of something else. 'Is there a garden of death?' I asked. 'Like at the City Chambers?'

'There is.'

I smiled grimly. Different city or not, the Mages were totally predictable. I could use that – in more ways than one.

Angus was right: Mungo was completely unruffled. When I apologised to him for taking control of his body yet again, he didn't react beyond a faint twitch of his long whiskers. I knew there was a good chance he didn't understand me – but I also knew he didn't fear me, and that had to count for something.

I crouched down and looked into his eyes before humming. *Belsh za tum.* The effect was instantaneous. The world spun and I felt a lurch of topsy-turvy nausea. The dizziness was momentary, and I blinked rapidly to adjust to my altered state. I tested Mungo's limbs. There was a flicker of satisfaction from his lingering consciousness; he enjoyed the stretch.

The floor trembled as an enormous pair of feet stomped towards me. Belle reached down and, pinching my tail between her finger and thumb, hauled me up into the air. The pain was excruciating and I squeaked in alarm, but she either didn't notice or didn't care. Her mouth moved, her booming voice making it hard to decipher her words. I squeaked again and twisted, my body hanging a terrifying distance from the floor.

Angus said something, '—down.'

'Why?' Belle enquired.

I breathed out as I finally tuned in to her words.

'I could stand on her. Squash Mairi,' Belle said. 'If the mouse dies, does she die?'

'Let's not test that theory. Put her down,' Angus said. There was a surprising note of command in his voice.

Belle tutted but thankfully returned me to the floor. 'Disgusting creature.'

I gazed at her ankles; how satisfying it would be to sink my tiny, sharp teeth into her exposed flesh. It wasn't a good idea; I needed to conserve my energy – and if I attacked her, she'd probably *would* stamp on me.

I twisted around, seeking an exit. There was a gap underneath the locked door that would likely suit. My paws skittered across the stone floor and I used the miniscule pits and troughs that were almost invisible to human eyes to propel my rodent body. It was easier than the last time I'd entered Mungo's body and far less disorientating – but it was still very odd.

I flattened my body when I reached the door and used my back legs to push myself through the gap. Mungo gave a brief flicker of resistance but it didn't last and he let me continue. I heard Angus shout something which might have been 'good luck', or it might have been 'off you fuck'. Either was possible.

Then I was on the other side of the door and free to explore the castle at will.

FIFTEEN

Angus had described the layout of the castle in detail, so I had an idea which direction to take. I also had my heightened rodent senses to rely on; while my sight and hearing were somewhat hampered by my size, my sense of smell was so acute that my nostrils were tingling.

I scurried down the first hallway, hugging the wall so that I could remain out of sight if anyone appeared. That was fortunate, because two guards had been posted next to the winding flight of stairs which we'd climbed up with our escorts. Neither of them were Mages, but I didn't doubt that they were there because of us.

Their gazes were fixed pointedly on the locked door, so it wasn't difficult to stay in the shadows and patter past them. At first I wondered why they weren't standing outside our room but, when the logical answer presented itself, I felt a thrill of shivery delight. The Mages were afraid that we'd communicate with the guards. Even though these were their own men, they didn't want to test their loyalty. If that were true, the resistance was having more impact than we'd dared to imagine.

The guards' presence meant I had no time to be nervous about descending the stairs. Whether the leap from step to stone step was dangerous for my little mouse body or not, I couldn't hesitate. Mungo didn't appear to be concerned; I guessed he was used to traversing staircases from his travels around the City Chambers.

I held my breath and jumped down the first step. I should have trusted Mungo's instincts, because it was far easier than I expected. I wasn't sure if the same would be true when I returned and had to climb *up* the stairs, and I reminded myself to keep plenty of energy in reserve. Then I flew down the remaining stairs at high speed.

By the time I reached the ground floor, exhilaration had overtaken anxiety. Nose twitching, I avoided the delectable scents of cooked food from my left and turned to the right. Mungo disagreed – naturally, he wanted to find the food – but he let me steer him away. As my confidence in him grew, so his confidence in me grew.

The door opposite the dining room lay ajar. I quested forward, using every rodent skill I could muster to decide whether anyone was inside. Before I'd rounded the edge of the door, I knew the room was clear. Angus had suspected that everyone, the Edinburgh Ascendant included, would be eating together. It wasn't always the case but, given the circumstances of the upcoming Challenge and my presence within the castle walls, he'd reckoned that the senior Mages would want to keep a close eye on everyone and maintain control. They couldn't afford any more defectors.

I allowed myself a tiny congratulatory hop and made a beeline for the grand desk in the centre of the room. Time to get to work.

I nipped easily up the chair leg, darted along the wooden arm and leapt upwards, embedding my little claws in the smart green leather of the desk top. I shook out my fur and gazed around. Huh. The Edinburgh Ascendant was a very mucky pup.

Before I could rein him in, Mungo launched for a plate balanced on top of several leather-bound books and narrowly avoided knocking over an inkwell. Nothing came between the wee mouse and food, not even a bid to save the country. Fortunately, there were only a few crusts left so I waited while he munched on them, enjoying a flush of warmth as he communicated hearty rodent gratitude. Then he let out a very un-mouse-like burp and I felt his demeanour alter as he let me to take control again.

He'd done me a favour by stopping for a snack. Thanks to the stack of books on which the plate was balanced, I was now higher than the other objects on the desk. It was never going to be easy to read written notes when I was this size, but my vantage point meant that I could see more of what was on the desk – and that included a sheet of paper with curling edges and beautifully inked calligraphy: *The Glasgow Ascendancy Challenge.* Perfect.

I leaned further and cricked my neck in a bid to read more of it, hoping that this piece of paper would give me the head start that I needed to stay alive in the competition.

Number of Challengers: 23

Shite. That was a lot. It had been twenty-four, but that number had been crossed out and altered, though that didn't make me feel any better. I leaned out a fraction further. There was a flicker of panic from Mungo but I sent a wave of reassurance. I was balanced. I wasn't going to fall.

First Challenge: Ga—

I couldn't read any more of the letters. I was too small, the angle was wrong and the writing was too big. I squeaked my irritation and pulled back. Perhaps if I shuffled to the right, I'd see more. I pattered over confidently, leaned out, leaned out a bit more. Just … a … fraction … more … and…

Mungo let out a high-pitched squeak of alarm. He pushed his consciousness forward again, but it was already too late; the book tipped over, taking me with it. I tumbled down, spun through the air, smacked into the side of the inkwell and sent it flying. Dark-blue ink splattered as I landed with a heavy thump onto the floor, slightly dazed and very annoyed.

I turned myself the right way up and sent an apology to Mungo. His smooth fur was coated in gloopy ink and there was a throbbing pain down my left haunch – his left haunch. It was difficult to tell where the mouse left and I began.

I did my best to hold onto my earlier confidence. It was fine. I'd rub off the worst of the ink, stretch a bit and everything would be alright. Except that was when the door opened and the cloaked figures walked into the room.

As before, it took me several moments to tune into what they were saying, but I understood the exact second when they saw the fallen inkwell and resulting devastation. Three sets of heavy feet strode over.

I panicked and darted for the furthest corner. I had to get out – if they spotted me, even in this body, I doubted I'd survive. Neither would Mungo. Fear clawed at my throat. I felt Mungo stiffen, then his little paws spun to the left. He took control and pulled us away.

'Someone's been in here! One of the servants? An intruder? A—'

There was a second voice: a woman. I'd have paused in shock, but Mungo was determined to keep going. 'A mouse,' she said drily. She was a servant. She had to be, she certainly couldn't be a Mage.

'You're sure, Frederica?'

Mungo's claws scratched at the floor and I winced at the

noise, but he wasn't going to slow down. He'd seen something on the other side of the room, and he was heading straight for it.

'Of course.'

My heart thumped painfully against my ribcage and I was breathing hard. One magic word designed to kill vermin and it would be over before it had even begun. I'd taken a stupid risk; I should never have come.

But Mungo was a survivor. When he twisted around a mahogany bookcase and shot diagonally across the floor I was certain we'd be seen, but then I saw the tiny hole at the foot of the wall where the ancient mortar had disintegrated. Once again, the wee mouse had made good. I hope that this time we wouldn't end up tumbling into an underground prison cell containing a tortured Afflicted soul because I wouldn't be lucky enough to find another Angus to help me escape. Not here. Not in this castle.

Mungo put on a final spurt of speed. The voices continued speaking – but then we were in the hole and away from the worst of the danger. Mungo chittered, reiterating his unhappiness at my clumsy actions. I'd never been told off by a mouse before, but I was genuinely chastened. I'd risked everything and got almost nothing in return. I had to be more careful.

Mungo's consciousness retreated again. It was dark and cramped, and I no longer knew where I was or where I was going. I couldn't risk getting trapped in any gaps or hidey-holes because sooner or later, I'd be forced to return to my natural form. It wouldn't go well if that happened in a mouse-sized space.

I noted a chink of light ahead; that would have to do. At least I could get my bearings again. I still wanted to visit the garden but it suddenly seemed too far away. It would be best to admit defeat, turn tail and return to the room-cum-prison cell.

I hurried towards the light and poked out my head, swivelling both ways to check the way was clear and sniffing the air. I recoiled slightly. Judging by the familiar, rotting scent, the garden was to my left and it wasn't far away. The staircase that led back upstairs was to my right. I knew which way I had to go, much as it galled me.

I heard more voices, although I couldn't decipher any words. If I took a slight detour, turned right but then curved the long way round and avoided the dining room and the Ascendant's office, I'd likely be safe.

I took off as fast as Mungo's paws would carry me; I didn't want to linger in these cold hallways. As before, I kept as close to the wall as possible. It was okay. I could do this.

The staircase came into view just as I heard footsteps behind me. Panic flared yet again, and I looked around for somewhere to hide. There was a shadowy spot behind a display cabinet less than five metres away that was perfect. I'd conceal myself there and wait for whoever was behind me to pass. I darted forward, using every dark shadow to my advantage, and scooted underneath.

The footsteps drew closer. Ten seconds, I estimated, if that. But then they stopped. There was a faint chuckle, followed by a quiet command. '*Ish var.*'

Oh no.

It didn't matter that I was underneath the cabinet, or that I was a mouse. The magical order took hold of my body and I was powerless to resist it. My four paws flailed uselessly. Shite.

No – I had to stop this. If I could hum and use that to focus my magical thoughts, perhaps I could squeak and do the same. I bit down hard and emitted a sharp, mousey cry, hoping to block the spell that was forcing me out. *Desh mar. Desh mar. DESH MAR.*

I threw everything I had into it, but it didn't work. A split second later, two hands reached down and scooped me up. Mungo freaked and pulled into a tight ball. I forced his eyes to stay open. I wanted to look my captor – or killer – in the face.

'That burst of magic would have worked if you hadn't let your fear get the better of you,' a voice said. 'I hoped that Laoch would have taught you better by now.'

It was the woman from the Ascendant's office – Frederica. And she knew. She knew who I was, or what I was. And she knew Laoch's real name.

I swallowed and stared upwards as she adjusted her hands, opening them so I could see her face. While the part of me that was Mungo tensed, expecting a final blow, the rest of me that remained Mairi could only gape. Frederica wasn't a servant at all. She was a slave.

I shouldn't have been so shocked because Laoch was not the only enslaved daemon at the Mages' disposal. Although I'd not met any others in Glasgow, it stood to reason that there would be more in Edinburgh.

I blinked at her coiled horns that were a shimmering, iridescent purple as opposed to the matt black of Laoch's. Her features were delicate, with sharp cheekbones that gave her an angular look heightened by curling tattoos that were identical to Laoch's own skin art. I'd studied his face often enough to know.

Frederica – although I doubted that was her real name – tilted her head and examined me. 'I'm not permitted to converse or communicate in any way with the usurper Mairi Wallace, the excommunicated Mage Angus, or their female companion,' she said after a long silence. 'My orders are explicit, and I cannot physically go against them.' Her bow-shaped lips curved into a small smile. 'Strangely,' she added with mild amusement, 'I am not forbidden from communicating with rodents.' She raised her eyebrows. 'No human bar one has ever known how to employ the magic to enter another being's consciousness.'

I was that one, but how had she known? How had she realised that Mungo was also me? As I considered the question, I reminded myself that I was adept at communicating without speech. I rose up on my hind legs and used my front paws to point to my chest in what I hoped was a questioning fashion.

She understood. 'I've lived within these castle walls for six years,' she said softly. 'No mouse has ever been so bold as to do what you did. I know who entered with you when you arrived at the castle, and I know where he is now. I can sense him, so I know you're not him. Plus,' she gestured down, letting me peer over the edge of her cupped hand, 'you left a trail.'

I looked down and saw the trail of tiny, inked pawprints. Oh.

'I'll clean those up for you.' Frederica smiled again, but this time it was a fleeting grin. 'It's too dangerous here. You should have stayed in your room. I cannot imagine why you would risk coming out like this, even in this body.'

I turned towards the putrid scent of the Mages' death garden and Frederica's eyes narrowed as she tried to make sense of my meaning. 'Why would you want to go there?' she asked softly.

I couldn't explain to her; it was too complicated to convey as a mouse.

Frederica sighed. Her jaw tightened, making her tattoos subtly alter shape and giving her features an even more angular slant. 'Very well,' she muttered. 'If you insist.'

She raised her hands and deposited me on top of her head between her horns. I felt Mungo's alarm return until we both realised that we could nestle on her scalp and hide in her hair. It wouldn't hold up to close inspection, but it would be more than enough if any Mages wandered by or engaged Frederica in brief conversation.

'Don't even think about leaving any droppings up there,' she hissed, turning away from the stairs towards the reek of the garden.

If I'd ever thought about what it would be like to travel on top of someone's head, I'd have imagined it would be a smooth journey. It wasn't. Every step jarred, and I slid from side to side. In the end, I had to dig Mungo's small claws into Frederica's scalp to avoid falling. I felt her wince slightly with pain, but she didn't complain. When we passed a group of grim-faced Edinburgh Mages, and she stepped aside and nodded her head in forced respect, I was glad that I had done so. I couldn't imagine their expressions if a mouse had slid down the front of her face.

We turned one corner and then another. When the hallway narrowed and we turned for a third time into a large courtyard, the scent of the garden was almost overpowering, even stronger and more unpleasant than the reek from the Glaswegian version. I couldn't repress a shudder at the thought of how many female corpses were buried there.

I peered through the strands of Frederica's hair and spied the glass dome. Aye: it was larger than the garden at the City Chambers, though it seemed to have the same sort of plants and over-sized insects inside. Good. I didn't know how the process worked – frankly, I didn't want to know – but I was aware that the Mages' inherent magic was waning and that the women's bodies were one of the ways the magical wankers boosted their powers.

Frederica wandered casually round the glass. A worker passed us, presumably a gardener who did the same work here as Billy had done in Glasgow. He kept his eyes downcast and didn't glance in her direction, but I felt his fear and tension and couldn't fail to spot his pallor. Was it Frederica who terrified him, or was his anxiety a permanent feature of his existence? Then he was gone, and Frederica was pushing at one of the glass panels to enter the garden.

The smell of death was horrifying. The earthy scents from the large plants in all their verdant blooming glory did nothing to hide the rot beneath their roots. These were shallow graves.

It wasn't only the bodies that created the nauseating smell, it was the unnatural magic that bound this place together. Mungo's consciousness shifted nervously and flickered at me. I did my best to reassure him and shuffled forward until I was almost at Frederica's forehead. I needed a closer look.

'Well?' she asked aloud. 'Why are we here?'

I gazed around until I spotted a tall bush with purple foliage. I raised my front paw, tapped her skull and she headed in that direction. When she reached the bush, I dug in my claws.

She hissed and halted. 'It would be better for both of us if you didn't actually draw blood,' she muttered.

Fair point. I retracted my claws, dipped my head and brushed the edge of her forehead with my whiskers in apology. Whether she understood or not, she grunted. It was the best I could do.

'Now what?'

I twisted my body, pattered round Frederica's right horn and jumped down onto her shoulder. Obligingly, she held out her arm so I could run along it and use my front paws to point at the purple bush. I needed a sample.

'You want this?'

I jerked my head and glanced back at her. She pursed her full lips then reached forward with her free hand and pulled off several leaves. She gave me a blank look of incomprehension, but I nodded enthusiastically. Perfect.

'Is that it?'

Nope. I darted back up her arm. Perched on her shoulder, I could see more of the death garden. There was an oleander shrub in the far corner with delicate flowers decorating its stems. I tapped my right paw and directed Frederica towards it. She sighed. 'This is not how I pictured my evening going,' she said. 'Walking around the Mages' green death hole and harvesting plants directed by a mouse.'

When she put it that way, I supposed it did sound nuts.

'This one?' she asked when she reached the plant. 'Tap twice for yes, once for no.'

I tapped twice and Frederica plucked a clump of blush-pink petals. I doubted I'd need more than one or two, but it would be handy to have some spare.

'Anything else?' she enquired.

Some stinging nettles would be perfect but I couldn't see any. I turned and checked the lower-lying plants. Perhaps the Mages didn't value nettles; they weren't pretty and could be found all over the wild, so their value wasn't high, but their uses were numerous and I was annoyed that I couldn't see any. I'd have to manage without them.

I attempted a mousy shrug to communicate that would be enough for now. I'd barely completed the action, when a deep voice behind us said, 'What the fuck are you doing in here?'

I stifled a squeak of alarm and shot up to conceal myself in Frederica's hair. She turned slowly while I flattened my body. When I peeked out and saw who had addressed her, my stomach sank: Aspen. That was all we needed.

Frederica was an ensorcelled slave, so she had to do what the Mages told her. She couldn't gainsay them, no matter how hard she might try to deny their orders. She also had to answer direct questions with the truth – although it didn't have to be the whole truth. Fur quivering, I held my breath and waited to hear what she would say.

'My Lord.' Frederica curtsied, keeping her head upright so that I didn't have to cling on to her scalp again. 'I am collecting leaves and petals.'

Aspen's eyes narrowed. 'For yourself, slave?' The other Mages I'd overheard had spoken to Frederica almost as if she were an equal; Lord Aspen spoke to her as if she were a cockroach.

'No.' Before he could ask her another question and force her into revealing the full truth, she added, 'I'm under orders to pick these. I have no idea why, or what they'll be used for.' She shrugged and I heard the smile in her voice. 'I do not understand magic in the way that the Mages do.'

I breathed out while Aspen rolled his eyes. 'Of course you don't. You're a female daemon. I don't know why we bother with you.'

There was another flicker of movement from behind Aspen and a shorter Mage with a rounded body appeared. Where Aspen was sallow, this one was ruddy. His eyes twinkled, but not in a kindly fashion. 'Well, well, well,' he said, 'look who it is. My favourite daemon.'

Even from the top of her head, I felt Frederica's body tense. She curtsied again. 'My Lord Mosse,' she murmured.

His pink lips curved into a nasty smile. 'Freddie darling, I've told you many times to call me Douglas.' He eyed her up and down, and suddenly I knew exactly what he was thinking.

'You ever shagged a daemon, Aspen?' Mosse didn't wait for an answer. 'Because if not, you really should.' He smirked. 'You know that we can make them do anything we want with nothing more than a single word.'

He glanced at the top of Frederica's head as if he were

staring right at me and my tension ratcheted up another notch. Oh no. 'And their horns are incredibly useful when you need something to hold onto.' He thrust his hips forward and backwards several times, his meaning unmistakable.

My gnawing fear was replaced by horrified anger. Oh, Frederica. Oh no. 'Their bodies are stronger than humans, and that means they can take more action. Sometimes I think they even enjoy it.' He leered. 'Ain't that right, Freddie? You like it when I—'

'Enough.' Aspen's voice was sharp. 'There's no need to be so crude. As a Mage, you should be above such base desires.'

My eyes swivelled from Aspen to Mosse and back again. They both despised powerful women, whether daemon or human, but they despised them for different reasons.

Mosse obediently ceased his taunting though he winked lasciviously at Frederica. I glared at him from my hiding spot, committing his face to memory. It was all I could do to hold myself back from delving for my magic and attacking him. It would have been a suicidal move but it would almost have been worth it.

'Come on,' Aspen snapped. 'We've got things to do. You promised me your support in the third round of the challenge.'

'If both of us make it that far,' Mosse responded with a smarmy, teasing note.

'Don't be facetious, man.' Aspen shook his head. He glanced at Frederica as if he'd almost forgotten she was there. 'Go on, bitch. Fuck off out of here.'

'Yes, my Lord.' She turned away and headed for the exit. I strained my ears to listen in to what Aspen was saying.

'I can promise you a good position in Glasgow once I'm Ascendant,' he continued. 'But that's dependent on your support.'

I listened harder but I couldn't hear Mosse's response. I

grimaced and focused on Frederica instead as she yanked open the door leading out of the garden. Her body remained rigid with rage, but I knew there was more to it than anger. Shame, humiliation ... maybe even some wholly undeserved guilt. I understood all of it, and I burned in the same way on her behalf.

The Mages couldn't continue like this. We couldn't let them.

CHAPTER

SIXTEEN

Although we didn't pass any Mages on the return journey, Frederica still didn't speak. She marched away from the death garden with her head held high, as if her posture could negate the humiliating experience she'd endured. There was nothing I could communicate that would make any of it better, so I remained still and sent out occasional bursts of reassurance in Mungo's direction.

Both the mouse and I knew that I didn't possess Laoch's stamina or power, and fatigue was already setting into my bones. As long as I got back to the room soon I'd be fine – but I wasn't so confident about the daemon who'd risked everything to help me.

We were almost at the chilly, winding staircase when I heard a clatter and Frederica stopped. I raised my head and saw a thin servant girl balancing a heavy tray complete with cloche, cutlery and an immaculate linen napkin. It looked as if she were about to drop it and send the contents splattering across the floor.

Frederica strode over and lifted it out of her hands. The

servant girl flinched. When I saw the red welt across her cheekbone, I did the same.

'Is this going up to the guests from Glasgow?' Frederica asked.

'Aye.'

'Then let me help you take it up the stairs.'

The girl's thin shoulders dropped in relief. Frederica balanced the tray on one hand and lifted the fancy silver cloche.

If I could have laughed, I probably would have. The napkin and cutlery might cost a year's salary but the food underneath the cloche could hardly be described as luxurious. It consisted of a thin gruel with a few unidentifiable and unappetising blobs floating on top. Even if it had looked tasty and nutritious, I wouldn't be eating any of it. If the Mages could send a conjured creature with poisonous spikes after me, putting something in my food to weaken me was hardly a stretch. How naïve did they think I was?

Frederica snorted, and half turned to block the servant girl's view. I understood immediately and hopped down to nestle beside the bowl of gruel. The daemon laid the tiny harvest from the death garden next to it and gave me a meaningful look.

Aye, I thought back at her, although I knew she wouldn't hear me. I will do whatever is within my power to destroy them, Frederica. I promise you that.

When she replaced the cloche, the sudden darkness was disorientating. I remained calm; Laoch's kinswoman had already done more than enough to earn my trust.

I felt the tray rise as Frederica ascended the stairs. It jiggled and jerked, coming to a halt when presumably Frederica was stopped by the guards. There was a brief murmur of voices and the tray started moving again. Finally it was lowered and I heard the rattle of a key. There were more muffled voices, more clanks and rattles, and then I was blinking up into the wide eyes of Belle and Angus.

I was back. Thank goodness.

Belle's skill at looking unimpressed was competition level. 'So you risked everything to gain nothing more than a few scraggly weeds?'

I shuffled down to the floor, stretched my legs and closed my eyes. I was so very, very tired. 'I learned that there are twenty-three people taking part in the Ascendancy Challenge.'

'Wowee,' she replied flatly.

'And,' I added, 'that the first challenge starts with "Ga".'

'Gasp.'

She was beginning to annoy me.

'Gauntlet,' Angus said. 'It makes sense. It's what I would have chosen for the first round.'

I opened one eye and looked up at him. Already I didn't like the sound of it. 'Why? Why would you have chosen that?'

He raised the bowl of gruel to his nose and sniffed. 'It seems fine,' he said. 'If you won't eat it, I will.'

I folded my arms. 'Angus...'

He clicked his tongue. 'You're so impatient. A gauntlet is by far the easiest way to knock out as many contenders as possible at the start of the challenge.' He crooked his finger at me. 'And that means you, lass.' He tilted the bowl and gulped down its contents in one go. Then he choked.

I wondered if he was about to keel over dead, but he simply wiped his mouth with the back of his hand and thumped his chest. 'Needs more salt,' he declared.

Belle heaved herself up from the floor and went to him. She lifted her hand, preparing to cuff him on the back of the head.

'Woman,' he said darkly, 'if you strike me, I shall not be responsible for my actions.'

I pushed my hair away from my eyes. 'We are all responsible for our actions,' I said. Was I the only grown-up in the damned room? I glanced at Laoch's silent body. He seemed well enough, but he was still deeply asleep. I was the only *conscious* grown-up.

Angus sighed heavily at the burden of having to explain. 'In the gauntlet, you will be asked to run from one point to another point. Along the way, you will be attacked. Anyone who crosses the finish line will be permitted to proceed to the next round.'

'Attacked?' Unsurprisingly, I didn't like the idea of that.

The old Mage waved an airy hand. 'Fireballs, magical traps, conjured monsters. That sort of thing.' He bared his teeth in a grin. 'If the Mages are looking to get rid of any undesirable challengers, it's the perfect way.'

And I was likely to be the most undesirable challenger. They'd throw everything they had at me to get me out of the Ascendancy Challenge as quickly and as cleanly as possible. 'Any tips?' I asked grimly.

'Run as fast as you can and don't get hit by anything.' He shrugged. 'It's pretty straightforward, darling.' That was easy for him to say.

'I can still smack you into oblivion,' Belle hissed.

'Go on then,' Angus replied. 'Give it a shot.' He lifted up the clump of leaves and petals from beside the bowl. 'What the fuck are these for?'

Temporary salvation. I hoped.

～

ALTHOUGH THE BED WAS NARROW, I slid onto it and curled up next to Laoch. I allowed myself one glorious moment to revel in the heat of his body next to mine and to smile at Mungo, who pattered up the leg of the small bed and hopped onto the pillow to curl up next to us. As soon as I closed my eyes, though, I was out for the count, falling into a dreamless sleep of the sort that only occurs when you're truly exhausted.

I woke up hours later to the dulcet tones of Belle and Angus competing in their own challenge, where they seemed to be doing their best to outdo each other's snores, Laoch's warm breath was on the nape of my neck and his arm was wrapped tightly around me. 'Mairi,' he whispered. 'Are you alright?'

A sheen of clammy sweat clung to my skin and my heart was thumping far faster than normal. For once it was nothing to do with Laoch's proximity; I knew that when I stood up, I'd feel a wash of dizziness.

I smiled slightly. 'Aye,' I told him. 'I'm fine.' I raised my head and glanced down at my arm. The scratch I'd given myself was red and swollen and there was a rash encircling my bicep. It was perfect: oleander for dizziness, dilated pupils and fever; grevillea for redness, rashes and itching.

I managed to get hold of some plants, I told him, using mind-to-mind communication. *Any Mage who sees me now will assume that the poison from that daft beithir yesterday is taking hold.* Anything I could do to make them believe I was less of a threat would work in my favour.

Great, he answered, sounding pissed off. *Apart from the fact that you actually ARE sick now.*

It's temporary. The effects aren't serious, and they'll wear off by the time the challenge begins. As long as I'm seen by a Mage or two in the meantime, a wee dizzy spell or two will be worth it.

Laoch growled aloud. *Where did you get the plants?*

I took a moment before answering. *I had some help.* I drew

in a breath and then sent him a mental image of Frederica. Laoch stiffened. *I don't know her real name. I only know what the Mages call her.*

Teasag. Her name is Teasag.

I licked my lips. *You know her.*

I used to. I thought—

I waited but he didn't finish his sentence. *Thought what?*

I thought she was dead.

I reached for his hand, entwining my fingers with his. *Oh, Laoch.*

She's alive. That's what counts.

I could feel his body quivering with rage. *She said she could sense you. She knows you're here. Can't you sense her?*

He shifted against me. *I was too tired before, and too afraid to try once I started to feel better. Hang on.* He lapsed into silence as his mind reached out, straining to sense his own kin. When he sucked in a sharp breath, I knew he'd succeeded. *There are five daemons here, Teasag included.* Laoch's pain vibrated through each word. *The oldest has been here for almost forty years.*

Even a day was too long to be a slave, so forty years was nigh impossible to comprehend. I wanted to tell him that if I survived the Ascendancy Challenge and won, we could free them, but I couldn't give even silent voice to such a thought. The likelihood that I'd survive the first round felt remote, despite all my planning.

Instead I turned so that I was facing him. Laoch's hand moved down to my hip while I reached up and gently traced the curling tattoos on his cheekbones. *Your markings are the same as hers.*

We come from the same area and our magical heritage is similar. Our families have long been entwined.

She risked a great deal to help me, I told him.

He smiled slightly. *That sounds like Teasag.*

Why do the Mages change your names?

Laoch didn't hesitate. *Power. It separates us from our identities and our heritage. They want to make us wholly theirs, as if they can erase who we are.*

I brushed away a lock of hair from his forehead. *Does it ever work?*

He placed his palm on the centre of my chest. *Nobody can take away what's in here.* Then he tapped my forehead. *Or in here. Even the supposedly weakest of humans know that, and the Mages know it too. That's why they are trying so desperately hard to grip more and more tightly. But nothing lasts forever.* He gazed into my eyes. *Nothing apart from love.*

There was an inexplicable stabbing sensation deep in my heart, and I swallowed hard. Unwilling to pursue this line of conversation, I nestled my head in the nook beneath his chin. *Should we be worried that the other daemons, Teasag included, will reveal your presence to the Mages?*

They'll only tell if they're forced to. We can't worry about what ifs. He paused for a moment. I knew then that he had understood that I was afraid of what was between us, given the brief future we probably had, and that was why I'd changed the subject.

What we should be worried about, Laoch told me, *is why we're sharing a tiny bed with a mouse.*

I let out an unladylike snort of laughter that made Angus jerk mid-snore on the floor. *I wish we could stay like this forever,* I sent out sadly. *Even with Mungo by our heads and Belle and Angus on the floor next to us.*

This time Laoch didn't hesitate at all. *Me too, Mairi.*

SEVENTEEN

Laoch was right about one thing: nothing lasted forever, not even peace.

It was mid-morning. Laoch, Angus and I were debating tactics for the upcoming gauntlet and Belle was occasionally throwing in unhelpful remarks when a loud knock came at the door.

We all heard the key turn in the lock. Laoch threw himself towards the far wall, concealing his presence through conventional rather than magical means. I tugged my sleeve upwards enough to display an inch of reddened skin and stood up shakily.

A moment later the door swung open, revealing two cloaked Mages. The first I didn't recognise but the second was the young Mage who'd volunteered the information that he'd also seen the mysterious hatched rune. He smiled in a friendly fashion, while his companion glared at me until I took a step forward and wobbled as a wave of dizziness hit me. Then he smiled, too. 'Are you feeling unwell?' he enquired.

'I've never felt better.' My voice was little more than a croak.

The friendlier Mage appeared alarmed. 'Oh dear. If you're not well, we could send for a doctor.'

I shook my head then instantly regretted the action when it made my dizziness worse. 'No. I'm absolutely fine.'

He moved towards me as if afraid I was about to collapse. Worried that he'd spot Laoch if he came any closer, I met him halfway. 'What can I do for you?'

'My name is Andrew, but you can call me Andy.'

'And my name,' his sour-faced companion said, 'is Francis, and you can call me sir.'

Andy jabbed him in the ribs. 'Ignore him. We thought you might like to get out for a couple of hours. Would you like a tour of the castle? We could show you around, if you like.' He wrung his hands in a manner that I felt certain was genuine, if rather old-fashioned. 'Only if you're feeling up to it, that is.'

Angus clapped his hands and joined us, beaming from ear to ear. 'What an excellent idea! I'd love a tour!'

Francis spat at Angus, 'You've been to this castle plenty of times. You're not getting any tour, traitor.'

Andy bobbed an awkward half-bow. 'My apologies, Mage Angus.'

'*Traitor* Angus,' Francis hissed. 'He no longer deserves the title of Mage.'

Andy looked embarrassed and avoided glancing at Angus again. 'Would you and your other companion like a tour, Miss Wallace?'

At that moment I could think of nothing I wanted less, but I needed as many Mages as possible to witness my weakened state. I also reckoned that there was more to this tour than fake hospitality. I wanted to know what the bastards were up to.

'That sounds great,' I said, this time managing to sound

more like a human and less like a frog with a hangover. 'Thank you so much. Belle? Would you like to come along?'

She was by my side in a jiffy. 'You bet your scrawny arse I would.' She grabbed Francis's arm and hooked it round hers, leaving Andy with me. Francis attempted to extricate himself with an expression of abject disgust, but Belle clung on and wrapped herself even more tightly around him. She was a canny soul; Andy was by far the softer touch and by distracting Francis she was helping me considerably. I might learn more about tomorrow's gauntlet if Andy let down his guard enough.

Taking care not to glance towards Laoch's hiding place, I looked at Angus. 'Keep the home fires burning.'

He curled his lip. 'Aye, I will.' He harrumphed loudly and crossed his arms. Angus was a better actor than even he gave himself credit for.

I followed Andy out of the door while Belle and the temporarily imprisoned Francis followed. Two new guards were stationed at the end of the draughty hallway. I evinced vague surprise at their presence but smiled at them. The nearest guard avoided my gaze but the other one, a middle-aged man with ginger hair that was only a shade lighter than my own, gave me a bashful grin.

'Hello,' I said. 'I'm Mairi. Who—?'

Andy, who was obviously under strict orders to ensure we didn't speak to anyone who might help us, interrupted quickly. 'People have lived on this rock since the Iron Ages,' he said, in an overly loud voice that contained only a hint of panic. 'But the castle has only been in existence for a thousand years. Several parts have been rebuilt over the centuries, of course. This is one of the older sections.' He swept me past the guards and down the staircase. I had to admit that it was far easier to descend as a human than a mouse.

'And how long have you Mages been ruling it?' Belle asked.

'One hundred and thirteen years,' Andy replied.

'Aye. Well that's one hundred and thirteen years too long, ain't it?'

I coughed. 'Do you live here?' I asked before she could say anything else.

'Of course. All the Edinburgh Mages do. Our quarters are over on the western side.'

'Do you have a kitchen near any of those quarters?' Belle asked. 'I'm bloody starving. I'll be a wraith soon if I dinna get anything to eat.'

'One can only hope,' Francis muttered.

In contrast, Andy looked alarmed at Belle's pronouncement. 'Of course. I'll take you straight to the kitchens for a sandwich, if you like.'

Belle sniffed. 'I would very much like.'

I stumbled on the bottom step and put a hand on the nearby wall to steady myself. I swallowed hard while, on cue, the Edinburgh Ascendant exited his study to watch me approach.

I'd not had a chance to study his features while I was in Mungo's body and, with my vision blurring somewhat, it was difficult to see much right now. He was thinner than I'd expected, but his face had the same pinched hardness that I associated with all the Mages. Even Angus and Andy had a similar look. Whether it was a by-product of their magic, a shared heritage, or simply that their faces mirrored their nasty work, I couldn't have said.

I wiped away some of the oleander-induced sweat on my forehead with my sleeve. I didn't have to fake looking ill; I suspected I'd overdone my herbal concoction, and I was feeling worse than I'd intended. But the Edinburgh Ascendant wasn't as transparent as Francis and he took pains not to react to my sick appearance.

'Miss Mairi Wallace,' he boomed as we approached. He spread his arms wide as if to embrace me. I couldn't imagine anything more horrifying. I moved to my left to use Andy as a barricade.

Belle had other ideas. She released Francis and bustled forward, almost throwing herself into the Ascendant's arms while the rest of us stared. The Ascendant, clearly nonplussed by her actions, blinked rapidly then adapted to the situation and hugged her back as if he'd planned to all along. Feeling as nauseated and dizzy as I did, it was hard not to look amused.

'I'm such a big fan!' Belle beamed. For someone who was terrified of both magic and the Mages, she was adapting quickly to her new role as a fearless revolutionary who was working against them. 'But I thought you'd be taller. You're kinda wee for the Ascendant. The Glasgow Ascendant was much taller.' She turned to me. 'Right, Mairi? This one looks as if a strong breeze would blow him over.'

Although his face remained stoically blank, I guessed that nobody had spoken to the Ascendant like that in years, decades even. He was probably raging inside. He wrestled back control of the situation, shoving Belle aside before he gazed at me. 'Dear me. You look rather unwell, Miss Wallace.'

'I'm perfectly fine,' I said, although I patently wasn't.

He clucked like a mother hen. I clenched my fists, holding back the temptation to strike him dead in the same manner that I'd killed his Glaswegian counterpart. I pasted on my sweetest smile. 'There is no need to be concerned.'

'There's every need to be concerned,' he replied instantly. 'You look terrible. If you need to withdraw from the Ascendancy Challenge, I'm sure nobody will hold it against you. It would be difficult for you to rise to the challenge even when you're feeling well. Given your current pallor, it would be unwise for you to participate.'

Uh-huh. 'I'm touched by your concern,' I said flatly, ignoring Andy's flinch at my tone. 'Truly touched.' My stomach lurched. If I suddenly threw up a spout of yellow bile over the Ascendant, it wouldn't be the worst thing in the world.

'Well, women are such delicate creatures. You ought to take care of yourself. It was only a few weeks ago that you didn't even possess the clarity to speak aloud. Am I right? You're obviously very fragile.'

He raised his hand, clicked his fingers and three servants immediately appeared from the dining room opposite. Of course: he was playing nice because he knew there were plenty of eyes and ears watching. He wanted his kind benevolence to be broadcast to the people of Edinburgh. The Ascendant clearly knew how to turn gossip and word of mouth to his benefit.

'Bring some water for Miss Wallace,' he ordered. 'And a chair.'

It took them about five seconds to follow his orders. I'd barely drawn breath when I was pushed gently into a velvet-backed chair and handed a glass of water. The third servant started to fan me with a folded napkin. I could well imagine the expression on Ailsa's face if she'd been asked to perform the same task.

I eyed the water dubiously. The Ascendant correctly interpreted my expression and chuckled. 'My dear girl! It's not poisoned. We would not do such a thing.' He gestured for the glass and I handed it to him. Smacking his lips, he took a long sip from it. 'You see? It's perfectly safe! We have no need to poison you – we invited you here, remember?'

He returned the glass to me. This time I drank from it, savouring every sweet mouthful. It tasted clear and fresh. Small mercies.

'I know what will help,' the Ascendant told me once I'd

finished every last drop. 'Some fresh air. Let's take a stroll on the ramparts. It will do you the world of the good.'

I felt rather than saw Mage Andy jerk. Ah – this supposedly off-the-cuff stroll was clearly planned.

'Some fresh air would be good,' I croaked. And then, for the eavesdropping servants' benefit, 'Thank you.' That I was gracious enough to show gratitude but didn't add any sort of honorific would not be lost on them.

The Edinburgh Ascendant offered me his hand but I pretended not to notice it and got to my feet without his aid. The nausea attacked me again and I was certain that my skin had turned an interesting shade of green. Good: the sicker he believed I was, the better. I shook myself in an attempt to look strong and followed him away from the hallways I'd traversed with Frederica – no, Teasag – and the death garden.

'You should be proud of yourself,' he proclaimed loudly, 'especially given that in other circumstances you'd be treated as a cold-blooded murderer and dealt with as such. You are a lucky girl. It is unprecedented for any non-Mage to be invited to participate in the challenge. In fact, it's unprecedented for any woman who does not work for us to spend a night within these walls. You are causing quite the stir.'

I murmured non-committally. He appeared determined to maintain a running commentary, though I didn't know whether it was to establish his authority or to ensure I had no chance to say anything that might cast him in a bad light. I didn't particularly care; the more he spoke, the more likely it was that he'd slip up and reveal something he shouldn't. I let him babble on, but he was too smart to say anything I could use. Most of his speech was a lecture on the castle's history.

'And of course,' he proclaimed, as we walked out onto the dizzyingly high ramparts, 'this is where the cannons used to be located so that invaders could be repelled. These days we use the ramparts for a different purpose.' My stomach churned yet again but the nausea wasn't a result of the plants I'd ingested. Not this time.

Belle, who was still behind me, let out an audible gasp. The Edinburgh Ascendant smiled. 'The view is quite something, isn't it?'

He knew very well that it wasn't the city spread beneath the castle that we were staring at. It was the line of gallows, the first three of which were occupied with hanging bodies.

'Sick fucks,' Belle muttered, her eyes avoiding the grisly display.

The Ascendant glanced at her then looked over her shoulder. 'Francis,' he said, 'shut that door, will you?'

The sallow Mage did as he was asked.

'There now.' The Ascendant smiled nastily. 'We will no longer be overheard.' He looked at Belle. 'You're right, madam. We are sick fucks. When your supposed leader here fails in her bid to mount a coup against our way of life, this is where you will end up. We'll reserve you a space.' He strolled over to the first corpse and touched it; it was almost a caress. I suppressed a shudder.

'You think you're so clever, Miss Wallace, murdering the Glasgow Ascendant, encouraging an insurgency against the only people who can defend this land against the ravages of the Afflicted.' He hawked up a ball of phlegm and spat it on the ground. 'You won't last two minutes in the Ascendancy Challenge, no matter how smart you think you are. And it's people like your little friend here who will suffer as a result, just like this fellow.' His face twisted into a vicious snarl. 'But you don't care about that, do you. You're too power hungry to give a shit about what happens to anyone other than yourself.'

His venom was almost overpowering, and it took all my

willpower to resist cowering away from him, but I stood my ground and met his gaze. 'I'm doing this because I care.'

Belle thrust her way forward until she was standing next to me, shoulder to shoulder. 'Aye! I dinna care whit happens to me as long as we put you fuckers in the ground. And we will do that, you mark my words!'

The Ascendant laughed coldly. 'I don't require magic to know you're lying through your teeth. You don't really believe you're going to beat us. There are too many of us. Regardless of what you did to poor Lord Noah, you'll never win – and we'll never lose.'

Aspen appeared from behind one of the massive stone bulwarks, his expression matching the Ascendant's. He flicked a hand and murmured a single phrase, '*Belz dar.*'

I felt the brief shiver of magic in the air, then the hood covering the hanging corpse disintegrated. I lifted my eyes unwillingly. When I saw the slack face of the poor soul displayed there, I wished I could unsee it.

Billy had suffered before he died; one of his eyes was missing and there were cuts and bruises all over his skin. I didn't know how long he'd tended the garden for the Mages in Glasgow, or what he'd done during the night that the City Chambers was attacked, but he didn't deserve this fate. Nobody did. Billy the Blawhard, that's what he'd called himself. I blinked back tears and looked away.

'This man was a loyal servant before you came along. He was friendly to you, and this was his fate.' The Ascendant glanced again at Belle. 'Is this what you want for yourself?'

I felt her tremble beside me but she said nothing.

The Ascendant nodded at Aspen. The Mage Lord repeated the same command: '*Belz dar.*'

The hood of the next corpse fell away. I didn't want to look but I had to; I had to bear witness to what the Mages had done.

Even so, when I looked the corpse in the face, my horror almost overtook me.

It was John McAllan. He'd known the risks when he'd given us shelter in his basement, but that didn't make this fair. None of it was fair. I couldn't begin to imagine how the Mages had found out about his involvement. His only offence had been selfless, brave kindness.

'Oh dear.' The Ascendant clicked his tongue. 'You look upset. You brought this on yourselves, you know. These deaths, along with countless others, are your fault. Lives cut short, missed opportunities – who knows what these men might have become if you had not interfered?' He shook his head in fake dismay. 'And that's to say nothing of your third victim here. *Belz dar.*'

Bile rose in my throat as the face of the final body was revealed. Belle turned away and retched. 'You didn't have to do that,' I whispered.

'Our job as Mages is to worry about the fate of all, not the fate of a few. We cannot afford any insurrection in these troublesome times, we have enough to worry about with the Afflicted. Our burdens are already too great. This child is dead because of *you*, not me.'

It wasn't clear how the boy who'd distracted the raven in the Glasgow street and then directed the Mages away from me had died. His eyes were open and unseeing, the white caul of death already upon them, although his face had no sign of the bruises or wounds that John McAllan and Billy had been forced to endure. But he was just as dead as they were.

Belle whimpered. The Edinburgh Ascendant smiled at her, then at me. 'If you withdraw from the Ascendancy Challenge with a public apology and a statement that you were wrong to challenge our authority, no one other than yourself will meet this fate. We're already close to finding your friends and family.

They will not die easily once they are captured. More innocent lives such as that of this poor child will be lost as a result of your foolish bid to destroy this country.'

I was shaking now as much as Belle, but I met his eyes. 'I will not withdraw.' My voice sounded stronger than I'd expected. 'I will not withdraw,' I repeated,

The Ascendant didn't look surprised. He turned to Belle. 'Then I will offer *you* this opportunity to walk away. It will never be repeated. You can leave here now and never return, and you and your husband will be granted clemency. If you decline my kind offer, I guarantee you will both end up here. There is no doubt that Mairi Wallace will lose the Ascendancy Challenge. Look at her. She is ill at the mere thought of it. This is your chance to escape, sweet innocent Belle.'

Belle staggered upwards and wiped her mouth. I'd never seen her so pale, and tears were running unchecked down her cheeks. Her voice shook but her tone was fierce. 'You should do your homework, Lord Ascendant. I am neither sweet nor inno- cent. I've known Mairi for years, probably longer than anyone else. She's stronger than you'll ever understand, and she won't give up no matter what you do to her, or to us. She *will* win the Ascendancy Challenge. And when she does, I will kill you with my own bare hands.' She pulled back her shoulders. 'I would like to go back to our room now.'

The Ascendant's smile disappeared and he stared at her, his lip curling. I realised that he wanted to remove Belle from the equation to isolate me as much as possible. 'So be it. You've made your choice and you will suffer for it.' He jerked his head at Francis and Andy. 'Get them out of here.'

As I turned, I noted Francis's smug swagger he moved forward to take hold of Belle, and Andy's white face and fixed stare. Then they opened the door and we were led away.

'If they were really close to capturing the others, they'd have offered proof,' Angus said.

I nodded. Neither my horror nor my grief had abated, but I was awash with clarity. 'Aye.'

Laoch's expression was dark. 'They must have gone to a lot of trouble to bring those bodies here from Glasgow so they could display them for your benefit. Executing children now.' He shook his head grimly, then glanced at Belle, who'd not said a word. 'You did well there, you know,' he said quietly.

Her lips tightened but she made no response. She wouldn't even raise her eyes to his.

'Did they notice that you're sick?' Angus asked me.

'They did.'

'Good.' He smiled approvingly. 'That will lull them into a false sense of security. They'll think they've undermined you physically with the poison and emotionally with the hangings.'

I passed a hand over my eyes. 'They *have* undermined me emotionally with the hangings, Angus.'

His smile vanished and he glared. 'Then for heaven's sake take that damned emotion and lock it away, lass! Emotion will hamper your ability to perform magic. If it gets the better of you, they'll win.'

Laoch's jaw tightened. 'Enough of that. Mairi knows that already and she needs to rest. We all do. Tomorrow will be a big day.'

The clanging of the dusk bell sounded and I couldn't help wondering if it would be the last time I'd hear it. 'Belle,' I said, 'nobody would blame you if you wanted to leave.'

Her head snapped up. She still didn't speak but her expression left me in no doubt as to her thoughts on the matter.

I sighed. 'Aye, okay, then.'

There was a knock on the door and we all jumped. Laoch hastily went back to his hiding place. I licked my lips and slowly walked over as the key turned and the door was unlocked. It remained closed, though, so I reached for the handle and opened it a few inches.

It was the Mages Francis and Andy. Again. What joy. I opened the door wider, suddenly terrified of what trouble they might bring. 'What do you want?'

'To give you your evening meal, of course,' Francis trilled. He held up a tray; it was yet another bowl of gruel. 'Mmm. Tasty.'

I wasn't going to thank him; I didn't have the energy to be polite. I handed the tray to Angus, then Andy passed me an identical one. As I took it from him, he pressed something into my hand. I tensed but managed not to react otherwise.

'How are you feeling?' Francis asked, unable to keep the satisfied smirk off his face. 'You look even more peely-wally than before.'

The effects of the oleander were starting to wear off, so I suspected it was the shock of the Ascendant's grisly revelations that were causing my continued pallor. I declared in an unnaturally loud voice, 'I have never felt better.'

He laughed. The Mages were obviously finding it hard to keep up the pretence that they'd not poisoned me. I curled my fingers around the thing that Andy had given me and passed back the second tray. 'Was there anything else?'

'Have a good night's sleep,' Francis sang. 'The challenge tomorrow will be so much fun.' He nudged Andy. 'Right?'

'Right,' Andy said, then he added, 'You should enjoy the meal while you can, bitch.'

Francis laughed, and I stared at Andy before closing the door. I heard the key turn immediately. I waited another beat until the sound of their departing footsteps drifted away, then opened my fist and gazed at what was concealed there.

Laoch and Angus were by my side in a flash. I put my finger to my lips, worried that Francis might still be in earshot. The tiny package was a small, folded piece of paper. I opened it up and read it silently.

You have been poisoned.

I rolled my eyes.

It's to weaken you in the first challenge.

Blow me down with a damned feather.

It will start earlier than you realise.

I straightened.

They will come for you at midnight.

I drew in a sharp breath; that titbit of information was genuinely useful. I scanned the last scrawled line.

There are hidden pits.

I frowned, not understanding what that meant.

Laoch's mouth flattened. He walked to the door, tilted his head then nodded at me. 'Nobody's listening.'

I supposed I should be thankful for small mercies. I passed the note to Belle, while Angus raised his eyebrows. 'It was the younger Mage who gave you this?'

'Aye.' I paused. 'He seems sympathetic to us. He definitely wasn't pleased by the executions. Do you know him?'

'No. I can tell you about most of the older Mages, but it's been a few years since I've been here so there are a lot of new faces. It might be a ploy,' he warned. 'The note might be another trap.'

I didn't think so. 'There's nothing in here that could lead to my death – in fact, the information suggests otherwise. The Mages don't know that I wasn't poisoned by the beithir.'

'But if you had been,' Laoch pointed out, 'you'd have

worked it out by now. It might be a bid to gain your trust then screw you later on.'

I considered his words. 'Nah.' I shook my head. 'As far as the Mages are concerned there is no later on. They are convinced they'll secure my grisly death in the first challenge.' I pulled a face. 'Let's face it, they might well do that despite everything we know.' I pointed at the note. 'I think we can trust it, and its bearer.'

I glanced at my companions and my stomach lurched with anxiety. 'And that means the gauntlet is due to begin far sooner than we thought.'

CHAPTER

EIGHTEEN

The knock came ten minutes before midnight. Naturally, I was up and waiting for it – I'd even had a decent sleep beforehand – but when the key turned and the door opened, I acted bleary and confused. I added an extra stagger for effect. I no longer felt ill; the effects of both the oleander and grevillea had worn off, but I needed anyone who saw me to believe I was sick.

'Wh – what?' I blinked and rubbed my eyes.

Of all people, Aspen was standing on the other side of the door. I gazed at him, wondering if he practised smiling with nasty, violent intent in the mirror or if it came naturally. 'It's time,' he said. 'The first round in the Ascendancy Challenge is due to begin. I will escort you to the starting point.'

I was getting better at acting. 'What?' I said again, adding a screech that was high-pitched enough to make Aspen wince. That was extraordinarily satisfying. 'It's the middle of the night! Nobody goes out at night, it's too dangerous. The first challenge is supposed to begin tomorrow!'

Aspen held up his hands. 'Calm down, dear,' he said. 'The

first challenge does begin tomorrow.' He smirked. 'It will start as soon as the midnight bell chimes.' He took out a pocket watch. 'We should get a move on if we're not going to be late. I'm competing as well, and I do not wish to fail because you caused a delay. If you're not ready, however…' His voice trailed off and he shrugged.

I glared at him. 'Give me one minute.'

He gave me a long, considering look. 'One minute, then. Any longer and I will leave without you, and your place will be forfeit.'

I almost snorted with derision. He wanted me to fail publicly; they all did. Even the Ascendant hadn't wanted me to back down when he'd shown me the gallows, he'd merely wanted to unnerve me. Regardless of Aspen's threats, the challenge wouldn't begin without me.

I closed the door to block him and turned to the others. 'This is it,' I said quietly.

Laoch didn't utter a word. He walked up to me, dipped his head and gave me a long, lingering kiss filled with meaning. I clung to him for as long as I could, until I felt his heartbeat thrumming against my body and his heat pressing into me. Then he pulled back and brushed my cheeks with the tips of his fingers.

Laoch moved to the side to avoid notice while I drew back my shoulders and re-opened the door. Angus and Belle joined me. Aspen was pointedly examining his fingernails. He glanced at my companions. 'They're not coming.'

'You cannae stop us,' Belle said. There was a quiver in her voice, but she was determined to stand her ground.

Fury sparked in Aspen's eyes at being gainsaid by a woman, but Angus stepped forward before he could reply. 'Aye,' he said. 'You can't stop us, and we are coming. We must bear witness.'

'She does not require you to do so. There will be others present who can do that in your stead.'

Angus looked delighted. 'If others are present, it is not a closed challenge and you cannot stop us from attending.'

A muscle jerked in Aspen's cheek; he'd been caught out and he knew it. 'Very well. On your own heads be it.' He moved aside to let us out. 'Follow me.'

I resisted the urge to glance back and glimpse Laoch for one last time as we trailed after the Mage who took off down the hallway at a tremendous pace.

This was it. It felt as if I were walking to my execution. Perhaps I was.

The cold stone walls and uneven floor were starting to feel familiar, and so were the guards at the end of it. Aspen passed them, his cloak billowing as he descended the winding staircase. Neither of them looked at him, but when I passed they both bowed.

A flash of alarm ripped through me. Any suggestion of disloyalty and both these guards would join Billy, John and the poor boy whose name I didn't know up on the ramparts. The Mages wouldn't hesitate to execute a couple more souls. But Aspen was too swept up in his own importance and didn't notice their gesture.

Tears pricked my eyes as I bowed my head in return. Many people bought into the Mages' lies – but not everyone. Not these men. There was more hope that things would change than I had realised.

We followed Aspen down the stairs, past the Ascendant's study and into the first courtyard. From there, he led us down a cobbled slope towards the castle's main exit. Torches lit our way, their flames flickering in the gentle breeze. It was a cold, crisp night and the stars gleamed while the moon hung full and pregnant, casting her glow over us.

I couldn't fully appreciate it, however. As soon as I tilted my head upwards, a raven shrieked and swooped towards me, claws outstretched. I ducked, more out of instinct than fear, and the bird wheeled away at the last moment. Aspen chuckled with what sounded like genuine merriment.

'Fecking things,' Belle muttered. She flapped her arms around her head as if to ward them off.

I didn't bother to conceal my words to Angus. Aspen would hear them no matter how much I whispered. 'Ravens?' I asked. 'At night?'

'It happens. They'll be using them to keep the audience in check and to ensure no Afflicted are approaching the challenge site. But the birds have poor night vision, so their usefulness at this time of night is limited.'

'He's right,' Aspen interrupted.

Angus rolled his eyes. 'Of course I'm right,' he muttered.

'The birds can't see well in the dark,' Aspen continued, as if Angus hadn't spoken, 'but they will sense you're a stranger. They will continue to fly down to check who you are and to make sure you're not a danger.'

On cue, another bird plunged towards me. This time I managed not to duck. I felt the tip of its feathers wing brush against my cheek before it veered away. I glanced at Aspen. 'But Lord Aspen,' I said softly, 'I *am* a danger.'

Angus nudged me with his elbow in warning, reminding me that I was supposed to be weak from my apparent poisoning. I grimaced inwardly then deliberately stumbled and nearly fell flat on my face on the hard, stone cobbles.

Aspen laughed aloud, his triumph audible. 'Yes, you're very dangerous,' he mocked and laughed again.

The castle gates were already open and more guards were flanking both sides of the wide stone opening. I paused, taking a moment to gaze out over the city. There were few visible lights other than a long strip of them at the foot of the castle hill. There: that was where the gauntlet would be.

No matter what precautions were in place, the Mages were taking a risk that the Afflicted would be drawn by the light and the noise and mount an attack. Maybe that was part of the challenge. I licked my dry, cracked lips and turned back to look at the castle where Laoch was hiding with Mungo by his side for emergencies. That was when I noticed the mark on the castle wall next to the entrance and let out a sharp cry.

Angus jerked, Belle darted behind him for cover, and Aspen looked around. 'What's the matter now, stupid woman? The challenge is almost due to start.'

I gritted my teeth and pointed. 'Look,' I said. 'That rune I told you about. There's one here on the walls of your own damned castle.'

'Don't be ridiculous,' he said dismissively.

I lurched forward and grabbed his arm. He shoved me away and raised his hand to strike my face. 'Look at it!' I pointed angrily. 'Get over yourself and *look*!'

Aspen glared at me then, without lowering his hand, followed my finger with his eyes. When he saw the rune, his jaw slackened. He dropped his arm, pushed past me and marched towards the symbol to examine it. 'This is nothing, merely crude graffiti.' He turned to the guards and started shouting. 'How long has this been here? Who did it?'

The guards exchanged glances.

'Uh…' one of them started.

Aspen stalked up to the stammering man, who couldn't have been more than twenty years old, and grabbed the front of his coat. 'Speak up, man!'

'Jamie saw it a few nights ago. None of us had noticed it before. We don't know who did it.'

'What is the point of having guards if you allow this sort

of thing to occur?' Aspen shook his head in disgust and scanned the group. His eyes alighted on an older man whose coat displayed red flashes on the shoulders to indicate his superiority. His mouth thinned then he jerked his head. *'Kall moy.'*

I knew that spell; I knew what those words did. The guard's eyes widened in fear and his hands automatically reached for his throat. His cheeks grew bright red, then purple. He choked and spluttered, unable to draw air into his lungs. It was like drowning on dry land, and it was horrific.

I watched for one desperate moment, then I pulled back my shoulders. No. It didn't matter who that guard was, I wasn't going to stand by while the Mages killed yet another person. I started forward, prepared to do whatever I could to stop Aspen, while the guard dropped to his hands and knees.

'No, lass.' Angus stepped in front of me. 'You need to save your strength for the challenge. I'll deal with this.'

I opened my mouth to protest but Belle was suddenly there next to me. 'No, Mairi,' she said. 'Do what you're told and let the old man sort this out.' She crossed her arms; for the briefest moment, I was transported back to the little tartan shop. I closed my eyes and Belle exhaled.

Angus started to speak. 'Aspen! Stop that!'

'It is not your place to interfere with this, traitor.'

'That's where you're wrong,' Angus said calmly. *'Del var.'*

The guard gasped aloud, gulping in air as more magic vibrated through the air. Aspen's spell broke with a snap, and he turned on Angus. 'I'm going to end you.'

'Please do.' Angus grinned. 'Expel all that magic of yours and leave nothing for the challenge. Go on. Do it.'

Aspen snarled, then pointed at the guard who had almost choked to death. 'Hit him. Make this traitor bleed.' He hissed through his teeth. 'End him!'

'You're telling the man you almost killed to attack me for saving him?' Angus asked sarcastically.

'I am in charge here.' Aspen marched over to the guard and kicked him on the shin. 'Do it. Kill the traitor.'

The guard struggled to his feet as his companions watched, wide-eyed. He looked at Aspen then he looked at Angus, and finally he looked at me. 'You're only a woman. You already look half deid. Whit can you do?'

Aspen let out a strangled snort of derision. I ignored him. 'I can win the Ascendancy Challenge.' My voice rang out clear as a church bell on a silent morning. Power throbbed behind every word. 'I can end their reign.'

'But will you?' one of the other guards asked in a quaking tone.

I gazed at them all. 'I make no promises and no guarantees. But I will give it everything I have.'

The first guard, the one whom Aspen had almost killed, wheezed, 'My maw could do magic. Nae much. She could light a fire, and once she saved a lad from drowning by using words to lift him fae the pond he was in. The Mages took her when I was ten years old and I never saw her again. I dinna ken what happened to her.'

He swallowed as he struggled to find the words. 'My wife is pregnant. If it's a lass...' He shook his head. With fumbling fingers, he undid the buttons on his coat and let it to drop to the ground. 'Shift's over, lads.' He turned his back on Aspen and stumbled away. The other guards watched him.

'Stop that man! Arrest him!' Aspen bawled.

Nobody moved. None of them joined the brave deserter, but none of them stopped him either. Aspen clenched his fists, his face almost as red as the guard's had been when he was struggling for air.

I recognised the look in his eyes: Lord Aspen was afraid. He opened his mouth to yell another magical command but suddenly a trumpet sounded, filling the air and forestalling him.

'Looks like the first challenge is about to begin,' Angus said. 'What will you do, Lord Aspen?'

The Mage's body started to shake. He raised his head and stared after the departing guard. 'I will come after you! You will be hung and drawn and quartered!' He gestured at one of the circling ravens. 'Follow that man. Do not lose him.' He glared at the other guards. 'And you lot! Do not think your inaction will go unpunished.'

The trumpet sounded again. Despite the odds stacked against me, suddenly it felt as if it were not a death knell but a signal that the tide was turning. Change was afoot.

Belle sidled up to me. 'You'd better win now, you eejit.'

Aye. I'd better.

CHAPTER

NINETEEN

We walked down the hill and across the bridge that covered the old moat. Well, Aspen, Belle and I walked; Angus skipped – several times. We pretended to ignore him and made it the rest of the way without incident. Even the ravens gave us a wide berth.

When we rounded the corner and saw the long street and the crowds in front of us, we all gaped, Angus included. 'It's been a good many years since I witnessed an Ascendancy Challenge,' he said to nobody in particular. 'I'd forgotten what a spectacle it is. The last one was more than twenty years ago. It ran to six rounds, but the first round is always the most exciting.'

Aspen sent him a cool look. 'You were always too much of a coward to participate.' He sniffed and stalked off to join a group of Mages that included the Edinburgh Ascendant. Aspen murmured to them, no doubt explaining what had occurred with the guards, and I saw several backs stiffen. The Ascendant jerked his head up to the castle as if he could see the aftermath of the confrontation with the guard from here.

I turned away and focused on the scene in front of me. It was terrifying. I certainly hadn't expected the gauntlet distance to be quite so great, neither had I expected so many people. I wondered if the Mages had dragged them here to witness my defeat, or if they were here voluntarily.

At least with the tall buildings at their backs, none of the Afflicted could appear unannounced and grab them from behind. Then I remembered how many Afflicted there were during the attack on the City Chambers. The Mages were taking a hell of a chance by holding this first challenge at night, whether the diseased creatures were becoming immune to sunshine or not.

I grimaced and turned to Angus. 'You don't think that part of the plan is to remind the people of Edinburgh that the Mages keep them safe from the Afflicted? Maybe they're encouraging an attack?'

'Under other circumstances I'd consider that,' he replied. 'But the Ascendancy Challenge is sacrosanct.' I certainly hoped he was right.

'I've never been out at this hour before,' Belle breathed, 'not since I was a teenager. Look at the sky. It's so ... dark.' She slipped her hand into mine. She gave me a confused frown, then realised we were holding hands and snatched hers away. 'Whit do you think you're doing?' She rubbed her palm down the front of her dress. 'Don't do that again!'

Uh-huh.

Angus squinted into the darkness. 'It looks as if the finish line will be Calton Hill beyond the other end of Princes Street. That's further than I expected.'

I pursed my lips. 'Can you see anything to suggest what sort of attacks to expect?'

He shook his head. 'No, but there will be Mages positioned down Princes Street who will use their magic to try and stop the gauntlet runners. They will have been selected because ostensibly they are impartial.' He glanced at me. 'But it's you they'll want to stop first.'

I pulled back my shoulders. I was ready.

'Stop that!' he hissed. 'You're sick, remember? Poisoned almost to the point of death!'

I let my shoulders droop and staggered against him. The crowd watching us from the starting line gasped before I let Angus help me straighten up.

'Better,' he said. 'If the Mages think you're going to collapse halfway down the gauntlet, they'll reserve their energy and mute their attacks. But they are not the only thing you have to worry about. I think I see a cage down there.'

Belle blinked. 'A cage?'

'It'll contain some beastie or other,' Angus said thoughtfully. 'Remember, lassie, defence is your best form of attack. And conserve your strength – I expect the worst will occur right before the finish line.' There was an odd note in his voice.

I glanced at him. Oh. 'You don't think I'll survive this first round, do you?'

'I think you will!' Belle interrupted loudly, though her words contrasted starkly with her expression.

'Wheesht, woman,' Angus said. He met my eyes. 'The odds are against you, lass, but do your best and who knows what may come afterwards. Or who. Even your presence is inspiring others. You can become a glorious martyr yet.'

'Funny how that doesn't fill me with excitement,' I muttered. 'Why are you still here if you think I'll fail?'

Angus sighed. 'Because after decades of doing the wrong thing, I've decided it's time to change.' He smiled faintly. 'Even if it makes a martyr of me, too.'

'I ain't being no fucking martyr,' Belle said.

'My dear, you will likely outlive us all,' Angus retorted.

There was a flash of light and for a second I caught a glimpse of several of the cages that Angus had mentioned. I tried not to focus on the creatures trapped inside them. Then the Ascendant's voice boomed out and I realised he was employing the same magic that Noah had used to speak to the entire city of Glasgow. Everyone in Edinburgh could probably hear him.

'The trumpet has sounded twice. When it sounds for a third time, the first round of the Ascendancy Challenge for the city of Glasgow will begin. This challenge is steeped in tradition and is designed to ensure you have the very best person at the helm. Our cities deserve the strongest and most intelligent leaders. *You* deserve that. *You* deserve a leader who will rule with compassion, but who will be prepared to make the hardest choices to keep you safe.'

He paused then resumed. 'Twenty-three competitors will vie for the position of Ascendant and, for the first time, one of those competitors is female.' He touched the centre of his chest. 'I want the challenge to be fair. I am prepared to allow a female to participate so we can settle the question once and for all whether women have the power to lead as well as men. All Mages believe wholeheartedly in a level playing field and we are proving that tonight to you, the good people of Edinburgh.

'You are here to witness the challenge. Do not worry. All our Mages will ensure there is no danger from the Afflicted. While we are here, you are safe.' He smiled beneficently and turned to me. 'I hope, dear Mairi, that you acquit yourself well and are not harmed during this dangerous and risky process.'

Amusement danced in his eyes as he addressed the crowd again. 'The first round is the gauntlet. Each candidate must make their way from the starting point to the end point at Calton Hill. All who survive will proceed to the second round.'

He bowed his head and clasped his hands together. 'Take your places at the starting line.'

I hung back, watching as the cluster of Mages moved ahead of me. Aspen untied his cloak and handed it to Teasag, who was standing meekly beside him. She didn't glance at me. Other Mages removed their cloaks, too; some were old, some were young – and right now, all of them were my enemy.

'God speed, Mairi,' Angus said.

Belle nodded. 'Gie it laldy.'

Angus raised an eyebrow. 'Laldy?'

Belle's lip curled. 'Good luck, lass.' Her thin lips flattened. 'You're going to need it.'

I'd make my own luck, but I acknowledged her words with a brief smile as I joined the others and took up position next to a lanky Mage with curling ginger hair.

'You know,' he said companionably, 'we've got a sweepstake going on how far you'll get. Drop dead at the hundred-metre mark and I'll win. I've got a few drinking debts to clear up, so you'd been doing me a real favour if you could last that long.'

His expression was earnest rather than threatening; he genuinely thought he was being friendly. I blinked several times and then, to remind them all that I was weak, poisoned and nothing more than a delicate female, I clutched my stomach, bent over and retched noisily.

'She'll never get that far, Roddy,' I heard another Mage laugh. 'You've already lost the sweepstake.'

'And you're going to lose the challenge too, you red-haired wanker,' said another more familiar voice with a harsh edge. I squinted up and recognised Mosse. My eyes narrowed; if I had the chance to take that bastard out, I definitely would.

The trumpet sounded for a third time. Laoch's face flashed into my mind for a final time, then a nearby Mage slammed his fist into the small of my back. I sprawled to the ground. Another Mage trod on my outstretched hand, his heel grinding down forcefully until there was a faint crunch of bone. I cried out at the sharp pain – at least of two of my fingers were broken.

I clenched my jaw and hauled myself back up to my feet. I didn't need to look at the Edinburgh Ascendant to know he was delighted.

'Come on, Mairi!'

I didn't know that voice; it was a stranger from the crowd.

Someone else shouted, 'Go, Mairi!'

Then there was another call, 'Run!'

I swallowed hard. Those people were counting on me.

I crossed the starting line and headed after the others. Come on, Mairi, give it your best shot. At least I didn't have to win this round; I only had to survive.

I'd barely taken three stumbling steps when, out of nowhere, there was a loud whoosh to my left followed by a blast of heat. I heard several screams from the watching crowd yelling at me to duck, but I was already back down on the ground. A half second later, a blazing fireball flew over my head. As soon as it passed me it dissipated into air, avoiding setting the audience alight.

I hissed under my breath. None of the Mages in front of me had been attacked by a damned fireball. What a surprise.

I heaved myself up. The safest course of action would be to catch up with some of the others; I'd be less likely to be pelted with fire if the other Mages might be burnt to a crisp at the same time. Holding my breath and ignoring the thrumming of my heart and the pain in my hand, I put on a burst of speed. The crowd cheered. I wasn't alone, I reminded myself. Most people here were on my side.

There were several flashes of light ahead and I felt the air molecules above my head start to snap together. I veered right and my foot slipped into a puddle. A streak of conjured lightning smacked down in the spot where I'd just been. Two for two, yet I was still standing, and I'd not expended any magical energy. But there was a long way to go yet.

I passed the first cage. It was empty, its door swinging open; whatever creature it had imprisoned was already on the loose. Then I heard a human screech. It was the red-haired Mage, and he was on the ground. Some sort of shaggy-haired wild dog with yellow fangs had a hold of his leg and was shaking it hard.

'*Ins veil!*' he screamed. '*Ins veil!*'

His pain and fear had gotten the better of him, and his emotions had weakened his magic. The more he attempted to conjure up the power he needed to throw off the beast, the less effective his words became. He raised his head and saw me. 'Help! Help me!'

I hesitated for a fraction of a second, then ran past him. He'd survive without me and I had my own problems to worry about. I put my head down and sprinted. The first group of straggling Mages was now only ten metres ahead.

I felt another of crackle of magic and my head swung around as I desperately searched for the source of the latest attack. I heard a guttering rumble and looked ahead in time to see a towering wave of murky water appear from the right and smash down on the heads of the cluster of Mages in front of me. Several were knocked over, but at least three of them muttered protective spells in the nick of time. The rumble sounded again. I held my breath and hummed. *Vaz.*

The crashing tsunami curved over my head and missed me entirely, though it drenched the watching crowd on the far side of the street. It appeared to have little force and did little damage except soak their clothes.

My eyes narrowed as I suddenly understood the game. The gauntlet was a long distance for a reason. In these early stages, the attacks were relatively easy to dodge or to block because they were trying to tire us out, to make us use as much magic as possible against simple assaults so that we had less energy to defend ourselves later. Given my supposed poisoning, they'd be expecting me to tire much faster than the Mages. Clearly, the key was to reserve as much strength as possible.

I could do that. I put on a final spurt until I drew level with the three Mages who'd not been flattened by the magical wave. Safety in numbers.

'Fuck off,' the nearest Mage spat. He veered towards me, collided with my shoulder and sent me briefly off course. I stumbled and he laughed coldly – but his amusement didn't last long. Another flash of lightning struck the spot where I'd have been if he hadn't knocked me. His body jerked and went limp, hovering almost comically in mid-air before collapsing completely. I ran around him. That was close.

The other two Mages next to me started to sprint, desperate to put as much distance between me and them as possible. I was the target of all the attacks, and they didn't want to be next to me. They pulled ahead for several seconds, then came to a sudden, stuttering halt as the ground in front of us revealed itself.

There was a gaping hole that had surely been created by magical means. I knew that falling into it would lead to certain death; it was too dark to see all the way down, but it would be a long drop. I swallowed hard. I'd have to use some magic to get across. There was no other way. I gritted my teeth, but at least I knew what to do.

Folis. It was the first magical word I'd learned and often the most useful. My body rose instantly into the air. The crowd to my left yelled their approval, and I smiled slightly as I used swimming strokes to shimmy forward. I had no idea what the other two Mages were doing; I was too caught up in my own brilliance. Unfortunately, that feeling didn't last long.

There was another rush of warm air from the right. I knew without looking that it was another fireball aimed at me. I dived to avoid it but I wasn't fast enough. The heaving ball of fire smacked into my thigh.

My clothes erupted in flames and I started to drop at high speed. Air whipped past me, and I fell past the edge of the chasm. The high walls of the hole closed in. I flapped frantically at the flames on my leg before humming in desperation. *Sel ez.* A gallon of water drenched me, soaking me to the skin and extinguishing the fire – but I was still falling. And faster now.

Folis.

Nothing happened. Shite. My panic was getting the better of me.

Folis.

I felt the magic jerk deep inside me, but it wasn't enough. I licked my lips and let Laoch's face fill my mind, then closed my eyes and tried for a third time. *Folis.* My body caught, suspended in the air. I was no longer falling – but I wasn't rising, either. Something was holding me down, some kind of strange block.

I opened my eyes and squinted upwards. Oh. From the far side of the hole, a face was looking down at me, its features framed in the flickering torchlight that was now a dozen metres above me. Douglas Mosse. His lips were moving, and I knew that he had cast a spell to counterbalance the effects of my folis magic. He saw me looking up at him, grinned and blew me a kiss before his face vanished. I was alone, hanging in the darkness, my magic draining away with every second I remained.

It was pointless attempting folis again; whatever Mosse had done, he was negating that particular spell. I had to think of something else, something the Mages wouldn't expect. I chewed on the inside of my cheek. My body slipped down a few inches, then a few more.

I could hear worried calls and cries from the crowd, none of whom knew me but who were all rooting for me. I blotted them out and concentrated. I couldn't panic. If I panicked, I'd die.

I slid half a metre further, then a full metre. My feet dangled into the darkness, and the dim light above my head was growing further away. Think, Mairi. Think.

I gazed at the walls of the enchanted chasm. Maybe I could climb out. I searched for a handhold or a foothold, but though there were some dribbles of water and some cracks, the rock was too solid, too smooth.

I noticed one long crack that started near my foot and stretched downwards rather than upwards. It was heading in the wrong direction, it wouldn't help – but then I spotted the tiny curling shoot poking out of it.

This time I allowed myself to drop until I was facing the little shoot. I reached out and touched it gently; even down here, in this dank, temporary hole, life had found a way. And this life belonged to the ivy plant, a strong climber that let almost nothing stop its ascent. It was also useful to have around if you had a cough. I smiled. As Laoch had said, a man can get rich from more than digging for gold.

I hummed. *Chelta.*

The first time I'd used that word it had taken days to work properly, but now I was a different person, stronger in so many ways. Magic poured out of me, flowed into the tiny plant, and almost immediately it began grow. It stretched upwards and outwards, clinging to the walls and finding cracks and holes that were too small for me to use, but which were perfect for the plant.

As soon as it had gained several metres and looked strong enough, I grasped it and curled my fingers into its thick foliage. It was good enough to hold my weight. I drew in a deep breath and started to climb.

It wasn't easy but I focused on moving one inch at a time. Sweat dripped off my brow and into my stinging eyes until I could barely see. My right hand, with its two broken fingers, made every second of my ascent excruciating. There were several moments when I felt it would be better to let go and plunge into the depths of the chasm, but I clung on. Every time the pain seemed too great, I pictured Laoch with his coiled horns, his flashing green eyes and his curling tattoos, and I kept moving. And eventually I reached the top.

By the time, I pulled myself over the edge and rolled onto my back, panting with the effort and crying involuntary tears from the agony in my hand, the crowd was completely silent. A single voice called out, thin and thready but filled with joy. 'There! There she is!'

There was an eruption of cheers. I tilted my head and looked over; people of all shapes and sizes were jumping up and down and cheering. I managed a weak smile.

Then I heard a voice I knew. 'Get the fuck up, lass! Get going!'

It was Angus. When I'd fallen, he must have scrambled through the crowds. I met his eyes, and he sent me a rude gesture in return. I wiped the tears from my cheeks and staggered up. I wasn't done yet.

The Mages in charge of administering the gauntlet challenge clearly hadn't expected me to emerge. I stumbled a good seventy feet forward before I was attacked again, this time by a slithering snake of jaw-dropping size. No doubt it had been trapped in one of the cages. I waved a hand towards it; there was enough scrappy power left inside me to hum it away.

I continued further and further down the street until the finish line was in sight. There was one final hill to crawl up and I'd be done. I'd almost made it.

When I saw what was right in front of me, however, I balked.

Three separate paths led up the hill. The first was blocked at several points by a wall of flame, and the second held shifting dark shapes that no doubt belonged to more of the beasties brought in for the gauntlet. Only the third path appeared clear and I headed straight for it – but then I stopped.

Thanks to the flickering flames, I could see some of the Mages who'd made it this far and not a single one was on the third path. It looked like the easiest route, but I recalled what the young Mage, Andy, had written in his note: *There are hidden pits.*

The gigantic hole I'd fallen into hadn't been concealed. What better way to stop me than by creating more pits that the Mages knew about but I did not? I doubted any of them had believed I'd make it this far, but they'd have been wary enough to create a final hurdle in case I did.

I gazed at the open pathway, then at the other two. Shite. Fire, then. It was my best option.

I started uphill. I'd gone only five metres when a raven cawed overhead, taunting me. It swooped down, skimmed the air in front of my face, then wheeled towards the clear path and back again to draw my attention to it. It wanted me to go that way, so all the more reason to brave the flames. I wasn't sure I had enough energy left to deal with the creatures.

It didn't take long to reach the first fiery barricade. The heat was immense and there were at least three more sections where I'd be forced to plunge through flames to get to the finish line. I only had so much magic left inside me. I hesitated, searching my brain for the right thing to do. I couldn't conjure up enough water to extinguish the flames four times, although I'd manage once or maybe twice. I needed something that would use less energy but allow me to pass unharmed.

As I considered, an idea flashed into my mind – and I hummed with all my might.

Sel ez. Water. *Fel zor.* Armour.

I wasn't sure it would work, so when it did it was the strangest sensation. Icy-cold water doused me from head to toe. Instead of sloughing off as it should have done, it clung to me, covering every inch, even my eyes, nose and throat.

The water made my vision blurry. I could still make out shapes and the fire, but everything was indistinct. I tried to breathe – but gulped in liquid. Oh no.

I reached inside myself to check my reserves. There was next to no magic left. My stamina was all but gone. It was this or nothing.

I took one step; the water sloshed around as I moved but it remained with me. I took another step, and another. Deprived of oxygen, my lungs were already starting to burn. I squeezed my hands into fists then I plunged through the first flaming barrier. The water hissed and spat, but the strange liquid armour held true.

I sprinted upwards, pumping my legs harder. I dimly heard the crowd yelling and ravens screeching, but there was only me and the finish line now and I pushed forward, through the next fiery wall. I was starting to feel dizzy but I had to keep going, had to keep moving upwards.

Clouds of steam rose when I ran through the second-to-last bank of flames. Dots danced in front of my eyes and I closed them tight. I kept putting one foot in front of the other as quickly as I could, and was only vaguely aware of crossing another fiery section.

And then I could hold it no longer. I released the spell and the water cascaded down and away from my body. It evaporated almost instantly on the hot ground. I wiped my eyes, slowed my steps and looked around.

The first thing I saw was the Edinburgh Ascendant. His expression was tight and his eyes were stony. Lord Aspen was standing by his shoulder, his narrowed gaze suggesting he'd finally realised I'd been faking my illness. Beside Aspen was Douglas Mosse; he made no effort to hide his hatred and disappointment. He bared his teeth in a snarl as I gulped in air and massaged my chest with my uninjured hand.

'You're last,' the Ascendant bit out. 'By quite some distance.'

I opened my mouth to answer but water dribbled out instead of words. I spat and coughed a few times, then managed to speak. 'I didn't have to win to clear this round. I only had to survive.'

I surveyed the cluster of Mages. Ten – no, eleven were left. My stomach flipped in triumphant delight. I'd done it: I'd proved a woman could keep up with them. I'd already beaten more than half their number. Regardless of what happened next, that would count for a great deal.

'Beginner's luck,' Mosse hissed. He rubbed a blackened burn mark on his cheek, and I saw blood on his hand. He'd not emerged unscathed.

Aspen, who'd been far ahead of me throughout the gauntlet and whose appearance was undamaged, continued to watch me. Most of these Mages were fools. Mosse was a bastard, and the Edinburgh Ascendant was a sadistic peacock. Aspen was the one I had to watch out for. His pride had been seriously dented before the gauntlet thanks to the defiant guard, and he wouldn't forget that. Neither would he misjudge my abilities again.

When I held his gaze, neither of us looked away. Even when one of the younger Mages interjected to tell us that a group of the Afflicted were approaching the other side of the hill, we continued to stare at each other. The connection was only broken when the Ascendant instructed a group of waiting guards to take me away and clear the area and they stepped in front of me and blocked my view.

As other guards appeared holding a broadly grinning Angus and Belle and led us away, the crowds below continued to cheer and shout.

Sooner or later, I thought, we'd all pay for this night. One way or another.

CHAPTER

TWENTY

The door slammed shut behind us and I immediately glanced at the far corner where Laoch was hiding. He pushed away from the wall and gave me a crooked smile.

Angus looked from Laoch to me and back again, then waved his arms between us. 'She's alive! She made it!'

Laoch's expression didn't alter.

'It's amazing,' Angus persisted. He turned to Belle for confirmation. 'Right?'

'Bloody amazing.' She was still beaming from ear to ear. I'd never seen Belle smile like that before, apart from the time when the MacDougalls' tartan shop went out of business. It was almost scary.

Angus gestured to Laoch. 'Why aren't you amazed?'

Laoch continued to gaze at me with the same smile. 'Because it's not amazing that the strongest, most powerful person I know survived the Mages' best efforts to kill her. Of course Mairi survived. There was never any doubt.'

I looked into his eyes and realised with a jolt that he was telling the truth. Unlike Angus, Belle and even me, Laoch had never doubted for one moment that I would return. A warm sensation filled the pit of my belly and spread through my body. 'It was only the first round,' I said quietly. 'And we've lost our advantage. The Mages know what I'm capable of now and they must realise I've not been poisoned.'

Angus sniffed. 'You really are a pessimistic creature.'

Laoch's face darkened before he gathered me in his arms. *If you died*, his voice whispered in my head, *I would feel it. We are entwined, you and me. Without you, I don't exist.*

My mouth dried and an odd shiver rippled down my spine. *Laoch, I...*

'Let's see to those wounds before you bleed all over this room,' Belle said. She rolled her eyes and added sarcastically, 'This bonnie, bonnie room.'

Laoch gently released me. 'Your hand,' he murmured.

I nodded. 'I think my fingers are broken.' I squinted at it. The first rays of dawn were appearing and their soft light made my swollen, bruised fingers look even worse than they felt.

'Dinna forget your side,' Belle pointed.

'I'm a bit burned, too.' I pulled up my wet shirt to expose the puckered red skin in all its scalded fury. Laoch's mouth tightened.

'And,' Angus added cheerfully, 'there are all the other minor cuts and bruises, any of which could become infected and destroy the lass at a moment's notice.'

If looks could kill, Laoch would have murdered Angus on the spot. I sighed and took a step back, then stumbled and almost lost my balance. Laoch reached for me again but I clenched my jaw and waved him off. I wanted to prove to myself that I still possessed some strength, even though my knees were on the verge of buckling and I was feeling more and more lightheaded by the second.

I staggered over to the small bed without help then sank down, taking the weight off my feet with a surge of relief.

'You're exhausted,' Laoch muttered, his voice ragged with concern.

'Aye, well that's no surprise, is it? The more weird, complicated spells you teach her and the more she uses them, the more drained she'll become,' Angus replied. 'She doesn't haven't the stamina for your magic. And now everyone knows the sort of things she has up her grubby sleeves.'

Confusion clouded Laoch's face. 'What do you mean? What spell?'

The old Mage gave him a look of disbelief. 'What spell?' he scoffed. 'You did notice that she looks like a drowned rat, right?'

Laoch folded his arms across his broad chest. 'I assumed that some swimming was involved,' he said evenly

'Swimming? *Swimming?*'

I half closed my eyes. I should have been annoyed that they were talking about me rather than to me, but I didn't have the energy – plus I was used to being treated as a mute object instead of an actual person. Frankly, I hoped that they'd all shut up and leave me in peace.

'Mairi,' Belle explained reluctantly, 'made some kind of suit for herself out of water to help her get past some flames. If she'd been smart, she'd have noticed that there was another pathway to the side that was clear of fire, but she was never very observant.' She sniffed. 'Next time, she ought to look more closely at her surroundings.'

'A suit made out of water?' Laoch's voice popped into my head. *Mairi? What is this about?*

I would have to explain after all. It was probably easier to answer aloud and let them all hear. 'I combined two spells,' I said, dragging the words out of my mouth. 'Armour and water.'

Several seconds passed and nobody said anything. I opened my eyes to see Laoch and Angus staring at me open-mouthed, while Belle frowned with baffled incomprehension.

'Two spells.' Angus ran a hand through his straggly grey hair. 'Two spells together?'

I nodded. 'Aye.'

'*Sel ez*?' Laoch asked. 'And what? *Fel zor*?'

'Aye.' I gazed at him. 'So what?'

'Combining two spells is impossible, lass,' Angus said.

I felt a flicker of irritation. Obviously, it wasn't impossible.

'That's not entirely true,' Laoch murmured. 'There were a few daemons in my grandmother's generation who could combine magic to create new effects.'

'You daemons are fucking odd, though.' Angus paused before adding slowly, 'You said grandmother.'

'Yes.'

'Not grandfather.'

'It was only female daemons who could display such power.'

Belle snorted. 'Big shocker. Women can multi-task. Men cannae.'

I was too tired to continue the conversation. 'The second challenge round will probably start soon. I need to rest. Can one of you please bind my fingers together? And then can all of you leave me alone to get some sleep?'

Guilt flashed across Laoch's face. Angus still appeared profoundly shocked, but also curious, about my apparent revelation. Belle was already rummaging around in one of the bags. She pulled out a white shirt and started tearing strips off it.

'Hey!' Angus shook away his amazement to glare at her. 'That's my shirt!'

'Well, I ain't using one of my blouses,' she sniped back.

Laoch pushed past both of them and sat down next to me. 'Here,' he said gently. 'Let me help you get these clothes off.'

As he reached for the first button on the still-wet shirt, there was a knock on the door and we all froze. My stomach lurched. No; surely it couldn't be a summons to the second round this quickly. But I knew it could be. Aspen had looked fresh and so had several of the others. The Mages would want to capitalise on my exhaustion and continue the challenge as quickly as possible.

Laoch's fingers squeezed mine with warm reassurance before he headed for his hiding place. I stood up and tried to look ready for whatever was to come before nodding to Angus.

'Aye?' he bellowed towards the door.

The key turned and the door swung open. I held my breath, only releasing it when I saw Andy standing nervously outside. He was clutching something in his hands and biting his bottom lip. 'Hello.'

I willed my legs to carry me close enough to greet the young Mage. 'The second round?' I asked, injecting a dose of unreal brightness into my voice.

Andy blinked. 'Huh?' He shook his head. 'Oh. No, that won't start until after midday. You've got time to recover.'

I peered at him. He seemed to be telling the truth but I couldn't be too sure.

'Why are you here then, laddie?' Angus enquired. 'You don't have any food with you. If you're checking on Mistress Mairi the Magnificent here, you can see that she's perfectly fine.'

Mistress Mairi the Magnificent? I managed to avoid staring

at Angus and kept my focus in Andy, who was shuffling his feet and swallowing hard.

'That … that's not why I'm here.' He thrust out his hand and opened his palm to reveal a small tin. 'I thought you might need a bit of help with your wounds. This is my own concoction – it's good for all manner of ailments.'

Belle bustled forward and snatched it from him, lifted it to her nose and sniffed. 'It reeks,' she declared loudly.

Andy offered an embarrassed shrug. 'It's not got the nicest smell,' he agreed. 'But it does work.'

I eyed the tin. Belle, who was clearly thinking what I was thinking, unscrewed the lid and passed the tin back to Andy. 'You try it first.'

His brow furrowed. 'Why would I—?' His voice trailed off. 'Oh. Okay.' He hooked out a glob of the foul-smelling ointment with his index finger and rubbed it onto his hands. I leaned forward and smelled the air; it did indeed smell foul, but I detected a faint whiff of lavender, calendula and, quite possibly, sheep dung. I'd used all of those in my herbal treatments. I suspected that Andy's offering was genuine and that he was trying to help.

He held up his hand to indicate it wasn't turning purple or green or dropping off his wrist.

I nodded. 'Thank you.'

'You're welcome.' He shuffled his feet again and twitched. There was more that he wanted to say.

I came right out with my question. 'What's the next challenge?'

'Uh, riddles.'

'Uh riddles? What's "uh riddles"?' Angus asked.

I glared at him. 'Enough of that,' I muttered. Angus glared back at me but subsided. I returned my attention to Andy. 'Do you know anything more?'

'No. I'm sorry. I'm not in the inner circle, so I'm not privy to that sort of information.'

'You're not taking part in the Ascendancy Challenge, either.' I hadn't seen him during the first round.

He gave a shocked laugh. 'No! I wouldn't want to be the bloody Ascendant. Who would?'

Who indeed? I smiled slightly. He still had something to say, but it appeared he was going to need more of a nudge to say it. 'Is there anything else?' I asked softly, trying to look encouraging.

Andy looked even more nervous. 'I wasn't at the challenge,' he said. 'I didn't want to watch. I heard about what you did, though. That magic.' He shook his head. 'Where did you learn that spell?'

I decided I might as well be truthful. 'I made it up on the spot by combining two other spells.'

He took a half step backwards. 'That's ... that's ... impossible.'

Angus snorted, but kept his mouth shut this time.

Andy glanced down the hallway, as if checking that the coast were clear, then looked back at me. 'You might just do it,' he whispered. 'You might win.'

'That's the plan,' I said cheerfully, although I was somewhat flummoxed by his words. They were not what I'd been expecting.

He reached into his breast pocket and took out a wad of folded paper. 'Here. You should have this.' He ran a shaky hand through his hair. 'I wasn't at the challenge because I went to the library. I took that page from one of the old books.'

'You damaged a book?'

His cheeks grew pink. 'I thought you should see it, and I didn't think I could smuggle the whole book up here.'

My curiosity got the better of me. I awkwardly unfolded

the piece of paper, trying not use my damaged fingers, while Belle and Angus shuffled either side of me to peer over my shoulders. When I saw what was inscribed on the paper, my body went rigid and I forgot about my pain and exhaustion.

'It's your rune,' Angus said aloud. I realised he was speaking for Laoch's benefit; the old Mage did have his uses on occasion.

'It is,' I said grimly. But it wasn't the depiction of the rune that was chilling, it was the translation underneath.

'*He Is Coming*,' Angus said. 'That's what it means?'

'According to the book, yes,' Andy told him. 'The rune's language is ancient, at least two thousand years old. Probably more.'

'And the book?' I asked. 'Is it some kind of dictionary?'

Andy shook his head. 'No. It's an old book filled with prophetic theories about the end of the world as we know it. We were supposed to be engulfed in fire ten years ago. Ninety-eight years ago, there should have been a great flood that swamped Europe for generations. The author, who's long since dead, writes about the prophecies as if they're nothing more than intriguing delusions. There's no sense that any of them are to be believed.' He licked his lips and dropped his voice. 'But we've all seen that rune.'

'Have you told the others about this?' Angus asked. 'The other Mages, I mean?'

'I tried,' Andy said, 'but they don't want to know. All they care about is the Ascendancy Challenge and...' His eyes flashed with guilt and he didn't finish his sentence.

'Getting rid of me,' I said.

'Aye.' He looked down. 'Sorry.'

Belle spoke up. 'Are you telling me that as well as waiting to be hung, drawn and quartered by the Mages, I need to worry about the end of the fecking world as well?'

I gazed down at the ripped page. *He Is Coming*. But who was *He*? Anxiety scratched at my bones. 'Who's to say? We have other things to worry about.' I smiled at her – but I also carefully re-folded the page and tucked it deep in my pocket where it would be safe.

TWENTY-ONE

Mage Andy had been right on one count: it was barely a shadow past noon when they came for me again.

I'd been half-expecting to see Aspen but instead of his glowering visage, two different Mages appeared at the door. They weren't familiar, and they didn't want to communicate in anything more than monosyllabic grunts. They should have realised that I enjoyed silence.

I smiled brilliantly at them. In truth, I was feeling good. Angus had bound my fingers with surprising expertise and Andy's potion, which was imbued with some sort of healing magic as well as the herbs, was working wonders. Fatigue flickered around the edges of my body but I knew had the energy to continue. I'd rested and I'd healed – at least in part. I was ready for the next challenge.

Belle, Angus and I traipsed along the hallway, past the guards and down the winding stone staircase. When the two dour Mages led us past the Ascendant's study towards the first courtyard, I thought that we were heading out of the castle again. Once I saw the narrow stands packed with people and the series of random doors in the courtyard's centre that led nowhere, I realised I was wrong. The second challenge was clearly taking place here.

The two Mages directed me towards the other Ascendancy candidates. Few of them glanced at me as I approached. Aspen and Mosse were deep in murmured conversation; most of the others were silent, their heads bowed in apparent contemplation.

Unwilling to appear cowed, I spread my arms in greeting. 'Good afternoon, gentlemen!' Nobody answered. I guessed they weren't among Mistress Mairi the Magnificent's fans.

Belle and Angus were led to the stands and seated in the centre, where they were surrounded by Mages instead of the ordinary folk who lined the back rows. A moment later there was another trumpet fanfare. Startled, I jumped slightly and heard Mosse snicker.

The Edinburgh Ascendant strode out from the same door I'd just used, flanked by Teasag and three more black-cloaked wankers. 'Ladies and gentlemen!' he boomed. 'Esteemed Mages! I welcome you all to the second round of the Glasgow Ascendancy Challenge!'

There was a smattering of applause, mostly from the watching Mages. If the Ascendant was dismayed by the lack of enthusiasm, he didn't show it. 'This round measures our candidates' intelligence, as well as their ability to think quickly. Anyone who rises to the position of Ascendant must be of sound mind. They must possess a keen intelligence and they must be able to make quick decisions.'

He nodded, stroked his chin and puffed out his chest. 'I had to take part in a similar contest when I participated in the challenge for the great city of Edinburgh, and I passed with flying colours. My tenure as your Ascendant proves how vital these skills are to any leader. I have shown that to you, my good people. The Glasgow Ascendant needs to show it to their people also.'

He paused and waited for the crowd to applaud dutifully again. I noted that some of the less enthusiastic audience members were joined by Mages and nudged sharply into reacting appropriately. I also noted that the Ascendant wasn't using the same voice amplification magic as before. My surprising survival was likely the reason for that, and I stifled a smile.

The Ascendant continued once the next round of forced clapping had subsided. 'You will see that there are three sets of doors. In this second round, each candidate will be tested individually. They will be given a series of riddles. Under timed conditions, they must answer each riddle and then step through the door. Answer correctly, and the candidate will pass through without incident. Answer wrongly, and the candidate will be ... punished. It does not appear to be a dangerous challenge but, believe me,' he smiled happily, 'it is.'

Uh-huh. Answer wrongly and I'd die in front of a watching crowd in the manner the Mages wanted.

'To ensure fairness, the audience will be magically screened from view once the challenge begins. They can see the candidates, but the candidates will not be able to see them. This will ensure that there is no cheating and that each candidate is given the same opportunity as the others. It is important that everything is kept fair and equal.'

Out of the corner of my eye, I saw Mosse's mouth twitch upwards. The Mages would leave nothing to chance. My friends and I had surmised that the preferred winners already knew the answers to the riddles.

Aspen was impassive, a couple of the participating Mages appeared confident, but there were several who looked scared.

Those were the less favoured ones who hadn't been provided with the answers. They weren't the competition I had to worry about.

'While the candidates wait their turn,' the Ascendant said, 'they can watch but not hear the proceedings.' He turned and bowed to us all. 'Good luck to each and every one of you.' His voice dropped and his lips moved as he murmured an incantation. The air shifted and my ears popped.

I saw the crowd clap again but this time I couldn't hear them. Curiously, I waved my arms in front of my face, and the Mage next to me did the same. We'd been struck deaf.

I swallowed the sudden choke of terror. I'd coped with worse, so I could cope with this. I swung my gaze back to the Ascendant. He was speaking to one of the Mages by his side, but he could have been reciting a nursery rhyme or telling a joke for all I could tell.

My eyes fell on Teasag. She felt the weight of my gaze and looked across, her expression troubled. I knew she doubted my ability to succeed. She looked me up and down and her brow furrowed abruptly, then something flashed across her face and her shoulders relaxed.

I exhaled.

Teasag knows, I communicated to Laoch.

Mungo's small furry body twitched against my bare skin before Laoch answered. *I thought she might sense me. Don't worry. Unless she's asked a direct question about my presence, we're safe.*

I licked my lips. *We're still cheating.*

This time Laoch didn't miss a beat. *So are they.*

I forced myself to relax. The trumpet player raised his instrument and sounded a note but I heard nothing. Then Aspen was beckoned forward.

With his shoulders pulled back, his head upright and his

black cloak swirling around his ankles, he emanated power. He also knew how to sway people to his cause. When he reached the starting point, he bowed courteously to the Ascendant, to the competitors, and finally to the crowd. Somehow he managed to appear humble without looking obsequious, and he hid his cold, sadistic edge well.

If Aspen won the Ascendancy Challenge, it would be a disaster for Glasgow. Blood would run in the streets on his command. Whether I survived or not, I had to do everything I could to ensure that he was not the winner.

I felt a secondary crackle of magic and the audience vanished from sight as the Ascendant had promised. Aspen acknowledged their concealment with a sharp nod before turning his back so that none of us could read his lips. He tilted his head to one side as the first riddle was read out to him.

He didn't answer immediately; in fact, he put on such a good show of thinking hard and working out the answer that I almost believed he didn't already know it.

I risked another communication. *Could you hear the riddle, Laoch?*

His response was swift. *I could not. And stop talking to me. Someone might pick up on it. I'll do the speaking.*

Aspen must have finally responded because he reached forward and twisted the doorknob, then stepped through the first door. When nothing happened and it was clear he was safe, he made a show of touching his chest as if he were relieved. Even the Mage next to me bristled at the act. He shook his head and turned away, unwilling to watch further.

I kept my gaze on Aspen as he completed the second riddle faster than the first, then took his time over the last one. He smiled when he stepped through the final door. The Ascendant strode up, shook him by the hand and clapped his shoulder. One down. Ten to go. Including me.

The next four Mages, Mosse included, completed the challenge without incident. Every time, the Edinburgh Ascendant marched up after they stepped through the final door and shook their hands. Things changed, however, when the sixth Mage was beckoned forward.

I recognised his face from Glasgow, although I struggled to remember his name. He'd definitely been one of the less memorable occupants of the City Chambers, and he didn't appear to be in favour here. I had already glimpsed the sweat on his brow and his shaking hands. I was certain this was the first candidate who hadn't already been supplied with the answers.

He took his place at the marker in front of the first door and the first riddle was read out to him. I could no longer see his face, but I saw his buttocks clench as he strained for the answer. Suddenly, he relaxed. He had it. I breathed out on his behalf. He gave the answer, stepped through the door and moved onto the next spot.

He was more confident now and he held himself differently. He was beginning to believe he could do this. However, when the second riddle was put to him, he tensed again and no answer was forthcoming. He shifted his weight from side to side as the seconds ticked by. The Ascendant gestured that his time was running out and he had to answer. Eventually he must have said something; he stepped forward, twisted the doorknob and stepped through.

For a moment, nothing happened and the Mage's body sagged in relief – but that relief was short-lived. There was a loud clanging sound, then a dark cloud formed directly above his head. A streak of lightning flashed down and smacked into the centre of his skull. The Mage crumpled instantly, convulsing on the ground.

I stared in horror. Shite.

Two more Mages appeared to drag the hapless candidate to the side and immediately begin chest compressions. The rest of us could only watch. When he didn't revive, the Ascendant strode forward and muttered an incantation. The young man's body jerked and his eyelids fluttered open. Without further ado, he was moved away so the next candidate could take his place.

My mouth was dry. Considerable efforts had been made to save that Mage's life, and would probably also be used for the others, but I doubted the same efforts would be expended on my behalf. They'd put on a good show for the audience, of course, but it wouldn't be good enough. If I got any answers wrong, I would be toast.

I tried desperately to think of any magic that would dispel the lightning, but whatever I came up with wouldn't be enough. The strike I received would contain the force from several Mages to make sure it killed me.

The next Mage passed through both the first and second doors without incident, but he faltered at the third door and didn't even try to answer. His arms flailed and he shook his head, but when his time ran out and he still hadn't stepped through the final doorway, the lightning struck him. It took even longer to revive him than the first man.

I curled my fingers into tight fists and continued to watch. What the Mages were prepared to do to their own kind only hinted at what they would do to the rest of us.

The eighth candidate bypassed the challenge completely. Instead of taking his spot and waiting for the first riddle, he walked up to the Ascendant, bowed his head and offered his withdrawal from the competition. The Ascendant nodded understandingly and clapped him on the shoulder – and as the Mage turned to walk away, he was also struck by a bolt. Nobody was allowed to resign; you were either in or you were out. I gazed at his limp, convulsing body until he was dragged away.

The last two Mages were quick-witted and made it through, albeit by the skin of their teeth. The final one had less than a second to spare by the time he blurted out his answer and threw himself through the last door.

Three had been knocked out. Seven had passed. And only I remained.

Relax. Stay confident, Mairi. You can do this.

The Ascendant beckoned me forward. I raised my head, pushed back my shoulders and moved ahead. I immediately stumbled, my toe catching on nothing at all. I still couldn't hear anything, but I could see the derisive smirks on the faces of the Mages who were administering the challenge. Damn it. I straightened up and offered a rueful smile, trying not to look too embarrassed. It was the best I could do.

I moved to the position marked in front of the first door. The Ascendant's lips were moving, but the spell that had rendered me deaf still hadn't been removed. I waved my hands and pointed to my ears, indicating that I couldn't hear, but nobody appeared to notice. My stomach tightened and I gestured again, then my ears popped painfully. I winced.

'…lies but we are not judged by size. What are we?'

What the fuck?

I stared at the Mage delivering the riddle. 'I only heard the last part,' I bit out. 'Can you repeat it?'

'Each riddle is only to be spoken once. The hearing spell was removed in time, as it was for the other candidates. You have fifty-two seconds remaining to give us your answer.'

Bastards.

Laoch's voice echoed in my head. *I didn't hear it all,* he communicated grimly. *Something touching, we bear truth and lies, but we are not judged by size.*

That was more than I'd been allowed to hear but it was better than nothing. I chewed the inside of my cheek and thought hard.

'Thirty seconds,' the riddle master said cheerfully.

I glanced again at Teasag. Her mouth was closed and her hands were by her sides. She was bound by her enslavement and forbidden to communicate with me, but I thought I registered sympathy in her eyes. Damn it.

My mind raced. Truth. Lies. Touching. What could it be? My panic was growing. I didn't know and I couldn't work it out, not under this sort of pressure. Not with only half a riddle.

'Fifteen seconds.'

I felt the Ascendant watching me, his delight growing. I wouldn't even get through the first door. I was fucked. I...

Words. Say it. Say words.

I spat it out. 'Words!'

The riddle master pointed to the door. 'Go on, then. Walk through.'

I had no idea whether Laoch was right or not, but I couldn't hang back. With my heart in my mouth, I reached for the doorknob and felt the cold metal burn my skin as I twisted it. Then the door opened and I stepped through.

A second passed, then another. No lightning. I was still there.

I looked at the Ascendant and saw that his earlier delight had vanished. I'd done it – at least, Laoch had.

The riddle master lifted his chin. 'I am the beginning of the end of time and space that surrounds everything and every place.'

I closed my eyes. The beginning of the end of time. My eyes flashed open. 'E,' I said, both loudly and distinctly.

The riddle master pointed to the door and I walked through it.

Well done, Laoch murmured.

I smiled slightly, although I was far from relaxed. There was a scorch mark on the stone cobbles in front of me where one of the fallen Mages had been hit. I sucked in a breath and waited for the final test. A cool breeze filtered through the courtyard; goosebumps rose across my skin and ruffled my curls. I swallowed hard, then I listened.

'An old evening singer bringing delight to city dwellers. I bellow with bending voice and many sounds, an actor proclaiming an entertainer's song to people far and wide.'

I stared at the riddle master. Was that it? He smiled placidly and folded his arms. I closed my eyes again to block him out so I could focus on what he'd said, but no answer flashed into my mind. Not this time.

'Thirty seconds.'

I got nothing, Mairi.

I grimaced. A minstrel? No. That was too obvious. Who sang in the evening? What sang in the evening? There was the warning bell at dusk, but it wasn't entertaining – not by a long shot. I hissed and squeezed my eyes shut tighter while a raven screeched its dark joy somewhere overhead.

'Fifteen seconds.'

I lifted my head and looked at the Ascendant. He was wary, his gaze watchful. I glanced at Teasag and then at the riddle master. Behind him was a cluster of Mages, Aspen included; having completed their own challenges, they were now allowed to watch mine.

Aspen raised his eyebrows. Only a few seconds remained.

The raven that had called out flapped down, landed on Aspen's shoulder and started to preen its feathers. I watched it while the riddle master uttered his final warning. 'Five seconds.'

I met his eyes. 'Nightingale.'

I knew I had answered correctly from the way the Mages' bodies altered and the atmosphere shifted. I didn't smile this time, but I did open the third and final doorway without being directed to do so. I stepped through.

As I did so, the Ascendant's eyes narrowed, his expression both thoughtful and calculating.

CHAPTER

TWENTY-TWO

'I thought you'd fucked it there, lass,' Angus said. 'We all did.' He wasn't the only one. I'd very nearly ended up as a nasty burn mark on the castle's cobbles.

I sank onto the narrow bed and ran a hand through my hair, drawing a ragged breath as the reek of singed Mage rose again to my nostrils.

'Those eejits ain't playing around,' Belle observed. 'They were happy to see their own kind smashed doon. They must want that Aspen fellow to win.'

Angus nodded. 'Aye. He's the favourite for sure. You'll need to take care of him.'

I blinked. Did he mean...?

Angus recognised my expression. 'I mean watch out for him, not kill him, lass.' He grunted. 'Although killing him wouldn't be the worst idea in the world. If we could get away with it.'

'She killed the Glasgow Ascendant,' Belle said. 'She can kill Aspen.'

'I got lucky with the Ascendant,' I retorted. I doubted it would happen again.

'I've killed a Mage myself. Wi' my own bare hands!' Belle held out her palms. 'I can kill Aspen!' She nodded. 'I'll save us all.' She made a stabbing motion, vicious glee lighting her eyes.

'We're not going to win by killing anyone. We need to be smarter than that.' I reached into my shirt, gently cupped Mungo and drew him out. His tiny nose quested upwards and he sniffed the air as I stroked him with light fingers. 'Thanks, Mungo,' I whispered. 'For everything. It's safe now, Laoch. You can come out.'

Mungo's whiskers twitched, but then Angus's hand shot out, cupping mine and the wee mouse. 'Wait,' he hissed. 'Someone's coming.'

I stiffened. Angus withdrew his hand and I returned Mungo – and Laoch – to their hiding place next to my heart. I turned to face the door as the key turned and a cluster of glowering Mages appeared.

Aspen strode in first, his expression set in a dour mask though that didn't stop his moustache quivering. It appeared to have a life of its own. He barely glanced at me. Instead, his gaze swung around the small room, including the spot behind the door where Laoch usually hid. His jaw tightened and he beckoned the waiting Mages. 'What are you waiting for?' he snapped. 'Get in here!'

They marched in, and almost immediately started muttering incantations and rummaging around. Two Mages headed for the bed and tossed the mattress; three of them got down on their hands and knees and began knocking on the floor; three more did the same on stone walls. Uh-oh.

'Is there a problem?' Angus enquired.

Aspen didn't answer. He frowned towards the hallway. 'Frederica! Get in here!'

The first frisson of anxiety trembled through me as Teasag slowly walked into the room. Our tiny room was becoming incredibly claustrophobic with so many warm bodies inside.

Belle, apparently still emboldened by her memories of stabbing Mage Ross, bustled forward, manoeuvring through two of the Mages to plant herself in front of Aspen. 'Whit do you think you're doing? Are we no' to be allowed some privacy?'

Aspen glanced at her with undisguised loathing. He tilted his head and I felt a sudden icy chill. '*Ins veil.*'

Belle's body lifted in the air and she was thrown backwards. She smashed into one of the kneeling Mages and sent them both flying. I sprang towards Aspen but Teasag, of all people, stepped in my way and shook her head. 'What's the meaning of this?' I demanded.

Aspen's lip curled. 'Don't tell me you don't know.'

'Clearly I don't.'

He rolled his eyes while his moustache, seemingly still with a mind of its own, bristled in contempt. 'You're a cheat.'

My stomach gave a sickening lurch but I held on to my irritated expression. 'Why do you think that?' I asked. 'Because you can't believe that a woman could pass two of your silly Ascendancy Challenge rounds?'

From the floor, Belle groaned. Angus helped her up as she wheezed and coughed.

'You have minimal education,' the Ascendant scoffed. 'You grew up in an orphanage. Your employment has consisted of working in a tiny tartan shop and being a servant. You didn't answer those three riddles correctly without help.'

I wouldn't have needed any help if I could have heard all three of them in their entirety. 'Or maybe,' I said flatly, 'your clever riddles weren't as difficult as you thought. After all, you managed to solve them.' I paused for a beat. 'Did you have help?'

Aspen scoffed loudly, but his moustache quivered yet again. He clicked his tongue and pointed to Teasag. 'Well?'

'I can see nothing out of the ordinary, my Lord.'

'The bitch is in cahoots with one of your kind. Is he here?'

I held my breath. She was enslaved and unable to lie. This could be very bad.

Teasag turned, completing one entire spin on her heels. 'I cannot see him.'

I released my breath.

'What about invisibility?' Aspen barked.

'My Lord?'

His jaw tightened. 'Can you daemons perform invisibility spells?'

They could; the first time I'd met Laoch, he'd rendered me invisible so that Mage Ross wouldn't see me. 'We have that capability,' Teasag answered. I tensed. 'However,' she continued, 'it is difficult to maintain for more than a few minutes. There was no invisibility spell cast during the last challenge round. I guarantee it.'

Aspen gave her a hard look, tapped his chin with his long fingers and spoke again. 'Was there any daemon in the audience today?'

My knees trembled. Aspen's question was direct, so Teasag had to answer it truthfully. Then I realised there was still a loophole: Laoch had been with me, not in the audience. We remained safe – for now.

'No.'

All of a sudden, a strange sound escaped Angus's lips. Everyone looked at him, even the group of Mages who were continuing to examine every inch of the small room. He doubled over and gasped.

'Angus?' I asked, alarmed.

He made another odd noise, clutched his stomach and wheezed repeatedly. Before I could step towards him, it became clear what he was doing. He was laughing, and it burst out of him as if he'd been holding it in for too long.

'A daemon! In the audience! Doing what?' He chortled. 'Bypassing all that magic to communicate the answers without anyone noticing?' He raised his head, tears of mirth streaming down his grey cheeks. 'How would he do that? Telepathy?'

I stiffened, but Angus continued to laugh uproariously. 'Oh, my days!'

Aspen's moustache had finally stopped twitching but his expression broadcast his fury. He wasn't used to being the butt of anyone's joke, especially a supposed traitor's. 'Has anyone found anything?' he roared.

The Mages stopped their search. 'No, my Lord,' one answered. The others shook their heads.

'Then get the fuck out of here!'

They gathered themselves up and hastily departed. I watched as Teasag quietly attached herself to the group and left with them.

Now only Aspen remained. He looked at me with flinty, cold eyes. 'You've done something,' he said. 'I don't know what, but I will find out. Don't think your minor success means anything. You won't make it through the next round. And your friends, not to mention the whole city of Glasgow and anyone who displays an iota of sympathy for you and your cause, will suffer greatly when you are gone.' He glared. 'I guarantee it.' He swept out, slamming the door closed behind him before the key rattled in the lock.

For one long moment, Angus, Belle and I stared at each other, then Angus wiped the tears from his cheeks and I turned to Belle. 'Are you alright?'

She nodded shakily, her earlier bravado all gone. Until now, she'd allowed herself to forget her terror of the Mages but with Aspen's attack it had returned threefold. Her lips parted and she gave a squeak before sinking to the floor.

I looked at Angus questioningly. He hesitated, his brow furrowing in momentary concentration, then shook his head. 'They've gone,' he said. 'They're not listening.' He breathed out heavily. 'If that daemon lassie hadn't been so canny with her answer, and if Aspen had been more circumspect with his questions, we'd be in a very different situation. All he requires is a scrap of proof that you've not been following the rules and we're all dead.' He gave me a warning glance. 'He may manufacture his own proof. We're on shaky ground indeed.'

Indeed. I reached for Mungo; I needed to see Laoch properly again. But then I heard stomping footsteps outside and the key turned yet again. I froze. Would this never be over?

It was Teasag. She stared ahead, without looking any of us in the eye. 'The woman and the traitor are to collect their belongings and come with me.'

'We will do no such thing!' Belle burst out, though her voice shook.

'The woman and the traitor are to collect their belongings and come with me,' Teasag repeated.

I swallowed. She wasn't permitted to communicate with us, so she'd obviously been granted one statement and that was all she could say.

'I'll stay here, if it's all the same to you,' Angus declared.

Teasag's eyes closed momentarily. Strain was etched on her face. If Belle and Angus refused to go with her, she would be obliged to employ brute force. That wouldn't go well for any of us, her included.

'Do as she says,' I said quietly.

Angus's head whipped towards me.

'We can't refuse,' I told him. 'We have no power here. You can leave me, it'll be fine.' Because I wouldn't be alone; I still had Laoch. 'They want to isolate me. I doubt they'll hurt you. You'll likely be safe until...' My voice trailed off.

Angus folded his arms, his expression making it clear that he wouldn't go anywhere. To my surprise, Belle shuffled next to him and touched his arm. 'They'll drag us oot of here one way or another. Leave Mairi in peace. She's used to being on her own.'

Teasag seemed relieved; a tiny smile lit the corners of her mouth.

'Go,' I urged. 'Stay safe.'

Angus harrumphed. 'Easier said than done, darling.' But he turned away, scooped up his bag and stuffed his clothes into it. I hugged both him and Belle, startling myself as much as them.

'I'll see you both at the next round.' I managed a tight smile.

'Keep your wits about you, lass,' Angus warned.

'And then some,' Belle added. Then they were gone.

WHEN IT FINALLY SEEMED SAFE for him to emerge from Mungo's body, Laoch was tired, though his exhaustion wasn't as worrisome as it had been last time. I stroked Mungo, murmuring my gratitude towards the wee mouse, then wordlessly turned to Laoch. I wrapped myself around him and buried my head in his chest.

It's becoming too dangerous. You should leave this city while you still can, I told him.

He didn't hesitate. *And you know I'm not going nowhere. Not while you're here.*

Aspen almost...

Aspen almost nothing. He's panicking. Laoch cupped my face. *All the Mages are. You've already done better than they expected.* He smiled down at me. *You're proving yourself to be quite the force, Mairi. You're in the final eight now.*

He's still suspicious. When they come to take me for the next round, you should stay here and use Mungo again. Just in case.

A muscle jerked in his jaw. *I'm growing tired of hiding.*

I need to know you're safe. If the Mages get their wish and I die…

Laoch's emerald eyes flashed. *You will not die. You're too strong now. You can win this, Mairi. Look how far you've already come.*

I worried my bottom lip. *Is it far enough, though? If I'm killed in the next round, will it have been enough for the resistance and other people to complete a revolution that will improve everyone's lives?*

Laoch stiffened and emitted a growl from deep inside his chest. *I have already told you. You will not be killed in the next round. You will not die.*

It remained a very real possibility. He had to realise that. *Laoch—*

No. His tone brooked no argument. His face softened and he gazed into my eyes. *You still don't believe it, do you? You don't believe that I love you.*

A twist of discomfort knotted in my belly. *Laoch, I know you care for me. You've done more for me than anyone, and I trust you completely.*

Liar.

I jerked.

If you trusted me, you'd believe my feelings. I wish you felt the same way about me as I do about you, but I'm aware that it's different for humans. You need more time, and I won't ever pressure you. Your feelings are yours, Mairi. His gaze was steady. *But my feelings are also mine. I did not lie when I told you I loved you, and I do not lie now. I don't know everything there is to know about you, but I know enough.*

He placed his hand flat on my chest, his fingers resting directly over my heart. *My soul sings when you are near. I spent years as a slave to the Mages and during all that time I never felt peace until you came along. I didn't fall in love with you instantly, but it didn't take very long. You're the last thing I think about before I go to sleep and the first thing I think about when I wake up. You don't need my protection, but I want to give you it. Always. I want to be a better person so I can be who you deserve. I can't imagine a future without you in it, and when you talk about dying as if it's nothing, it makes me feel physically ill.*

I pulled away from him and stepped backwards. Laoch's face closed off. *I've frightened you. That wasn't my intention.*

I shook my head and spoke aloud because it was important to me to do so, especially with him. 'You didn't frighten me. *I* frightened me.' I swallowed hard. 'Because that's how I feel about you. It shouldn't make sense, but it absolutely does.' I stared into his emerald eyes. 'I love you.'

He searched my face. When he realised I was telling the truth, his body relaxed. I reached up and traced the curling tattoos on his cheekbones with the tips of my fingers. He smiled with deep satisfaction. 'Well then,' he murmured. 'That settles that.'

He dipped his head to my ear. 'I like this country, and I want to see it free from the yoke of the Mages. I'd love to have my revenge on them for what they did to me, as well as count-less others. But I love you more, so don't you dare die. I need you too much.'

I smiled back at him, then I kissed him until there was nothing left in my head apart from Laoch and me. We existed together, not apart.

If only things could remain that way.

CHAPTER
TWENTY-THREE

My eyes travelled along the packed stands as I searched desperately for Angus or Belle. Neither of them were visible. I clenched my jaw and glanced at the other candidates who were flanking the Edinburgh Ascendant. I stilled. There was no sign of Aspen. Where the fuck was he? And where were Belle and Angus?

Mosse and the Ascendant smirked at me; they knew who I was looking for. I could only pray that they hadn't actually killed Belle and Angus and had merely forbidden them to attend. Surely even the Mages wouldn't be so brazen – not yet – but I couldn't put anything past them.

With Laoch back in our room, and without Belle and Angus, not to mention the dozens of powerful Mages planning my death, my confidence was leaking away. It was only a few hours since Laoch and I had lain in each other's arms and repeated our love for each other. I did what I could to recall that feeling, but knowing he couldn't be by my side only made me feel worse.

'Gie 'em hell, lass!'

I started. That had come from the watching crowd. I turned and spotted a raven spiralling down from the sky towards a young man. A second later, three Mages grabbed hold of him and dragged him away.

My mouth thinned. They wanted the crowd here to act as witnesses, not as support. The man shrieked and kicked out, but one of the Mages muttered something and a moment later his face went slack and his eyes rolled back in his head.

The people around him watched, stiff and silent, their hatred for the Mages palpable but their fear holding them back. I remembered the guard who'd walked away despite knowing his actions would probably lead to his death, and I looked again at the faces turning towards mine. Their expressions were full of hope and expectation, albeit mingled with desperation.

There were guards and patrolling Mages to keep the audience in check, but anyone with eyes could see that most of those people were on my side. They wanted me to win. The bravery of that young man and that guard, not to mention Billy and John McAllan and the poor nameless boy, could not be set aside no matter what the Mages did.

Laoch's green eyes flashed into my mind and I nodded to myself. I wasn't alone, not even remotely.

I cleared my throat and then I yelled. Until that moment, I'd never believed such a sound could come out of my mouth. 'Halt!'

Everyone was staring at me, and I fought back the flush that rose up my cheeks. I pretended not to notice Mosse rapidly moving towards me to shut me up. This would be a lot easier if I knew the damned magic for projecting my voice.

'The Ascendancy Challenge is steeped in tradition!' I shouted.

Mosse was already reaching for me.

'Many people here believe it in wholeheartedly! The Mages have allowed me to participate, even though I am female, even though I am not one of them. They are truly gracious!'

Mosse's hand fell away. There were plenty of derisive snickers from the crowd.

'I am sure,' I continued, 'that their grace extends to allowing every audience member to remain, regardless of who they want to win. Each candidate has their own supporters, and those supporters must be allowed to stay and voice their support. I would expect nothing less from the men who rule this land!'

As if on cue, a woman's voice rang out. 'And they are great men!'

Out of the corner of my eye, I saw several Mages stand up straighter.

'I speak as an intelligent woman,' she shouted. 'No female should be permitted to rule any part of Scotland! We do not have the capabilities that a man has. We certainly do not have the capabilities that a Mage has. They have kept us safe from the Afflicted for this long. We need to trust them!'

I sought her out. My gaze eventually landed on a well-dressed woman who was looking immensely pleased with herself. I had to remember that there were still plenty of people who bought into the Mages' lies. Unfortunately for this particular woman, her outburst played right into my hands.

'Lord Aspen for Glasgow Ascendant!' she screamed.

But Lord Aspen still wasn't here. I pushed away my anxiety and turned to the Edinburgh Ascendant, ostensibly addressing him alone although I kept my voice loud enough for everyone to hear. 'You see? This grand lady should be entitled to voice her support for whomsoever she wishes, in the same way that the young man over there who was attacked should be entitled to voice his support for me!' I pointed across. The man in question was being manoeuvred down a set of stairs towards the arena exit.

It was enough. Several people started to yell, 'Let him go! Let! Him! Go!'

More took up the chant; the mood was changing. Several more ravens appeared overhead, swooping down with danger-ous, black-winged intent, but too many people were shouting now. I felt the same frisson in the air that I'd felt that night at the City Chambers when all hell broke loose.

'They won't be shouting for you when you're lying dead in this dirt, bitch,' Mosse spat at me. Maybe not. But they wouldn't be shouting for him, either.

The Edinburgh Ascendant raised his hands and called for silence, but the crowd continued to yell. I saw the anger in his face and registered the shudder of magic as his lips moved in incantation. His voice rose above the noise. 'A mere mistake! Everyone here is free to support whoever they wish!'

He turned magnanimously towards the Mages who were holding the young man, and they nodded and deposited him on a seat. His head lolled to one side, so one of the black cloaks muttered something and his body jerked as he returned to consciousness. The crowd quietened, at least slightly.

I wrestled back control and yelled again. 'The Edinburgh Ascendant is most gracious! Perhaps he will also be gracious enough to allow my friends to return. They were taken away yesterday, and I have not seen them since.'

'Shut the fuck up,' Mosse commanded, his voice vibrating with rage. A few members of the crowd heard him and murmured disapproval. Dissent was growing by the minute – and not only back in Glasgow.

I stood even straighter. 'I've spent my life in silence,' I told him. 'I won't do that any longer.' I stared at the Ascendant again; I could perform for the crowd as well as he could. My words were as good as his. 'Where are my friends?' I shouted. 'There are only two of them and they mean you no harm. Why have you taken them from me?'

The Ascendant bared his teeth in a forced smile. 'An oversight, I am sure.' He waved his hands. 'Find the girl's ... friends and bring them here.'

Two Mages immediately took off. I curtsied. 'Thank you. I'm a woman, though. Not a girl.'

For a moment I thought that Mosse would hit me. Instead he curled his hands into fists. 'You'll get yours, girl,' he muttered. 'Sooner than you think.' He stalked away to re-join the others.

The Ascendant continued to smile. He reminded me of a feral tomcat that used to hang around the orphanage: soft fur, big gooey eyes – and waiting for the first opportunity to bite your hand off. 'Where is Lord Aspen?' he enquired.

'He is attending to another matter. He will be here before the next round begins,' Mosse answered, bowing.

'He had better be,' the Ascendant snapped. He shook himself before he continued speaking, making his jowls judder. 'It is clear that we have made some innocent mistakes,' he said, still projecting his voice magically so that the audience could hear him even if the city as a whole could not. 'Minor matters only. It is not our intention to make the Ascendancy Challenge unfair. I know how important it is that all our candidates have an equal chance. We would not have extended the warm invitation to Mairi Wallace if that were not the case.'

Tendrils of dread snaked through me. What did the damned Mages have planned this time? I had no idea what the next challenge would entail, but from the Ascendant's slick words, I guessed it wouldn't be easy.

'To prove that we are being fair, and that the grand tradition of our Ascendancy Challenge remains sacrosanct, we have made some changes to the next round,' he boomed.

From the corner of my eye, I saw Belle and Angus shuffle forward. I checked them over to see if they'd been harmed. Belle's expression was tight, her mouth puckered, but she appeared well; Angus had an angry welt across his cheekbone. I stiffened but he shook his head, indicating that now was not the time to mention it.

'You're well?' I muttered when they moved beside me.

'They've mostly ignored us,' Angus replied.

Belle snorted. 'Mostly.'

He sent her a sidelong look. 'We're fine.'

I'd expected the Edinburgh Ascendant to display impatience at the delay to his speech while I spoke to my companions, but I'd under-estimated his ability to dissemble. He smiled beneficently and stretched out his arms to indicate that he'd done as I'd asked and he was being nothing but kind towards me.

A moment later there was another flurry of movement and Aspen appeared, his chest rising and falling. The Ascendant threw him an irritated look for his lack of good timekeeping, and Aspen bowed low in apology.

The Ascendant's mouth tightened as he nodded at Aspen to move into position. 'We will delay no further,' he proclaimed. 'To keep things fair for Miss Wallace, who is unable to perform magic to the Mages' standard, we are preventing the use of *any* magic in this next round.'

My curiosity about Aspen's late appearance vanished in an instant and my blood turned to ice. I might not possess the abilities or stamina of someone who'd been a Mage for decades, but I wasn't far off and I could match most of these bastards. They were denying the use of enchantment for a reason.

'This not only helps Mairi Wallace,' the Ascendant continued, 'but also the citizens who ultimately will be led by the eventual winner. After all, even a powerful and potent Mage cannot rely on magic alone. We must have other tools at our disposal to hold back the Afflicted and ensure the safety of Scotland's people. Consequently, the magical powers of all candidates will be nullified during the third round.'

I clenched my jaw. 'Can they do that?' I hissed in a low voice. 'Can they take away our powers?'

Angus's expression was dark; if anything, the welt on his cheek appeared even harsher. 'Aye. It's only temporary, and it's not an easy thing to achieve. It will take the combined power of many of the non-competing Mages to complete such a feat – and even then, it's a dangerous action. But they can do it. Do not doubt that, lass.'

The Edinburgh Ascendant smiled broadly. He'd seen my expression. 'The eventual winner must be strong of body as well as mind,' he said, while the crowd leaned forward, most of their faces as grim as mine. 'Therefore the third round will be a simple challenge of hand-to-hand combat. After this, only four candidates for the position of Glasgow Ascendant will remain.'

My heart sank into my boots as I gazed at the other seven candidates. Aspen was the oldest but even he wasn't much more than forty years old, and I had no doubt that he was much stronger than me. Without magic, I didn't think I could beat any of my fellow competitors.

'Tha's no' fair!' someone shouted from the crowd. A raven flew down towards the woman who had yelled, but this time she was not approached by any of the eagle-eyed Mages.

'Aye!' another voice called out. 'It's no' fair at all!'

'I can assure you it's very fair,' the Ascendant said. 'And to prove that, each fight will cease upon first blood. We are not looking for bodies, we are merely searching for the winner.

Various weapons will be made available. Everyone has an equal chance.'

I exchanged glances with Belle and Angus. First blood only. As if. If I didn't win my bout, I'd die here.

A sigh escaped my lips. In theory, I had the advantage because I'd survived most of my life without magic – but I'd not been in a fight since I was a small child, and then it had been more of the hair-pulling variety.

The white-bearded Mage by the Ascendant's side cleared his throat before starting to read out the names of the paired competitors. 'Lord Aldridge will meet Mage Ferguson. Mage Stewart will meet Lord McDonald. Lord Aspen will meet Mage Kent.'

My head dropped further.

'Lord Mosse will meet Mairi Wallace. The third round will begin in a moment.'

Another day, another opportunity for almost certain death. I thought again about Laoch and how it had felt to have his arms wrapped around me, while Belle studied her feet and Angus looked directly at me.

'Any last words?' he asked.

CHAPTER

TWENTY-FOUR

I stood in a cluster with the other seven candidates. It was no comfort to know that Mosse had probably originally been paired with Aspen and expected to throw the fight in his favour. Mosse was, without doubt, the strongest Mage physically and such a win would have worked very well for Aspen's public image. Instead, Aspen was going to fight the weediest looking Mage, and I was going to fight Mosse.

Even with his black cloak covering most of his body, I could see his taut muscles and large frame. I was almost half his size. I reached for my hair, tying it into a tight bun. It was about all I could do to prepare.

I counted forty Mages who filed out from behind the Edinburgh Ascendant and formed a circle around us. Strength definitely came in numbers. I shook my head in dismay while each one of them placed a hand on the shoulder of the Mage next to them. The oldest looking one murmured, '*Desh mar tum.*'

The air stirred. I'd already considered – and discarded – the idea of blocking the nullification spell. I was the only person who could use magic without speaking aloud, but whether

237

they heard me or not, the other Mages would know in an instant if I tried to do such a thing. Hell, they were probably hoping I would so they could detach my head from my shoulders for cheating. I had to play along and take my lumps, even if I could not yet think of a way to beat Mosse.

I stood still and held my breath. And that was when I felt the unnatural and highly unpleasant effects of the magic.

I wasn't the only one who was disturbed by what was happening. Ferguson and Stewart, the Mages on either side of me, gasped audibly. I squeezed my eyes shut. I hadn't expected it to hurt, but it did. It really did. It felt as if someone had punched a hole in my stomach and was pulling out my intestines inch by inch rather than the magic deep inside in my body.

Tears pricked behind my eyelids. I'd been drained of magic before, but that was a result of my own action and had occurred over time, not all at once like this. I felt violated, empty. I'd take a dozen fiery gauntlets and fierce skin-shredding monsters over this sensation any day.

My breath was ragged and my bones screamed with pain. The only saving grace was that, when I forced my eyes open and gazed around the circle of Mages whose power was fuelling the magic-draining spell, I could see them wilting. At least half a dozen of them were ashen grey. At least this wasn't a feat that one Mage could pull off alone; if it were, I'd have been fucked long ago.

A Mage fell to his knees, then another and another. Those who were still standing hurried to fill up the gaps and avoid any break in power, but soon there were too few of them to make up for their fallen comrades.

The Edinburgh Ascendant barked out an order and the circle fell apart. Several Mages collapsed and the pain shooting through my body ceased instantly – but I knew without checking that I no longer had enough power inside me to perform even the weakest of spells.

'Look at Aldgate,' Mage Ferguson muttered through gritted teeth. 'Look at him.'

He wasn't talking to me but I followed his gaze. Aldgate was the old, white-bearded Mage who had incanted the nullification spell. He was flat on his back and three Mages were bending over him. The Ascendant marched over, looked down then shook his head. 'He's already gone. Leave him.'

My mouth dropped open. He'd died? Because of this? They'd sacrificed one of their own for this damned spell? I swallowed hard and looked at Angus. His face told of his sickened shock.

'You're monsters,' I whispered. 'You're all monsters.'

By my side, Ferguson stiffened. '*You're* the monster. This wouldn't be happening if it weren't for you.' He moved away from me, as if he'd be contaminated by my proximity.

I considered his words. He was right: the Ascendancy Challenge wouldn't be happening without me. This magic-free round wouldn't be happening without me. Mage Aldgate wouldn't be dead without me. But I wasn't going to feel guilty, whether I was the cause or not. None of this was my fault.

'The first fight is between Mairi Wallace and Lord Mosse,' the Ascendant declared, as if there weren't a dead Mage lying by his feet.

What? My head whipped around. I'd thought we were last. Next to me, Ferguson snickered. 'Die slowly, bitch. Your first blood drawn will kill you.'

I ignored him and took a step forward. As soon as I did so, my legs wobbled. So that was why Mosse and I were going to be the first to fight; they didn't want to allow me any time to get used to the sensation of being drained of magic.

I wasn't the only one with shaky legs. Mosse, who'd also

stepped out from the cluster of waiting candidates, looked very pale.

Aspen clasped him on the shoulder. 'Good luck!'

The other candidates called out good wishes. If they thought their words would upset me even more, they were sadly mistaken. The watching crowd took up the same call, but most of them weren't yelling for Mosse: they were shouting for me.

'Mairi! Mairi! Mairi!'

Mosse leaned towards me. Despite the physical effects of the magic-draining spell, his voice was laden with venom. 'Imagine how quickly that enthusiasm will turn to despair when you are dying at my feet. They'll soon realise that no-one can fight us successfully. Not even you.'

I didn't look at him. I stood ramrod straight, praying that my knees wouldn't give way, and pulled a long draught of cold air into my lungs. The trumpet sounded and both Mosse and I were beckoned to a roped-off area in front of the seated audience. Mosse was taken to one corner while I was pointed to another.

The cobbles were slick with the last of the dew from the night before and I knew I would struggle not to slip and slide in my cheap shoes. I eyed the straggly weeds, finding life through the cracks in the cobbles in several places, then I curled my hands around the rope and gazed at the small pile of weaponry. There was a heavy mace, a rusting sword and a small dagger. I didn't need to hold the mace to know that it would be too much for me – I doubted I could raise it above my hips. The dagger was too small – I wouldn't be able to get close enough to Mosse to wound him. I had to grab that sword, even though I'd never used one before .

I glanced at my opponent. Mosse would likely go for the

mace; it would be the easiest way to crush my skull with one blow.

Laoch was right, I thought calmly. I wasn't going to die. I was going to beat Mosse. I was going to get past the round. And then—

'Wait!'

I looked around. That was Aspen. What was the bastard up to now?

The crowd hushed, and I risked a quick glance at Belle and Angus, who had been ushered to the furthest corner. They looked wary; even the Ascendant appeared confused.

'Lord Aspen?' he asked. 'What is it?'

Aspen smiled and I knew exactly what was about to happen. My legs turned to lead and my heart hammered painfully against my ribcage. No. Please. No.

'We have been remiss,' Aspen said. 'I believe Mairi Wallace requested that her friends be permitted to join her for this round to witness her participation.'

'Yes, yes.' The Ascendant looked impatient. 'What's your point, Aspen?'

The Mage's smile widened. 'We must ensure sure that *all* of Miss Wallace's friends are present. It's only fair. Frederica? Get over here.'

Teasag appeared from behind another group of watching Mages and Aldgate's cooling body. Her expression gave nothing away. I stared at her, willing her to say something, do something, but she had to follow Aspen's order and march to his side.

'Daemons are tricksy creatures,' Aspen said. 'You have to ask them the right questions or they'll find a way to avoid answering you properly.'

I looked at Teasag. There was a tense stiffness to her body and something deep reflected in her eyes. Pain: she was experiencing a great deal of pain, likely both physical and emotional. My eyes dropped to her cupped hands, and my own agony seared my chest.

The Ascendant tapped his foot. 'So?'

Aspen looked at me. 'I finally asked the right question.' He nudged Teasag. 'Go on.'

She sighed deeply and opened her hands. There, in the centre of her palm, lay Mungo curled into a tight ball.

I couldn't stop myself crying out. For a horrifying moment I thought the wee mouse was dead and Laoch with him. I moved away from my position inside the fighting ring, but several Mages immediately came towards me, indicating that I should not take another step.

I had no magic inside me and I was outnumbered by at least two hundred to one – but I'd take them all on if I had to.

The Ascendant looked from me to Mungo and back again. 'It's a mouse. What of it?'

Mungo's tail twitched and I gasped. He was alive – he was still alive! I started forward again. As I ducked under the rope, ignoring the Mages' stark warnings, a gust of wind smacked me off course. I twisted my head and saw Angus staring at me, shaking his head in alarm. Beside him, Belle was flapping her hands.

'This is no mere mouse,' Aspen said. 'Look at the upstart. Look at her face.'

Everyone who'd not already been watching me turned. I bared my teeth. Aspen's moustache trembled with barely held delight. He reached for Mungo, grabbed his tail and hauled him up into the air.

'Leave him!' I screamed. 'Leave him alone!'

Mungo blinked at me. I shook my head and ducked under the rope again, this time aiming for the other side. Screw

Angus and the Mages and everything else; I wouldn't allow this to happen.

This time it wasn't Angus who stopped me. There was a burst of power and a loud crackle. The crowd gasped, and so did several Mages. Mungo dropped to the ground squeaking and scurried away as fast as his legs would carry him.

Run, I sent after him. *Run as fast and as far away as you can.*

Nobody looked at the wee mouse now because in his place was Laoch.

The world seemed to stop. I could hear nothing and see nothing beyond Laoch's bowed head. He looked up and met my eyes. 'Scotland needs you as much as I need you,' he said. 'No matter what, Mairi, you have my heart. Never forget that, whatever they make me do or do to me.' He smiled sadly and added in the gentlest of voices, 'It's time to fight.'

'Laoch!' My cry was strangled. 'Laoch!'

Aspen snapped his fingers. 'Maxwell, bring them here.'

Another daemon appeared, one I'd not seen before. From his silver hair and white tinged horns, this was the older slave Laoch had mentioned. There was sweat on his brow and his eyes were brimming with tears, but he could not refuse a direct order.

When I saw what he was carrying, I pushed past the Mage in front of me.

'No, Mairi.' Laoch shook his head. 'No.' His voice echoed inside my mind. *You can't win like this, you can't stop what's about to happen. All you can do is win the Ascendancy Challenge. I believe you can, Mairi. I truly do. This is bigger than you or me. Save yourself, then your country.* He paused. *And then you can save me. I love you.*

Maxwell held out the cushion to Aspen as I came to a stuttering halt and watched helplessly while slave cuffs were snapped around Laoch's wrists and neck.

'Do you have anything to say for yourself?' the Ascendant enquired. He was addressing me but I only had eyes for Laoch.

'Nicholas,' Aspen commanded, 'you are answerable only to me, the Ascendant of Edinburgh and the other forsworn and loyal Mages. You are not to communicate in any manner, either spoken or unspoken, with Mairi Wallace or her companions. Is that understood?'

Laoch and I continued to gaze at each other.

'You will not look at her again, Nicholas.'

Laoch's head twisted away and I closed my eyes. I'd stood back while the Mages executed my friend Isla, and now I was standing back while they enslaved my love for a second time. They obviously thought this act would destroy me.

They thought wrong.

'Well, that was interesting indeed,' the Ascendant said. 'You'll have to find out what that spell is. It would be most amusing if we could all transform ourselves into mice.' He chuckled. 'Let's get started with the next round, shall we? Enough delays.'

I heard the sound of running feet and opened my eyes. It was Mage Andy, holding a book and panting for breath. 'Wait!' he gasped. 'There's something you need to know. There's—'

'Save it for later,' the Ascendant ordered. 'I don't want to stand here all day. I'm going to need a cup of tea and some cake before too long.' He patted his stomach. 'Well, girl? Back to the enclosure with you. Let's get this over and done with.'

CHAPTER

TWENTY-FIVE

I did my best to keep my eyes away from Laoch and the cruel cuffs biting into his skin. I couldn't bear to see his emerald gaze dulled yet again by the yoke of slavery. Aspen, however, wanted me to look at him.

Before the trumpet signalled the beginning of my fight with Mosse, Laoch shouted out, his voice hoarse, 'You're going to lose, bitch!'

Aspen murmured to Laoch. 'Again.'

'You're going to lose, bitch!' Laoch called. His face was filled with sorrowful apology but he could no more gainsay Aspen's orders than I could scale the walls of Edinburgh Castle.

The crowd started to chant my name, softly at first but then with growing intensity. They might not understand what had happened with Laoch, but they knew I was shaken and they were willing me on. I raised my chin. I'd win this for them and I'd win it for Laoch. The Mages had given me no choice.

I love you, I told Laoch, though I knew he couldn't reply. Not now.

Keeping my expression blank, I turned to Mosse. His smirk

already contained a triumphant edge. I ignored it and straightened my spine. Bring it fucking on.

The trumpeter raised his instrument to his lips and the audience fell silent. I waited, my fingertips brushing against the rough rope surrounding the enclosure. I glanced again at the small pile of weapons and again at Mosse's face and overpowering body. I exhaled. A moment later, the trumpet sounded.

Mosse sprang forward, lunging not for me but for the weapons. As expected, he snatched up the mace and I saw the veins in his forearm bulge as he hefted it upwards. I sent a forlorn glance towards the sword and darted away.

The heavy weapon would slow him down. While I certainly wasn't stronger, I could move faster so maybe I could tire him out. As long as I stayed far enough away from him, I'd be safe. For now.

I blotted out the sound of the crowd and the sight of Laoch standing helplessly and focused solely on my body. I had to stay low and balanced.

Mosse charged, the mace high above his head. I ran away from him to the far corner. Telling myself not to become trapped in one small space, I hesitated for little more than a second before running again, looping round the enclosure and out of Mosse's reach. He roared and followed me, his footsteps thundering on the cobbles. I slowed slightly, allowed him to catch up and then, when I felt the air shift as he swung the mace, I picked up speed yet again and moved out of the way before he could land his blow. Without my soft body to cushion the hit, the tip of the mace clattered to the ground, and I heard Mosse grunt in exasperation. I danced forward, twisting my head in time to see him raise the mace again.

'Run, bitch,' he spat. 'I'll catch up sooner or later.'

Aye, he likely would. I should have run for that sword when

I'd had the chance; much as I'd like to escape his mace swings forever, I was only going to win this damned fight if I made him bleed. I couldn't run from him for hours. All the same, I allowed my feet to carry me past the sword and dagger, then turned and watched Mosse barrel towards me. His face was growing red with exertion. My strategy was having some effect.

I waited a beat and turned to my left. Mosse reacted immediately and twisted to head me off. I changed my mind and spun right, but as soon as I took my first step I felt my foot slide out from underneath me.

The world slipped sideways and I dimly heard several members of the audience scream. I landed with a thud on the hard, damp cobbles while Mosse yelled in delight and lunged towards me. I gritted my teeth, rolling away from him as fast as I could in a bid to escape. Unfortunately, I wasn't quite fast enough.

Mosse towered over me. He raised the mace yet again and brought it slamming down. I rolled left and its rusty head clanged into the spot where I'd been laying. Mosse heaved it up, brought it down for a second time. I rolled to the right.

'Get the feck up, Mairi!' I heard Belle scream.

I clenched my jaw. Not yet, not just yet.

Mosse wheezed; he was moving more slowly. When he hefted the mace upwards, the fingers of my right hand grabbed hold of the ragged green leaves sprouting next to me. I yanked out as much of the plant as I could and rolled for one final time, away from the mace's dangerous reach. Then I scrabbled upwards, digging my heels in to avoid slipping again.

The mace was already in the air as Mosse swung it with both hands. I jumped back, narrowly avoiding it, and he swung it once more. I closed my fingers into a tight fist, crushing the leaves as I darted away from him.

I pulled back, then sprinted towards the dagger and the sword. I reached out as if to grab the hilt of the dagger, and heard Mosse's harsh grunt from behind.

Belle had started to yell something, but I was way ahead of her. I pelted to my right, ignored the dagger and straightened up. A split second later, the mace left Mosse's hands and flew through the air. It whizzed past the spot where I'd been standing and clattered to the ground several feet away. I'd missed it by a mere moment. I'd relied on the fact that he always swung the damned thing from right to left; if he threw it in desperation to prevent me from grabbing a weapon, the same would be true. What he hadn't realised was that I already had a weapon.

I pivoted a full hundred and eighty degrees and started to sprint. Given that until now I'd been running away from Mosse, not towards him, it was the last thing he expected me to do. He'd already started forward to retrieve the mace but he faltered when he saw me coming. I knew it was because of surprise rather than fear but I took full advantage of his hesitation and pushed myself to my limits.

Mosse snarled and clenched his fists, preparing to throw a punch at my head. I knew he'd use his right hand first, so I veered left, opened my hand and leapt upwards. I smeared the green, gunky mess from the weed into his eyes while his other hand came at me. This time I didn't move fast enough and he hit the side of my head, making me stagger. But he was in no position to take advantage of my stumble because he was already screaming.

The hogweed that had been sprouting between the cobbles was little more than a sapling. Given its position in the courtyard, it would probably not have grown much even if it had been left alone. Fully grown, it was potent and dangerous to both skin and eyes. I wasn't sure what reaction a young plant like this would cause, though I'd suspected it would hurt if I smeared it in Mosse's eyes. I wasn't wrong.

As tears streamed down his cheeks and he frantically rubbed his eyes, I scooped up the sword and the dagger. This might be my moment to draw blood from Mosse.

His eyes were red-rimmed and sore from the hogweed, but he was still gazing at me with venomous hatred. The little weed's effects had been short lived. I hefted the dagger and, with only a second to make up my mind, I tensed and threw it straight at him.

It didn't work; there wasn't enough power in my arm and the dagger's blade was too blunt. It bounced uselessly off his arm and he bared his teeth. Mosse was too well-trained as a Mage to let his emotions overcome him. He swallowed his anger before he bent down and picked up the dagger, then he came at me again.

I clutched the sword's handle as Mosse charged. The blade felt awkward and heavy, even though it had to be at least half the weight of the mace. I waved it uncertainly. The pointy end looked sharp enough; all I had to do was thrust it in the right direction. I tightened my grip, my palms slick with sweat.

Mosse lunged with the dagger and the blades crashed together. I swung the sword towards him, but such was the force of Mosse's blow that he knocked it out of my hands. He held up the dagger and leapt at me.

There was no time to dive left or right; all I could do to avoid that rusty blade was throw myself onto the cobbles. Mosse's body cannoned into mine and I knew without looking up that he was preparing to plunge the weapon downwards between my shoulder blades. He'd learned from his earlier mistakes and had moved his legs to prevent me rolling away.

There was only one move left. I opened my jaw and sank my teeth into his ankle. Mosse dropped the dagger and howled, while an unpleasant metallic tang filled my mouth. I'd done it. I'd drawn his blood.

I spat it out onto the cobbles next to me and gestured pointedly, then I pulled myself upright.

The audience were on their feet and cheering, waving their arms around and jumping up and down. Belle was crying. Angus had cracked a smile. And when I looked at Laoch, who couldn't return my gaze but who was watching Mosse, the desperate warmth in his eyes almost floored me. Then his face flickered with alarm.

I craned my neck back. I'd won – but Mosse wasn't giving up. I should have known this would happen. Ignoring the wound in his leg, he was already reaching for the dagger.

I yanked myself away and scrabbled for the sword as he brandished the knife. 'You,' he gasped, 'are still going to die, bitch.'

The crowd were screaming at the Mages but they were holding back, waiting hopefully to see what Mosse would do.

I heard the Ascendant call, 'Lord Mosse! You must cease now. The round is over,' but there was neither energy nor power in his command. I might have won, but I could still die.

Mosse swiped the knife forward and its blade scratched my cheek. Blood welled up and trickled down as he threw back his head and laughed coldly. But then my fingers curled around the hilt of the sword and I brandished it with all the force I could muster, whacking his knees with the flat of the blade.

He lunged for me again as I brought the sword up and cut deep into his thigh before sprinting away from him in case he came at me again. He growled and started to run after me, but there was too much blood spurting from his thigh wound. His legs gave way, he fell to his knees and dropped his head. The crowd roared its approval.

Neither the Ascendant nor Aspen looked happy but they

knew it was finished. I didn't smile, though I felt a heavy satisfaction in the pit of my stomach. I couldn't be happy but I could be content with the outcome.

I looked for Laoch but he was no longer there; he must have already been ordered away. Only Teasag remained, although she wasn't looking at me but at Mosse. As the blood pooled around his legs and his head dropped further, her expression filled with grim delight.

Two Mages ducked under the rope and moved towards Mosse. A few flickers of healing magic and he'd be fine. He'd live to fight another day.

I glanced again at Teasag and my mouth tightened. Ignoring the approaching Mages, I shifted my grip on the sword and went back to Mosse. I twisted the weapon and struck down, landing the blade onto his exposed neck. As his blood sprayed across my face and clothes and splattered onto the cobbles, I finally met Teasag's eyes.

There. He wouldn't fight again.

CHAPTER

TWENTY-SIX

The two Mages held my arms and dragged me in front of the Edinburgh Ascendant. His eyes were cold. 'The rules were quite clear,' he said. 'The fight was to first blood only. You killed a man when he was down, when you had already won. We cannot permit such cold-blooded actions.'

I didn't look away; instead I wiped my bloodied hands on the front of my shirt and pushed away the horror of what I'd done. 'I was proving my candidacy,' I declared loudly, 'and meting out appropriate justice after Mosse did not end the fight himself after first blood. I was doing what you would have done in the circumstances.'

Angus stepped forward. 'The lass speaks true. She won the fight and Lord Mosse chose to continue. She was well within her rights to kill him.'

The Ascendant didn't look at him but waved a hand and murmured a brief incantation to silence him. '*Vair al.*'

My eyes narrowed but I didn't comment. Behind us, the

252

crowd were growing louder by the second. 'Mairi! Mairi! Mairi!'

Aspen whispered something in the Ascendant's ear. He stiffened, but gave a sharp nod. 'Take her back to her quarters.'

'There are three more fights to go,' I said. 'Surely I'm to be permitted to watch my competitors.'

He didn't deign to answer as the two Mages next to me pulled me away. 'Wait!' I called. 'My friends—'

'Fuck your friends.'

The Mages' grip on my arms increased as their efforts to heave me away doubled in intensity.

I spotted Mage Andy, white-faced, taking advantage of the break in proceedings to dart up to the Ascendant once more, but he was waved away before he could open his mouth. 'Help the bitch back to her room.'

'Sir—'

'Now.'

The Mages holding me dropped their hands and Andy took my upper arm in a loose grip. I made a show of tugging at his hold. 'Bastard,' I hissed at him, but I let him lead me away from the battleground.

As soon as we were out of earshot, I asked, 'Where is Laoch?'

Andy gave me a blank look. 'Who?'

I gritted my teeth. 'Nicholas. The daemon. The one they—'

'Oh.' He seemed baffled. 'They'll have put him to work, I imagine. Did he really come with you in the body of a mouse?'

Andy was on my side, as much as any Mage could be, but I'd still punch him if he didn't stop acting as if Laoch were nothing more than a trifling amusement. 'Find out where he is.' I clenched my fists. 'Please.'

'Uh, I'll try.' He glanced at me and comprehension lit his face. 'Oh. He means a lot to you. He won't be killed, then – that would be too easy, too final. This sort of thing has happened many times before. The daemon will be kept around to make sure you stay in check and—' His voice trailed off.

'And what?'

He looked away. 'And he'll be used as an example of the punishment other deserters can expect if they try to escape.'

'Meaning he'll be tortured?'

Andy rubbed his neck awkwardly. 'Aye. Probably.' He paused. 'I'm sorry.'

I shouldn't have been surprised. I should have been glad that Andy believed Laoch wouldn't be killed, but all I felt was burning rage. I breathed deeply, trying to calm myself. As long as I was here, I could still save him.

'What about me?' I asked. 'Will I be allowed to continue or will my throat be sliced as I sleep before the next round?'

'The next round will be the final round,' Andy said. 'And I don't have the faintest idea what the Ascendant will do to you before then.'

I translated that as meaning that the Ascendant would definitely do something. I opened my mouth to speak again but Andy wasn't done. 'The Ascendancy Challenge isn't what's important.'

It might not be important to him, but it certainly was to me. This time he didn't register my expression. His face filled with dismay. 'I've been doing some more digging.'

I stilled. 'He is coming.'

'Aye.' Andy swallowed hard and his Adam's apple bobbed in his throat. 'I've found another book that I think references who *he* might be.'

From the tone of his voice and his pale face, I already knew that 'he' wouldn't be anyone we'd be pleased to see. 'Go on,' I said grimly, rubbing at Mosse's blood which was drying on my skin.

'Cadal Righ,' he told me. 'A vicious bastard of a Mage from the last century or so. There have been nasty stories about him over the years that were never taken seriously, but the details fit.'

I squinted. 'I've never heard of him.'

'That doesn't surprise me – I'd not heard much about him myself. Cadal Righ tried to stage a coup and take over the Mages. He very nearly succeeded, but he was eventually beaten back and sentenced to death. He's only mentioned in a few old Mage books that wouldn't have been widely disseminated, the sort of books we like to keep away from the public.'

I snorted. Of course they did.

We crossed the final courtyard towards my little room. 'I don't see why a story about a single Mage relates to what's happening with the Afflicted now. If he was executed—'

'His execution never took place. He disappeared before it could happen.'

I pursed my lips. 'All the same, he must have died decades ago.'

Andy gave a grudging nod. 'There's been no mention of him for the last 120 years.'

I shrugged. 'There you go then.'

'There's a picture of him, an etching. He had a tattoo – a rune.'

'You mean—?'

'Aye. The same one that's been popping up all over the country.'

'His descendants? Have they taken up his cause?' As soon as the words left my mouth, they didn't feel right. That wouldn't explain the involvement of the Afflicted.

'Maybe.' Andy looked grim. His hand delved beneath his cloak and he pulled out a book, the one he'd been waving at the Ascendant before my fight. 'There's more. Cadal Righ disappeared in October 1892.' He tapped the book's cover. 'It's all in here but I can find no mention of a sighting of him after that date. And I bet you know what happened in November 1892.'

I did know: that was when the first of the Afflicted appeared. We'd been taught about it in the orphanage.

Andy stopped in front of the door. 'Before he vanished, Cadal Righ told his would-be executioners that one day Scotland would be his to rule.'

I stared at him. The door opened and four guards marched through, immediately surrounding me and blocking my view. I glanced at their hard, weathered faces and curled lips. I'd been lucky with some of the other guards, but I doubted any of these had empathy either for me or the ordinary folk of this country.

The first guard glared at me. 'You're to come with us. Now.'

'What's the meaning of this?' Andy asked. 'I'm supposed to escort this woman to her room.'

'Ascendant's orders,' one of the others growled. 'He wants her somewhere else now. Out of the way, sir.'

I pushed myself onto my tiptoes to try and catch Andy's eye. 'You should get the Ascendant and all the others to listen to what you've found. Use the books as proof. Cadal Righ might be nothing more than an old story, but we don't know. If the Ascendant ordered other Mages to search those old books with you, you might find out more.'

'I'll try,' he promised.

'Do,' I said. 'And find Laoch.'

The nearest guard backhanded me without any warning. I cried out and staggered as the pain bounced through my cheekbone and into my jaw.

'Hey!' Andy protested.

'Excuse us, sir.' The guard bowed towards him, grabbed me and shoved me through the door. The other three followed closely behind. The door was slammed shut behind us. I was not pushed towards the familiar staircase but past the Ascendant's study and down the draughty hallway towards the Edinburgh Mages' death garden.

A tremor of fear uncurled in my stomach and I started to resist, digging my heels into the stone floor. When that didn't work, I hummed and reached for the magic inside me, but there was nothing there. The magic that had been taken from me before my fight with Mosse hadn't returned. I was powerless.

My bones ached from the fight with Mosse, and I was still covered in his blood. My cheek throbbed where the guard had struck me. I was scared – but I wasn't going to be cowed. I thought of the crowd chanting my name; I'd come too far. If I were killed now, people would act, not just here but back in Glasgow as well, maybe in other cities, too. The Mages had created this situation, believing they could best me and easily draw a line under any rebellion, but they'd made things worse for themselves. I had to remember that, not only for my sake but for Laoch's too.

I stopped resisting and allowed them to lead me on. Magic or no magic, I still possessed some control. My death here would increase my power, not defeat it.

Approaching the garden with human eyes was different from seeing it through the gaze of a mouse; it looked smaller and less intimidating, although the decaying reek of death remained. My nostrils twitched and I had to repress a shudder.

I heard the click of footsteps from behind and the guards around me dropped into deep bows. I folded my arms and turned to face the Ascendant. 'I thought you'd be staying to watch the rest of the fights.' I was pleased that my voice remained strong and calm.

'Why?' He seemed genuinely curious. 'I already know who will win. The only surprise bout was yours.'

I dipped into a mock curtsey. 'Happy to oblige.' I glanced over his shoulder. 'Did you see Mage Andy? He was out in the courtyard. He has some information that I think you should know.'

The Ascendant threw back his head and laughed. 'He has some wild conspiracy theories, for sure. What he doesn't have is actual information.'

I persisted. 'The Afflicteds' methods are changing. The runes are all over the place.'

He rolled his eyes. 'So what? I didn't come here to talk to you about that.'

'Let me guess,' I said flatly. 'You came here to show me a few more hanging bodies.' I nodded at the garden. 'Or perhaps to dig up some female corpses that you've abused in order to enhance your magic. You want to scare me into yielding.'

He laughed again. 'Oh my dear, I already know you're not going to yield.' He nodded to the guards and they departed swiftly, leaving us alone. He leaned forward. 'I came here to negotiate.'

CHAPTER

TWENTY-SEVEN

I didn't believe him for a moment. If there was one thing I'd learned over the last few months, it was that the Mages never negotiated. They were too full of their own power and importance to concede an inch. I kept my expression blank, however, and indicated that I was listening.

The Ascendant smiled beatifically. 'You know, you did me a favour when you murdered Gerald.'

I was confused. 'Who?'

'The Glasgow Ascendant. He was never my favourite and having him out of the way has improved my position considerably. It meant that I could install the right person in his place.' He sighed. 'But you've changed all that.'

'My heart bleeds.'

There was a tiny tug at the corner of his thin mouth. 'I'm sure. I had high hopes for young Noah, you know. He'd have toed the line and done as he was told. But I adapted and decided Lord Mosse would be an appropriate replacement. All the arrangements were in place. Now Mosse is dead, I must adapt yet again. It's proving quite tiresome.'

I thought about the conversation I'd overheard. 'Lord Aspen believed that Mosse was in his pocket.'

The Ascendant's lip curled. 'Lord Aspen is a fool.' He shrugged. 'He'll win now, though. That man is Glasgow's future.'

I met his eyes. 'Not if I have anything to say about it.'

The Ascendant didn't argue; instead he pointed away from the garden. 'Come with me,' he said. 'I would like to show you something.'

I followed him down the last few metres of the dark corridor. At the very end, a dripping candle stood in a bronze sconce, its flame flickering. The light it cast was just enough to see a small oak door at the far side, locked with a rusty iron bolt. That didn't bode well.

The Ascendant slid the bolt, and the door swung open with a high-pitched creak loud enough to send judders down the spines of most normal folk. I peered around his shoulder and spied a narrow staircase leading downwards. Oh great: he was taking me to the castle dungeons.

'Do not be afraid,' he said in an almost caring tone. 'I'll keep you safe. I even made sure that the corners were swept free of spiders this morning. I know how you wee girls are frightened of creepy crawlies.'

'It's not spiders that worry me,' I replied icily.

The Ascendant gave me a measured look. 'No,' he said after a long pause. 'I don't suppose it is.' He smiled again. 'I do not imagine you know enough to incant the spell for casting light yet, do you?'

I knew it well, but that hardly mattered now. I splayed my hands. 'I do not currently possess any magic,' I reminded him. 'It was taken from me before my fight with Mosse.'

'Ah yes. I'd forgotten about that.'

No, he hadn't. I shrugged, suggesting that it wasn't important, although my stomach was churning. That hadn't been a throwaway comment; he was checking up on me. He wanted to know if I could wield magic again .

'*Altus ish moy*,' he intoned, pushing far more power into the simple spell than necessary. Was he trying to show off or to prove himself?

The entire staircase was flooded with light so bright that I was forced to shield my eyes. 'Oh,' the Ascendant said in mock surprise. 'Is that too much for you?'

'It's fine.'

A tiny smile toyed at the corners of his mouth as he started to descend. I remained where I was. One hard shove in the small of his back and he'd go flying. I might get lucky and he'd break his neck.

'I will not hurt you,' he called back. 'I give you my word.'

I gingerly took a step, then another and another. I had a horrible sense of foreboding about what was waiting for me below. I prayed desperately that it wasn't Laoch in chains.

The staircase curled further into the depths of the castle than I'd have thought possible. As we descended deeper into the rock, the air grew chillier and I rubbed my arms. I reached inside myself, searching for a shred of magic that might have reappeared, but so far there was nothing.

Finally the staircase ended at the entrance to a large, cavernous room. The floor was uneven and there was a smell of damp mould tinged with the unmistakable iron tang of old blood. I hissed a curse under my breath. If the Ascendant heard me, he didn't react.

'This way,' he said. He swept out his cloak and marched ahead past several large, empty cages. I could well imagine what they had been used for and I shook my head. Following this bastard down here had been a bad idea; I half expected at any moment to be shoved into one of the cages and left to rot.

The Ascendant stopped beside a wooden table surrounded by chairs and turned to face me. 'Take the weight off your feet, dear.'

'My name is Mairi,' I bit out. 'I am not your dear.'

'Forgive me. I spoke out of habit rather than design. Please, Mairi, sit.'

I gritted my teeth but obeyed. He took the chair opposite, settling himself before leaning back and smiling. There was no evidence of the snarling face he'd presented to me on the castle roof, and that only made me more wary.

'I will admit that we have made some errors, ' he said. '*I* have made some errors. We underestimated your abilities, and you have exceeded our expectations. I imagine that you have exceeded your own, as well.'

I didn't say anything.

'However, I do not believe that you have thought this through. You are in a strange city. You are on your own.'

I met his eyes. 'I am not alone,' I said evenly.

'We have your daemon,' he replied. 'He is ours to command once more. And you know that we have your friends, too. They will not live for much longer. I say this not as a threat but a statement of fact.'

'The people are on my side,' I spat. 'And there are a damned sight more of them than there are of you.'

The Ascendant sighed deeply. 'Aye. It is true that you have conjured up considerable feeling amongst the ordinary folk. We did not expect such strength of feeling. Not everyone is on your side, but most of them are.' He linked his fingers under his chin and regarded me carefully. 'And that creates a problem for all of us.'

I crossed my arms. 'It's not a problem for me.'

'Of course it is. You've proved you're not stupid. If they rise up like they did in Glasgow, hundreds will die, perhaps thousands.'

I kept my tone as calm as his. 'They won't need to rise up if I win the Ascendancy Challenge.'

'Even if you win, I am still in charge of *this* city. That will not change. Glasgow is only one place – and what do you think will happen there if you take charge? Hmm?'

'Freedom,' I said. 'For everyone.'

The Ascendant laughed. 'Freedom? Do you really believe that freedom is so wonderful? The freedom you talk about will lead to anarchy. If you take control of Glasgow, the Mages will leave. Where will your food come from? The farms belong to us. How will you maintain order when people are starving? People will be free, but they will still die. How will you keep the Afflicted at bay? You have no idea of the magical energy we expend to keep their kind in check and to prevent their terrible disease from spreading.'

'We have people with magic. You Mages aren't the only ones who can throw out a spell or two.'

'You're talking about women.'

'I am.'

'Angus told you, didn't he? He told you where the Affliction comes from. Give females power, and you will increase the numbers of the Afflicted. They will over-run Glasgow, and in less than five years there will be nobody left who is not diseased. You will not be able to stop it. You might think our methods are cruel, but we have ensured the safety and well-being of this land for decades. There is no other way.'

'There is always another way,' I bit out.

He raised an eyebrow. 'You know of one?'

'Not yet.' I clenched my jaw. 'But I will.'

'Revolution is easy. Ruling is entirely different.'

I didn't have all the answers, but there was one thing I was sure of. 'We cannot continue as things are now.'

'Agreed,' he said, surprising me. 'I did say I was going to show you something. Wait here a moment and I will retrieve it.' He pushed back his chair and stood up, then walked towards the far end of the huge room. Unfortunately he took the light with him, plunging me into darkness.

I remained where I was and watched him turn right and vanish behind a wall. I could see nothing beyond a dim glow of light where he'd disappeared. That was when I heard the snuffling.

I sat bolt upright. Shite. Something else was down here – an animal, or a long-forsaken prisoner. There was a grunt, followed by a cough and my blood ran cold.

I knew who that was, though I could scarcely believe they'd brought Noah down here. I stood up and tried to pierce the gloom with my eyes. He was somewhere beyond where the Ascendant had gone.

I tensed, expecting the worst, but then I heard footsteps and saw the flickering light from the Ascendant's spell return. As soon as he came into view, I yelled, 'Noah is here? You brought Noah here? Is he in a cage?'

The Ascendant was carrying a rolled-up sheet of paper. 'Of course we brought Lord Noah here. We can hardly have him running around the castle in his state, can we?'

'What are you going to do with him?'

He drew closer and gave me a curious look. 'Do you care?'

'No, but—'

He interrupted me. 'Well then.' He unrolled the piece of paper. 'Forget about poor Lord Noah for now. This is what I wanted to show you.' He spread the paper on the table and, against my better judgement, I looked down.

'A map?' I frowned.

The Ascendant clicked his fingers. 'You see? I said you weren't stupid. Yes, it's a map.' He jabbed at it. 'We are here. Glasgow is here. There is Perth and Inverness and Aberdeen.'

I stared at him. 'So?'

He pointed. 'This is the Isle of Arran. It's accessible only by boat. It's quite beautiful. So I'm told, anyway.'

'I don't need a geography lesson.'

'I'll give it to you.'

A geography lesson? 'Pardon?'

'I will give you the Isle of Arran in its entirety. It will belong to you and whoever you choose to join you. Any of your friends can go along – I'll even let you have your daemon. No Mages will set foot on it and you will have all the freedom that your heart desires. There are no Afflicted there at the moment. If your actions create more of them, or if you turn that way, then you will only have yourself to blame, but nobody on the mainland will suffer. It is by far the safest and the best option.' He beamed. 'You're welcome.'

I looked from the map to him and back again. 'What?'

'Arran is yours.'

My mouth was dry. I had not expected anything like this, not even remotely.

'All you have to do is publicly renounce your place in the Ascendancy Challenge. That will quell those eejits out there who seem to think that a revolution is necessary. Then you can leave, and the revolt will fade away without a figurehead to spur it on.' He nodded earnestly. 'The alternative is that Glasgow will not survive if you win. Scotland might not either. You get to live.' He paused. 'And so will everyone else.'

'Walk away?'

'Aye.'

'And live on this island for the rest of my life?'

'Aye.'

My lip curled. 'And leave you lot in charge?' I shook my head. 'Never.'

For the first time, the Ascendant's eyes flashed with anger. 'Do not look a gift horse in the mouth, girlie. This is far more than you could have expected when you started this crusade. It's far more than we wanted to give you.' He slammed fist down on the map. 'This way we all win.'

I closed my eyes, thinking of Laoch. I imagined he was standing next to me, with his hand on my hip. Then I looked again at the Ascendant. 'This way I win,' I said, my voice clear, 'and this way you win, but this is not a win for Scotland. It's not a win for the thousands of people out there. They will remain under the Mages' yoke and continue to suffer.'

'They'll be alive.'

'Unless they say or do something that pisses off one of your lot, and they're summarily executed for their trouble.'

He glared at me, his cheeks turning red. 'Am I to take that as a no?'

'That's a fucking no.'

His mouth tightened. 'So be it.' He snatched up the map and strode away towards the stairs.

I sprang to my feet to dart after him, but the Ascendant barked a single incantation over his shoulder. '*Ins veil.*'

My body was thrown up into the air and jerked sideways. Air whizzed past, my spine slammed against the back of one of the empty cages, and the jarring impact shuddered through me. I gasped for breath, certain I'd cracked at least one rib. I struggled up as the light surrounding the Ascendant continued to move further away and he disappeared towards the staircase.

'You can't kill me!' I croaked after him. 'And you can't leave me down here alone! If I am not present for the final Ascendancy Challenge round, the people of this city won't stand for it. Neither will the people of Glasgow!'

The Ascendant stopped then slowly turned. 'You talk far too much for a woman. You should learn your place. Don't worry, you will be at the next round. You just won't be there in the manner that you'd like to be. Once the good people of Edinburgh see what has happened to you, and Glasgow learns the truth, they will have no choice but to back down. They will understand why you cannot lead and why they were stupid to think they could take us on. You really should have chosen the island, you know. It was a genuine offer.'

He turned away once more. A moment later, I couldn't see him, but as the last of his conjured light disappeared, I heard his final mutter. *'Brashar.'*

There was the cold rattle of metal upon metal, followed by a faint snuffle and a grunt. That was when I finally accepted what was happening: I was trapped in dungeon with no magic and no light. And Noah, who was now wholly Afflicted, had been released from his cage.

The Ascendant didn't want him to kill me, he wanted Noah to infect me because then it truly would be game over and nobody could argue. He'd present my diseased state to the crowd before the final challenge. Hell, he might even parade me around Glasgow in a cage of my own so that nobody was left in any doubt.

Something the Gowk had said to me echoed in my head: *One person alone can spark a revolution* – but not if that person was Afflicted. The figurehead of the resistance would be nothing more than a pockmarked creature with barely a shred of sentient consciousness. Between that and the fear of their own Affliction, the revolution would fade away.

Aye. I was screwed.

TWENTY-EIGHT

I heard Noah groan, and his shuffling footsteps drifted towards me. There was a spluttering, hacking cough followed by what sounded like words, although I couldn't hear them precisely. I took a step and hissed with pain. There had to be something I could do or somewhere I could hide until my magic returned and I could fight him off. Maybe I could lock myself in one of the damned cages.

There wasn't a definitive reason why an Afflicted person might infect somebody healthy. Sometimes they only had to breathe the same air for a short time, although I knew of a boy from my old orphanage who was trapped in a derelict warehouse with three Afflicted for two days and he'd been fine. I knew of people who had been bitten by someone Afflicted and remained disease free, and I knew of people who'd been scratched slightly by someone Afflicted and turned within hours.

Given that I knew the Mages had been experimenting on the Afflicted they captured, I suspected they knew far more about how such infections were transferred. My best bet was to stay as far away from Noah as I could; after all, he had been contaminated very quickly.

Noah's croaky voice floated towards me. 'He...'

I gritted my teeth and started to limp. Surrounded by choking darkness, I couldn't see anything. I waved my arms in front of me, trying desperately to remember the layout of the room.

'...Is.'

I wheezed and stumbled forward. The less noise I made the better, but that was easier said than done.

'...Coming.'

My fingertips brushed against something. There. That was a cage. Relief washed over me and I felt my way along its exterior, searching for the opening.

'He ... Is ... Coming.'

I felt a gap and my fingers fumbled as I tried to find the catch. The cage rattled at my touch and I tugged at what I thought was the metal door. It wouldn't budge. I tried harder.

'He ... Is ... Coming.'

My hand curled around a heavy metal object. A padlock. Oh no. The cage was locked, and I had no way of getting into it. I sucked in a breath, feeling the wash of pain in my lungs. Maybe I'd get into the next one. Maybe not all of them were already locked.

'He ... Is ... Coming.'

Noah was getting closer. I located the next cage, moving faster now that I was more familiar with them. Damn it, this one was locked too. I heard Noah cough again, then suddenly he let out an ear-piercing howl. He was less than ten metres away.

I couldn't waste time trying to get into any more of the

cages. My best chance was to find the staircase and race upwards to the door, even though I knew it would be locked and I'd likely be trapped in a dead end.

The Afflicted were comfortable with the cloak of darkness, but usually there were stars or the moon or a few dull lanterns to offer at least some light. This dungeon wasn't like that; down here was smothering darkness. I hoped that Noah's vision was impaired and he wouldn't work out where I'd gone. It was a slim thread of hope but it was all I had.

I took another excruciating gulp of air then held my breath so my wheezing didn't give me away. As I tiptoed towards the staircase. Noah continued to groan and shuffle behind me, punctuating every few seconds with same refrain. *He Is Coming.* He didn't appear capable of saying anything else.

I thrust one hand in front of me and the other to my left, trailing my fingers from cage to cage and trying to walk in a straight line. I wished I'd paid more attention to how many cages there were when I'd entered, or how far it was to the staircase. It had taken the Ascendant maybe twenty seconds to walk from the spot where I'd fallen to the stairs, though he'd been moving considerably faster than I was. There was probably little more than fifteen feet to go. I picked up the pace. Noah was closer now.

The hand I'd been holding in front of me hit something: the wall. I'd reached the end of the room. Galvanised, I sidestepped. The gap leading to the staircase was along here somewhere. Any moment now...

Noah let out a screech, an inhuman, nightmarish sound that chilled my bones and froze my steps. The air beside me stirred and I turned my head. When I saw the weak glow of twin yellow lights less than a metre from my face, I squeaked aloud. Those were Noah's eyes – and he was staring straight at me.

I raised my hands in front of my face and braced for impact as Noah blinked. He drew closer so I not only saw his strange eyes but I smelled him also. The once-coiffed Mage was long gone.

His breath rattled. 'He. Is.'

I couldn't help it. 'Coming,' I said.

The eyes pulled back, tilting to a slight angle. I'd surprised him. Oh. *Oh.* I swallowed hard, then pointed my index finger and slowly drew a shape in the air: three horizontal slashes, followed by two diagonal ones. The rune.

Noah's eyes blinked again. 'He. Is.'

I finished the sentence again. 'Coming.'

'He.' He grunted. 'Is.'

My mouth felt like parchment. 'Coming.'

'He. Is. Coming.' Noah's eyes lowered and disappeared as he turned away from me. A second later, I heard his heavy feet scuffling upwards as he ascended the staircase.

My shoulders sagged with relief, and strange tears that I hadn't expected filled my eyes. I didn't understand what had just happened, but something had.

The loud noise of Noah's footsteps continued above my head, moving further and further up. He uttered the same phrase several more times until he was far enough away that it was little more than a muffled murmur. A moment later, I heard the same howling screech, followed by a thud. There was another thud. And another. And another.

It took me a few seconds to understand what was happening: Noah was trying to break through the wooden door at the top of the staircase. I stayed where I was for a moment then, against my better judgement, shuffled right, located the first step and climbed the stairs after him.

The closer I got, the more I could hear.

'He.'

Thump.

'Is.'

Thud.

'Coming.'

Thud followed by splintering crack.

'He.'

Thump. Another crack.

'Is.'

Thud. Hacking cough.

'Coming.'

The sound of breaking wood.

I pulled myself further up, gasping and wheezing but less concerned about my pain than with what was happening above me. When I rounded the final corner, there were already a few glimmers of light from beyond. Noah had punched through the solid wood of the door to the other side.

'He.'

He smacked the wood with his fist, breaking an entire section and making a thick plank buckle.

'Is.'

He punched the plank again, widening the gap.

I licked my lips. 'Coming.'

Noah paused and looked around. Now that dull light was drifting in from the corridor, I could see more of his face. A huge sore ran down his left cheek, his hair hung in knots and dirt was smeared all over him. His eyes continued to glow, lit by some mysterious magic from within, but his expression looked oddly cheerful rather than being filled with the mask of impotent rage I'd seen on the faces of other Afflicted.

I held my breath again and moved up until I was on the top step next to him. I took great care not to allow any part of my body touch his. I drew the rune in the air again, then pointed to the door and gestured down the stairs. Noah grunted and moved two steps back.

With my heart pounding, I reached through the gap that Noah had created. My fingers fumbled, but I eventually found the bolt and slid it across. The half-ruined door burst open, and I quickly stepped out.

Four pairs of shocked eyes were staring at me. 'Hi,' I said weakly. 'What brings you lot here?'

Angus raised his eyebrows, amusement glimmering. 'We came to rescue you.'

Andy shuffled his feet. 'I did as you said and went to find the Ascendant to try and get him to listen to what I'd found about Cadal Righ, but I couldn't see him in the courtyard. He'd already gone. I knew there must be a reason why he'd left the Ascendancy Challenge so early, and I thought you might be in trouble given the way the guards had dragged you away. I spoke to Frederica and she helped us find you.'

'She's no' been that helpful!' Belle sniped. 'The lassie will no' even look at us. She will no' even speak!'

'She's a slave,' I said. 'She's not allowed to speak to us.' I glanced at Teasag. She wasn't looking at me; she was gazing at the broken door. From her face, she already knew what was beyond it.

Noah took his cue. 'He. Is. Coming.'

Belle jumped back a foot. 'Whit was that?'

I scratched my head, unsure how to explain. Before words could formulate in my head, there was a loud rumbling and the floor under our feet started to shake.

Angus stiffened and his eyes narrowed. Andy whipped around, as if expecting to see a horde of Mages thundering towards us. The floor shook again, more violently this time. From not too far away, I heard screaming. The thick stone walls trembled as there was a thunderous boom. Belle cried out, covering her head with her arms to shield herself from whatever was happening.

Noah remained out of sight beyond the broken door. He cackled, 'He. Is.' He coughed. 'Here.'

CHAPTER

TWENTY-NINE

I took off down the corridor as fast as my broken body would allow. There was one thought in my mind and it was enough to spur me on regardless of my pain. The others took a moment to react but soon I heard their footsteps behind me.

'Mairi!' Belle screeched. 'Where are you going? Whit's going on?'

Without slowing, I half turned my head. Instead of answering her, I looked at Andy. 'Did you find him?' There was a snarl in my voice.

He blinked at me, pale-faced. 'Who?'

'Laoch!' I snapped.

Andy's confusion didn't clear. For fuck's sake. We'd already been through this. 'Nicholas! Where is he?'

'I don't know. I didn't have time to look for him as well.'

A spasm of anxiety tightened my bones. I turned away and kept stumbling forward.

I thundered past the garden, barely registering its sickly smell, then burst into the next large hallway close to the

Ascendant's study. My nostrils tickled with the faint scent of burning.

I frowned and spun into the Ascendant's room. He wasn't there, but the small, thin servant girl was staring out of the narrow window. She was shaking. I lurched up and peered over her shoulder. When I saw what she was looking at, my fear only increased. Oh God. Oh no.

'For feck's lass!' Angus wheezed. 'Will you stop racing around like a damned hurricane and explain what's going on?'

The servant girl stiffened as she became aware of my presence. She'd been too focused on the terrible scene outside to pay attention to what was happening inside. She leapt away from the window and cowered by the far wall, wrapping her arms tightly around her body. I didn't blame her.

I looked at Angus and gestured towards the window. 'See for yourself.'

His brow furrowed but he loped over followed by Andy, Belle and finally Teasag. Her expression suggested she already knew what she would see.

'It's broad daylight,' Andy said faintly.

Aye.

'They can't do that in broad daylight.'

Clearly, they could.

'How many of them do you think there are out there?'

I raised onto my tiptoes. It was a veritable army of the Afflicted, and they were heading this way. They weren't running or yelling; instead they were marching calmly towards the castle entrance as if in no doubt that it belonged to them.

'All of them,' Angus whispered. 'It looks like all of them.'

There was another loud rumble and once again the floor beneath us shook. It seemed as if the very foundations of Edinburgh Castle were being tested.

I looked at the servant girl. 'You know this castle well?'

She didn't answer. She stared at me, but then her mouth twitched. I nodded.

'Good,' I said. 'Find somewhere safe to hide. Do not come out until you are sure it is safe to do so. Do you hear me?'

She nodded jerkily. A moment later she picked up her skirts and darted out of the room.

'Andy.'

The young Mage was twisting his hands together, his jaw working uselessly as he tried to make sense of what was happening. He may have been the only person who'd expected this, but he was still stunned by it.

I tried again. 'Andy!'

He jumped and looked at me. 'Wh – what?'

'Teasag is not permitted to talk to me, but she'll talk to you.'

His hands turned over and over again. 'Who is Teasag?'

I counted to five in my head. He wasn't stupid, he'd merely been shocked into inaction. Andy swallowed hard and compre-hension finally lit his eyes. 'You mean Frederica.'

I nodded. 'Ask her where Laoch is – she can sense his whereabouts. Find out where he's gone.'

Andy turned to her and asked the question. She answered instantly. 'He's in the main courtyard.'

I was already heading for the door.

'Is this a good idea?' Belle quavered. 'All those other bampots will be there as well.'

'You can stay here if you like,' I threw over my shoulder. Someone in another room screamed and the castle quaked again. Belle screeched.

'I think we're going to come with you,' I heard Angus murmur

I stepped out of the study in time to see a familiar figure hobbling past. Noah swerved into the first courtyard. I tensed, then I followed him. He was dragging his left foot behind him but he wasn't allowing it to hamper his progress. He pressed on while I trailed after him, my fear and foreboding increasing with every step.

The main courtyard still contained the roped-off area where my fight with Mosse had taken place. If I squinted, I could see his bloodstains marring the uneven cobbles. But that was far from the most chilling detail.

The stand, which had been filled with people, now lay empty. In the far corner, there were hundreds of people pressed against the wall. Some were attempting to scale it, some were banging on a closed door. In the other corner, there was a large pile of rubble; where once there had been a solid stone wall, now there was a gaping hole. Through it, I saw the dirty, pockmarked faces of dozens upon dozens of the Afflicted standing on the rocky outcrop beyond the castle. They weren't trying to breach the gap; instead, it looked as if they were waiting for something. Or someone.

I spun around, searching desperately for Laoch. I caught a brief glimpse of one tall man with horns and my heart soared, then I realised it wasn't him, it was the older daemon. I cursed and turned my attention to the huge cluster of Mages in the centre of the courtyard. They were packed tightly together, facing the ruined section of wall, and they were chanting.

'*Finza. Finza. Finza.*'

They were attempting to close the gap. Despite their numbers and the vast power that emanated from them, they weren't making any progress. Their voices rose in a chorus and a few of the fallen stones shuddered, but nothing else happened.

Noah was already halfway across the courtyard, making a beeline for the destroyed wall. Andy shot out from behind me and darted after him. I lunged forward and grabbed the back of his cloak to haul him back.

'No,' I told him. 'Noah is keyed into this somehow. We need to watch and see what he does. It might help us understand what's happening.'

I didn't get the chance to find out. Another figure ran out from the shadows to my left. I gasped. Laoch.

I surged forward while Laoch's mouth moved and he muttered a spell. Noah's body jerked as his limbs spasmed then collapsed to the cobbles in an untidy heap. I turned towards Laoch, relief flooding through me. That was when I saw Aspen standing a metre beyond him.

'Nicholas!' Aspen barked. 'Get back here!'

To my dismay, Laoch obeyed.

I swung towards Aspen, while the other Mages continued their useless chanting. 'Your magic has gone, hasn't it?' I spat. 'That's why you're here, instead of with your buddies. Let Laoch go. He can help.'

'He's going nowhere.' Aspen's lip curled. 'This is your doing, isn't it?' He gestured at the wall and the blank-faced Afflicted who were standing silently beyond it.

Eejit. 'Even if I had the magic to control the Afflicted,' I hissed, 'I'd never put innocent lives in danger.'

'You're such a hero,' Aspen mocked. 'But you're not doing anything to help those people now, are you? Mages are doing the heavy lifting now. This is why you need us. This is why your revolution will destroy this country if it isn't stopped.'

Angus appeared by my side. 'It doesn't appear that any of the Mages are having an effect,' he said.

Aspen bared his teeth and snarled at him. He was afraid; Aspen was genuinely afraid. Not only that, but he had less idea about what was happening right now than I did.

'Listen,' I said, my voice low and urgent. 'Mage Andy found

something. There's a chance that this is something to do with an old Mage from generations ago called—'

I didn't get the chance to finish. There was a bright flash and the crowd of people on the other side of the walled court-yard shrieked. I craned my neck up and saw the clouds over-head change from fluffy white to blood red. Scores of ravens took to the air from the battlements, cawing and screeching, their wings flapping in alarm. They circled then took off in one tightly packed flock as if they'd decided to cut their losses and leave while they still could. I shuddered. What now?

Belle shuffled towards me and whimpered. 'Mairi—'

There was a crack of thunder and a voice boomed out. 'My name is Cadal Righ. This is *my* castle. Scotland is *my* kingdom. And I am here to claim what is mine.' There was a pause. Then, '*Ins veil.*'

There was a loud whoomp. A moment later, the chanting Mages were scattered, blown backwards by the force of the spell. People screamed. I jumped back out of the path of a flying body. A Mage landed at my feet, his eyes staring unseeing towards the terrifying red sky.

'Over my dead body!' The Ascendant picked himself up, shook himself off and strode towards the ruined gap.

'That can be arranged,' the voice boomed again.

From the other side of the castle wall, the Afflicted started to part into two columns. A man appeared, striding past the scores of diseased folk before stepping carefully over the broken stones and into the courtyard.

He was barely an inch over five feet. His skin was paler than any I'd ever seen, and his eyes were rimmed with red. He was wearing a Mages' cloak but it was in a style I'd not seen before, and the edges were frayed and tattered. He smiled at the Ascendant with thin lips that were as white and pale as the rest of him.

'*Viz na*,' he intoned.

For a moment, nothing happened. The Ascendant didn't move and neither did Cadal Righ. Then there was an odd ripping sound.

It wasn't fabric that was ripping, it was flesh. As we watched, the Ascendant's clothes and skin peeled away. I saw blood and bone and far more of the Ascendant's internal organs than I could ever have wished to see. Bile rose into my mouth and I retched as the Ascendant's body collapsed in a bloody heap. It had taken less than three seconds.

'Anyone else?' Cadal Righ spread out his arms and smiled patiently.

'What do we do now?' Belle muttered. 'What the fuck do we do now?'

To my surprise, it was Aspen who answered, though his response barely audible. 'We run.'

I didn't move. My feet seemed to be rooted to the spot. There was something more evil and destructive than the Mages after all.

And this time I didn't think there would be a way out.

About the Author

After teaching English literature in the UK, Japan and Malaysia, Helen Harper left behind the world of education following the worldwide success of her Blood Destiny series of books. She thanks her lucky stars every day that she's able to do so.

Helen has always been a book lover, devouring science fiction and fantasy tales when she was a child growing up in Scotland.

She currently lives in Edinburgh with far too many cats – not to mention the dragons, fairies, demons, wizards and vampires that seem to keep appearing from nowhere.